Needlework

Needlework

a novel

Julia Watts

THREE ROOMS PRESS
New York, NY

Needlework
A NOVEL BY Julia Watts

ISBN 978-1-953103-07-9 (trade paperback)
ISBN 978-1-953103-08-6 (Epub)
Library of Congress Control Number: 2021935394

TRP-090

Publication Date: October 5, 2021
First edition

Young Adult Fiction: Ages 14+
BISAC Coding:
YAF031000 Young Adult Fiction / LGBTQ+
YAF058190 Young Adult Fiction / Social Themes / Prejudice & Racism
YAF058080 Young Adult Fiction / Social Themes / Drugs, Alcohol, Substance Abuse
YAF018070 Young Adult Fiction / Family Siblings

COVER DESIGN AND ILLUSTRATION:
Victoria Black: www.thevictoriablack.com

BOOK DESIGN:
KG Design International: www.katgeorges.com

DISTRIBUTED IN THE U.S. AND INTERNATIONALLY BY:
Publishers Group West: www.pgw.com

Three Rooms Press
New York, NY
www.threeroomspress.com
info@threeroomspress.com

For the families we come from
and the families we make

*"If you don't like the road you're walking,
start paving another one."*

—Dolly Parton

Needlework

Chapter 1

"Look! It's Mommy!" Caleb hollers from the back seat.

We're coming back from shopping for winter clothes at the Walmart—two pairs of off-brand jeans and three new shirts apiece, cheap plaid flannel. Is Walmart where I would choose to buy what I put on my body if I lived somewhere with other shopping choices? No. But sometimes you just have to accept reality, and for now, Walmart is reality. I reckon it beats going to school naked.

"Oh, Lord, not again." Nanny steers the car to the side of the road where Mommy is standing holding a sign that says "Homeless and Hungry Please Help."

"Caleb, you stay in the car," Nanny says. "Kody, you get out and help me."

"Yes, ma'am." I unfasten my seat belt.

I know that from Nanny's point of view, Mommy has picked the absolute worst spot to beg. The Walmart is right beside the interstate exit where everybody can see it, and everybody in Morgan, Kentucky, does their shopping at the Walmart. This means that everybody will see Mommy, which will cause Nanny the maximum amount of embarrassment. If Mommy was standing with her sign in downtown Morgan, where most of the stores have shut down and there are just a few offices and a sad little flower shop, nobody would see her.

Mommy sees me right away and smiles. Her teeth look bad. "There's my handsome boy!"

Nanny's not having it. She grabs Mommy by the arm and says, "Get in the car, Amanda."

Mommy jerks out of Nanny's grip. "Mama, I've got to make some money."

"Jobs is how people make money," Nanny says. It's kind of a low blow. Mommy has held a job at every fast-food restaurant in Morgan and has gotten fired from every single one of them. Sometimes for stealing but mostly for just not showing up regular.

"You know there ain't no good jobs in this hellhole," Mommy says.

"Any job's better than begging on the side of the road," Nanny says. "What would people from church say if they seen you with that sign? Homeless and hungry, my foot. I stocked your refrigerator on Saturday. The refrigerator that's in your *home*."

I think any of Nanny's church friends that drove by would be pretty familiar with our situation. It's old news that my mother has "problems," and so Nanny is raising me, and my Uncle Jay and his wife Tiff are raising Caleb. Who I worry about are the people from out of town who are getting off the interstate and seeing our little family drama: *Look! Hillbillies fighting on the side of the road! How quaint!*

I guess we at least provide them some entertainment.

I decide to be the peacemaker. I put my arm around Mommy's bony shoulders. She seems so small, partly because my last growth spurt put me a head taller than her, but mostly because there's a lot less of her than there used to be.

"Come on, Mommy," I say, gently pushing her forward. "Caleb's in the back seat. You want to see Caleb, don't you?"

When she hears Caleb's name, her expression softens, and you can almost imagine for a minute that she might be somebody's mother.

I lead Mommy to the car and open the door. She slides into the back seat next to Caleb and says, "There's my baby! Give me some sugar!"

I jump into the front passenger seat and Nanny guns it and peels out onto the road. We could be in an action movie.

"Hey, you wasn't supposed to do that!" Mommy says. "I just wanted to say hi to Caleb."

Caleb has his head leaned on Mommy's shoulder. He's still little—not even ten—and has chubby cheeks and dark-lashed blue eyes. He really is a cute kid. "We bought stuff for lunch at Walmart's, Mommy," he says. "If you're hungry, you can have lunch with us. Nanny's making sloppy joes."

"I love me some sloppy joes," Mommy says. "But do you know what I really, really love?"

"What's that?" Caleb says with a giggle in his voice.

"Sloppy kisses!" Mommy says and leans over Caleb—she's not wearing her seat belt—and starts covering his face with big, loud smooches. Caleb giggles like a maniac.

When Mommy pays attention to Caleb, it's almost pitiful how happy it makes him. It's like he can't get enough of her.

I used to be that way. But more often now, it seems like I'm getting too much of her. Too much of her problems, too much of the raw, buzzing need that's taken over her whole personality. When Mommy said to Caleb, "You know what I really, really love?" I had to bite my tongue to keep from saying *Drugs. You love drugs. You'd love a full bottle of Oxys more than you love anybody in this car.*

"Take it easy around them curves," Mommy says as Nanny drives us down the winding roads that lead to her house. "I've got a sick stomach today."

"Dopesick," Nanny says under her breath.

"No," Mommy says, sounding mad. "I think I ate a bad taco yesterday, is all."

"If you ate at Taco Tico, there's no doubt you ate a bad taco," I say. Taco Tico is our sad local version of Mexican fast food. "Bad tacos is the only kind they've got."

"You got that right," Mommy says. "And I used to work there so I know how nasty it is. I don't know why I can't stay away from Taco Tuesday."

Nanny makes a left into the holler. It's such a small road that you have to know it's there to turn onto it. We drive down the tree-lined gravel road, turn right at the mailbox that Mamaw painted with pictures of cardinals, then pull into our driveway. Nanny used to live in a trailer, but now she has a modular home. It's kind of like a trailer but it doesn't have wheels and it looks more house-like. When Nanny bought it, two flatbed trucks came, each with half the house on it. They unloaded the halves and fastened them together to make a whole house. It reminded me of this old Fisher-Price house from when I was in the toddler room at church. It was hinged so you could open it up and play with the little figures in the different rooms.

As soon as they hear the car, the dogs come running. Me and Nanny rescue dogs that have been abandoned on the side of the road, so we always have a mess of mutts, usually unfortunate looking hound dog/Heinz 57 mixes. Right now there are three bitches: Dolly, Loretta, and Tammy. The male dog we rescued along with Tammy, who's too lazy to get up off the porch to greet us, is George Jones. Nanny teases me because I name all the dogs after classic country stars.

"Now you girls settle down," Nanny fusses at the dogs when she gets out of the car. "It ain't time to eat yet."

"That's right," I say, scratching Dolly behind her ears. "And you country divas have got to watch your figures."

The house isn't fancy, and Nanny's decorating taste isn't the same as mine (if it's got Jesus or a Bible quote on it, she's slapping it up on the wall), but it is super clean. Every Saturday morning, Nanny cooks us a big breakfast, sausage and eggs and biscuits and gravy, and we clean the house from top to bottom. After that, we usually just lay around and watch sappy movies and maybe stick a frozen pizza in the oven when we get hungry.

As soon as we're in the house, Caleb turns on the TV to cartoons, and Mommy says, "Mama, is it all right with you if I take a shower?"

"Get you a clean towel out of the hall closet," Nanny says. "Me and Kody will start lunch."

Nanny unwraps a pound of ground beef and drops it in a skillet while I work on putting the groceries away. That's the thing about Walmart—you can pick up your cheap groceries and your cheap school clothes in the same place.

"I'm glad she's taking a shower," I say, putting cans of soup and vegetables in the pantry. "She kind of stinks. Caleb don't seem to notice, though. He still hangs all over her."

"Well, you know Caleb," Nanny says, poking at the ground beef in the skillet with a spatula. "He's blinded by how much he loves her. I guess that blindness includes his nose, too. Oh hey, don't put that can away. I need it."

I look down at the can I'm holding. It has a picture of a fat sloppy joe on it and is labeled Manwich. I hand it to Nanny. "What kind of name for a product is that?" I say. "Manwich. Is that supposed to sound appetizing?"

"I don't know," Nanny says. "I never really thought about it. It is a peculiar name, though."

"Manwich," I say in a big, booming voice. "The favorite food of cannibals everywhere."

Nanny laughs. "The things that come out of your mouth, Kody."

Mommy comes into the kitchen barefoot, her wet hair slicked back from her face. She has on a pink track suit. Nanny's favorite. "I borrowed some clean clothes," Mommy says. "Once I got clean, I didn't want to put on the same old dirty stuff."

"You can borrow any clothes you want as long as you leave me enough so I don't have to go naked," Nanny says, pouring the Manwich sauce over the ground beef. "Now, Amanda, do you need me to go to town tomorrow and pay your water bill?"

Of course that's why she wanted to shower here. Nanny catches onto some things faster than I do.

"If you don't care to . . . " Mommy says. She shakes her head to get the water out of her ears, which puts me in mind of a wet dog.

"Well, I do care to since I'd rather have the money for something else, but I can't have you living without running water."

"You could just give me the money, and I'll pay the bill tomorrow. Save you the trouble."

Nanny doesn't look up from the stove. "Amanda, you know good and well that if I gave you money, you wouldn't use it to pay no water bill."

Mommy doesn't argue. Probably because she knows Nanny is right.

We all sit down at the kitchen table. Caleb is a big eater. He picks up his sloppy joe and gets sauce all over his face. I eat mine open-faced with a knife and fork. Nanny picks at her food and watches to see if Mommy's eating, which she isn't much. She eats a few potato chips but mostly ignores her sandwich.

"Me and Kody's started piecing a quilt in the evenings," Nanny says, probably just to have something to say. "It's slow going, but I reckon we might have it ready in time for the spring church bazaar."

Caleb looks up from his almost empty plate. "Uncle Jay says Kody ought to be going deer hunting with him instead of staying home and sewing ruffled curtains with Nanny."

For the record, I've never sewed ruffled curtains in my life. I'm open to trying it, but I ain't done it yet.

Mommy reaches out and touches Caleb's arm. "You tell that brother of mine that Kody don't need to be out hunting no deer. Kody is my artist. And you"—she touches his nose with her fingertip—"are my athlete."

Caleb loves this, of course, but I kind of like being called an artist, too. That's the thing about Mama. Most of the time, there's not much to her except for being high or being sick because she needs to get high. But sometimes, you get these glimmers of who she is underneath.

After everybody's eaten all they're going to eat, Caleb says, "Mommy, you want to watch cartoons with me?"

"Sure, puppy. Let's go."

She and Caleb cuddle up on the couch, and Caleb turns up the TV way too loud. I help Nanny load the dishwasher. When we're done, I say, "If it's all right with you, I'm gonna go to my room for a few minutes and listen to a few songs."

"You and them old records," Nanny says, but she's smiling. The records I listen to were Papaw's before he died from the black lung, and I know she's glad I love them and that they're not just shoved in the back of a closet somewhere.

I love my family, but it feels good to go to my room and close the door.

Papaw died when I was real little, and I didn't discover his record collection till I was twelve and Nanny and me were going through all the stuff in the trailer, getting ready to move into the modular home. Shoved into a corner of the closet was an old LP player and two milk crates full of vinyl records. When I asked Nanny about them, she said, "Them was your papaw's. I could probably sell them, but he loved them so much I don't have the heart to get rid of them."

I slid one of the albums out and looked at the picture on the cover. A dimple-cheeked gal in a tight red sweater with big blonde hair and the biggest bust I'd ever seen. I was looking at my salvation even though I didn't know it yet. But I did know enough to ask, "Can I have them?"

Nanny shrugged. "I don't see why not."

And so now the turntable and the records are in my room, right next to my bed so I don't have to get up to switch from Side A to Side B. There are albums by lots of the male country music greats: Porter Waggoner, Buck Owens, George Jones, Roger Miller, Kenny Rogers. I like all those guys, especially Roger Miller because he's hilarious, but my real love is the girl singers. I love Loretta's sassy lyrics and that she's from the middle of nowhere in Kentucky like me. And I love how nobody can sound sadder than Tammy Wynette when she sings about something like her d-i-v-o-r-c-e. But there's one country diva that reigns supreme over all the others, past and present, and that is the buxom blonde whose picture I saw first on the day I discovered Papaw's record collection.

Dolly Parton.

Papaw had Dolly's *My Tennessee Mountain Home, Porter Wayne and Dolly Rebecca,* (an album of duets between Dolly and Porter Waggoner), *The Best of Dolly Parton,* and *A Real, Live Dolly* which is a recording of a concert she gave in her hometown of Sevierville. I play these albums all over and over again, even though the songs about dead children make me cry.

I love Dolly's voice—how bright and clear it is. I love her songs about growing up poor in the mountains, about being different from everybody else. I know most sixteen-year-old boys probably don't lay in bed listening to fifty-year-old Dolly Parton records, but I'm not like most sixteen-year-old boys. I can't explain it, but I feel like Dolly would understand me.

I put *The Best of Dolly* on the turntable, lay on my bed, and fall into a "Jolene"-induced Dolly trance. A lot of kids at school listen to country music, but just the new Top 40 stuff, meaning that they basically drive around in their trucks while listening to songs about guys driving around in their trucks.

I don't have a truck, and Nanny couldn't afford one even if I wanted it. What I would like is a computer, but we can't afford that either, and even if we could, we live too far out in the country to have a reliable internet connection. That, plus Nanny thinks the internet is the world's biggest source of sin.

She may have a point.

I'm on Track #4, "Touch Your Woman," when Nanny hollers, "Kody, your mommy's leaving! Come tell her bye!"

Mommy didn't even last twenty minutes watching cartoons with Caleb. Her visits are always like this. She asks for money but doesn't get it, so she takes what she can get—a hot shower, a little food if she can eat it—then gets restless and moves on because we don't really have what she wants.

Mommy is already standing by the front door. Caleb is clinging to her like a baby koala bear.

"You taking off?" I say, hoping this will be a hint to Caleb to peel himself off of her.

"Yeah," Mommy says, not meeting my eyes. Mommy lives about a quarter mile up the holler in the hand-me-down trailer Nanny gave her, the one Nanny and me used to live in.

"You want me to drive you?" I just got my license a couple of months ago, and Nanny's a scaredy cat about me driving her car, but sometimes she'll let me go short distances.

"No, I'll walk," Mommy says. "I've got a friend coming over to the house."

I know what kind of friend she means. The kind who'll sell her pills or share some pills with her for the right kind of favor. "Okay, bye," I say.

I must sound cold because she pulls a sad face and says, "No hug for your mommy?"

I lean over and give her a quick hug. "Bye, Mommy."

After she's gone, Nanny lets out a sigh, like she'd been holding her breath the whole time Mommy was there. "Kody, you wanna drive Caleb home?" she asks. "I told Jay I'd have him back in time for basketball practice."

I'm kind of surprised. Nanny's usually stingy with the car, and Uncle Jay and Aunt Tiff live on the other side of town.

Compared to the distances Nanny usually lets me drive, this is practically a cross-country trip. "Sure," I say. "You ready to go, Caleb?"

"How come Nanny ain't taking me?" he asks.

"I'm wore out, honey," Nanny says, and I'm sure it's true. Worrying about Mommy takes its toll on her. Plus, she's sixty-three years old, and she puts in forty-five hours a week at the uniform factory, making shirts for mechanics and coveralls for construction workers. It's hard to believe that at night, when we're watching TV, she wants to sew for fun. "Come give your nanny a hug," she says.

Once we're outside, Caleb says, "Can I sit in the front seat?"

"Back seat's safer," I say. Nanny always makes him sit in the back.

"Oh, come on," he says, starting up a whine.

"All right, just this one time," I say. "But buckle your seat belt. Don't be like Mommy."

Caleb's quiet while I start the car, but I can feel his mood darkening. I've noticed this happens after he spends time with Mommy. He's super happy when he's with her, all giggles and hugs, but once she's gone, a little black storm cloud settles over his head. It's like Mommy is a drug he has to come down from.

After a couple of minutes, Caleb says, "Why are you mean to Mommy?"

"I'm not," I say.

"You are, too," Caleb says. "You don't hug her unless she makes you, and you go listen to your stupid music instead of spending time with her."

"Well, that was because I wanted to make sure you got enough time with her all to yourself," I say. On the side of the road on the way to town, a scrawny brown dog is rooting through garbage. I make a mental note of where he is. Nanny and me might go back for him later or at least leave him some food if we can't catch him.

"Do you love Mommy?" Caleb asks.

"Of course I love Mommy." We pass the white aluminum-sided church where we go every Sunday. "I just don't love the choices she makes."

Caleb is quiet again, then he says, "Like her not raising us?"

"Well, that was the court's decision," I say. "But yeah, that's the kind of thing I'm talking about. The things she chooses to do that make her unfit to raise us."

"At least she ain't in jail like Daddy," Caleb says.

"That's true." Most of the time I don't call Robbie, the man who knocked up Mommy, "Daddy" even though Nanny makes me and Caleb go visit him two or three times a year. As far as I'm concerned, he's just a sperm donor, but Caleb calls him Daddy even though Mommy's brother, Uncle Jay, has been way more of a father to him.

As we get to the outskirts of town, I say, "Hey, I've got a little money. You want to drive through the Dairy Queen?"

Caleb's eyes get big. "Yeah. I want a Blizzard, the kind with smooshed-up Oreos."

I wasn't planning on making such a big investment. "I ain't got enough for Blizzards, buddy, but I can get us a cone apiece."

"A cone would be good, too," Caleb says.

That's one thing about growing up the way we have. You're used to settling for less.

But even if they're cheap, the ice cream cones are sweet and good. We ride through downtown, past the court-house and the flower shop and the funeral home, past the empty storefronts that used to be stores in the days before Walmart.

After he's demolished his cone, Caleb says, "Kody?"

"Yeah?" I'm still working on my cone, holding it with my left hand and driving with my right. Nanny would have a fit if she saw I didn't have both hands on the wheel.

"How come you like to do girl things?"

This again. "I don't," I say. "The things I do are boy things because I'm a boy and I'm doing them."

"But the things you do with Nanny—sewing and crocheting and making candy—them's girl things."

"Who says?"

"Uncle Jay. And the Bible."

"Is that so?" I pop the last bite of cone—which is always the best bite—into my mouth. "I don't know where it says in the Bible that a boy can't cook or sew. And all them men in the Bible went around with long hair wearing robes that looked like dresses."

"Yeah," Caleb says. "But that was because pants and barber shops hadn't been invented yet."

"Caleb, I don't like hunting or fishing or football, but I like you. Do you like me even though I like different stuff than you do?"

"Yeah, I like you. It's just—"

"Let's leave it at that then, okay?" I say before he can say anything else.

"Okay," he says.

I pull into Jay and Tiff's driveway and park behind Jay's old white pickup truck with its "MAKE AMERICA GREAT AGAIN" and "FRIENDS OF COAL" bumper stickers. Jay worked in the mines before he and just about everybody else got laid off. Now he works at the oil change place out by the interstate.

Tiff answers the door. Her hair is up in a messy bun and she's wearing a t-shirt that says *Southern 'n Sassy*. She's barefoot, and her toenails are painted light blue. I hand her the Walmart bags with Caleb's new clothes in them.

"Shoot, did you buy out the store?" she asks.

"Not hardly," Caleb says. "If you bought out Walmart's, you'd have to bring everything home in a hundred eighteen wheelers."

"That's probably true, buddy," Tiff says and grabs Caleb in a little half hug. Caleb isn't crazy about Tiff the way he's crazy about Mommy, but he likes her. He says she's pretty and nice, which is true.

"Thanks for bringing him home, Kody," Tiff says. "You wanna come in and get you a Mountain Dew or something?"

"I'm good," I say. "If I'm out too long with the car, Nanny'll have a conniption fit."

Jay appears in the doorway. He looks a lot like Mommy around the eyes, but where she's super skinny, he's pretty well-padded around the middle. "Your nanny was the same way when I was your age," he says. "Say, you missed deer season again, but next time it rolls around, I'm gonna get onto you about going out with me and Caleb."

"Just keep asking me," I say. "One day I might take a notion to do it."

I'll never take a notion to go out in the cold at the crack of dawn to murder one of God's beautiful creatures, but if I sound agreeable, it'll shut Jay up.

"Hey, have you seen your mommy?" Jay asks.

"We had lunch with her at Nanny's today," Caleb says.

Jay meets my eyes. "How did she look?"

I mouth the word "bad," then say, "She was begging at the interstate exit again."

"Did she eat anything at lunch?" Jay asks.

"A little. A few potato chips."

"Okay. Well."

I understand why these are the only words he can come up with. With Mommy's problems it's like there's so much to say but nothing more to say at the same time. Between driving her to the Christian counseling center and doctor's appointments and watching her like a hawk, we've tried all we know how to try. If we had more money it might be different, but we don't. What good does talking about it do?

"I'd better get going," I say.

I have one more stop to make before I go home, but it's a secret. Soon I'm back at the spot where we found Mommy this afternoon. I pull into the Walmart parking lot.

A lot of the time when I do my secret shopping, I don't even look that carefully as I make my selection. The most important thing is to grab the stuff and get out of the aisle before anybody sees me. I go to the self-checkout because automated cash registers don't ask questions.

Once I'm back in the car, I actually look at what I've bought—a tube of lipstick called Plum Passion, some eyeshadow that looks like glittery copper, and a mascara that promises lashes that will be "chunky, not clumpy." I gaze on the items' beauty for a moment and feel a little rush of bliss.

But I know what I have to do. I take all the items out of their packaging and stuff them into my jeans pockets. I put all the packaging and the receipt in the Walmart bag and throw it in the nearest trash can.

Why does my secret shopping make me feel better? Maybe it's a reminder that there's beauty in the world because there's beauty in my pockets.

There's beauty around me, too, but the mountains are scarred up from mining like a beautiful woman with a black eye from a beating. The winding country roads are beautiful, too, but they're often cluttered with trash.

Which reminds me. There's a big bag of dog food in the trunk of the car. I pull over at the place in the road where I saw the dog snuffling around in the garbage. There's no sign of him now. I call "here, boy" a few times. I hear some rustling in the woods, but he doesn't come out. I open the trunk of the car and reach into my pocket for my pocketknife. I pull out the mascara on the first try but then find the knife. I cut open the top of the bag and dump a pile of dog food far enough away from the road that he can safely eat it.

I hope he comes back and finds it. I might not be able to save him, but at least I can help him hang on a little longer.

seventeen, I know it'd just about kill Nanny if I did the
[...]e. She was good enough to take me in when Mommy
[...]dn't take care of me, so I at least owe it to her to graduate
[...] high school.

[...]don't blame the kids who don't try, though. It's hard to
[...]here and know what you're trying for. There are no more
[...]-paying jobs. When Nanny talks about downtown
[...]an being busy, with a movie theater and a soda foun-
[...]and everybody coming to town with money in their
[...]ts from their good-paying jobs at the mines or the mill,
[...]e a fairy tale, just one more story from an old person
[...] the good old days.

[...]st of the mines have closed down, and the one big
[...]facturing plant we had here shut down here and moved
[...]xico. And no matter how excited those Future Farmers
[...]erica get, there's no real money in farming anymore.
[...]ok around to see what the grownups are doing, and it
[...] seem like you have much to look forward to. Will you
[...]get by drawing a little check from the government
[...]nonth? Will you put on an ugly blue vest and become a
[...]rt worker bee? Or will you be like my mommy, living
[...]gh to high instead of paycheck to paycheck?

[...]e find a way out. A few with enough money and enough
[...]o go to college. The ones who join the army and risk
[...]their asses shot off so they can see the world beyond
[...]nty. I probably don't have the brains and definitely
[...]ve the money for college, and I don't have the courage
[...]es to even make it through basic training.

[...]luate next year, and if anybody asked me what I'm
[...]do after high school, I would honestly say that I have
[...] Fortunately, nobody ever asks.

Chapter 2

MORGAN COUNTY HIGH IS FOR COUNTRY kids. Town kids
go to Morgan City Schools, so that's where you get the kids
of the doctors and the lawyers and the professors at Randall,
the local Baptist college. You wouldn't think people in a little
mountain town in Southeastern Kentucky would have anything to be snobby about, but the Morgan City School kids
think they're way better than the Morgan County ones.

The five hundred or so students at Morgan County
High are the kids of the miners or laid-off miners, the
sawmill workers, the farmers, the unemployed, the meth
cookers, and the "drawers" who eke by on a monthly government disability check. The upside of this student
population is that nobody's a snob about who wears what
or has what because none of us have much. The downside
is that if you're a boy who's not crazy for high school football or UK basketball and who doesn't dress in head-to-toe
camo on the first day of deer season, then you might as
well come to school in a strapless gown and a tiara.

But at least when I walk through the door on the first day
after winter break wearing my stiff new Walmart jeans, everybody else is wearing Walmart jeans, too.

I wander down the crowded halls towards homeroom, past clumps of football players, Future Farmers of America, cheerleaders, and tough girls. Like wolves, kids travel in packs. I tell myself I'm a lone wolf, not a solitary elk or bunny rabbit.

In home room, I exhale in relief when I see Lexy Jo, L.J. to her friends, who waves me over to the empty seat next to her. L.J. goes to my church and is super religious but in a way that's sweet, not scary. She looks like she always does—no makeup, her ash brown hair pulled back in a ponytail, wearing Mom jeans and a Christian t-shirt. This one says *Keep Calm and Pray*.

"Hey, you," I say.

Even though L.J. is sixteen like me, there's something comforting and old ladyish about her, like she's the world's youngest mamaw. Even her hugs feel grandmotherly. She's well-padded enough to feel extra comfy, and she always smells like talcum powder.

I pull out of the hug, sit at the desk next to her, and look around the room. Two giant Future Farmers of America are taking turns shoving each other in the chest, but they've got smiles on their faces, so it's not a fight. They're just too manly to hug, I reckon. A cloud formation is in the back of the room where a couple of skinny, pasty kids—the kind with sad little fuzz-'staches on their upper lips—are vaping. They're trying to be sneaky about it but failing.

"Looks like Haley Simmons has been putting on some weight," L.J. says.

Since L.J. isn't thin as a rail herself, it seems weird for her to call out another girl on her weight. I look over to where Haley's sitting and immediately see what L.J. means. Haley's wearing a baggy t-shirt to hide it, but there's no denying that she—as Nanny would say—has a bun in the oven.

"Bless her heart," I say. Haley's the sam when she had me.

"Maybe we can get some people at th baby clothes for her," L.J. says. "And m money to buy diapers. Them things is ex

That's what's so great about L.J. If sh trouble, she jumps right in to figuring o help. There are a lot of so-called Christ a lot from L.J.

"I wonder who the daddy is," L.J. say my business."

"I don't know. She might not know

L.J. play slaps my arm. "Kody, that's

"No judgment," I say. "I'm just sayi always liked the boys, and the boys hav

"All eyes on me!" says a booming n the room. It's balding, squatty Coac the psychology class I took last yea your schedules so everybody be qu name. After you get your schedule, l where you're supposed to be at. An till the bell rings."

Coach Braden's only teaching te A lot of other teachers here are the and the teachers here have a lot most don't. They're just putting retire, graduate, or drop out.

I'm not exactly setting the w point average, but I do try. In so subject's interesting. In most I tr to. Also, because Mommy drop

But I try in school anyway. Maybe I'm just trying to make Nanny proud by doing better than Mommy did, but that's setting the bar pretty low.

In the cafeteria, I sit down across from L.J. and unwrap my peanut butter and jelly sandwich. Nanny still packs me a sandwich and an apple every day just like she did when I was in kindergarten. I'm grateful. I can't even stand the smell of cafeteria food.

"How's it going so far?" I ask.

L.J. dips one of the cafeteria's mystery nuggets into a puddle of ketchup. "Algebra II like to killed me. And it's just the first day. Why do I need to know how to solve for x to be a children's worship leader?"

"Good question." I take a bite of my sandwich. "Unless you want to witness to the children using quadratic equations." L.J. wants to go to this Bible college in Tennessee once she graduates, but she'll need a full scholarship to pay for it.

"Believe me, I don't," she says. "Hey, I ran into Haley in the hall and told her I was praying for her, and you know what she said to me?"

I shake my head. Whatever Haley said, I know it wasn't good.

"She said, 'I don't need your judgment, church girl.' I told her I wasn't judging her. I was praying for her, and she said, 'Same difference.' I wanted to explain that it wasn't, but she just turned her back and walked away." L.J. dips another nugget. "It kinda hurt my feelings."

"Don't let it," I say. "She's got to be having a hard day feeling like everybody's eyes are on her and her big belly. I kinda like it that she called you 'church girl,' though. That could be your superhero name."

She grins a little. "What?"

"Church Girl! It's your superhero identity. You could wear a spandex outfit with a flouncy skirt and a big cross on your chest. You could carry a King James Version and Bible Blast bad guys until they'd pray for forgiveness."

L.J. smiles. "I can't decide if that's sacrilegious or not."

"How could Church Girl be sacrilegious? She's clothed in the Gospel Armor!"

She gives in and laughs. Sometimes I wonder why L.J. wants me for a friend, as different as we are. But then I remember I can always make her laugh.

* * *

THE BEST PART OF MY DAY is always between 4 and 6 p.m. Nanny doesn't get home from work until 6:15, so once the school bus drops me at the head of the holler, I have two hours of glorious privacy. Sometimes thinking about having this time ahead of me is the only thing that gets me through the school day.

After I greet the dogs and put down my school stuff, I get a glass of juice from the fridge and a cookie or two from the cookie jar, then go straight to my room. I put a Dolly album on the stereo—today it's *The Best Of*—and turn it up so loud the neighbors would complain if we had any neighbors. Our closest neighbors are a pasture full of Hereford cattle, and I know in my heart that they love Dolly as much as I do.

Once my soundtrack is going, I get my secret box from under my bed. I shuck off my ugly Walmart clothes, including my socks and underwear, and take the first item out of the box, a butter yellow satin kimono embroidered with butterflies. Butterflies are Dolly's favorite, so I was excited when I found the kimono at Goodwill one day when

Nanny let me take the car out. Then I take the other items out of the box and arrange them on my dresser: foundation, blush, eyeshadow, eyeliner, mascara, powder, half a dozen shades of lipstick, and a cheap wig that's really more yellow than blonde (I bought it on clearance at Walmart after Halloween).

While Dolly sings, I paint.

I don't have much in the way of facial hair yet, so a thin coat of foundation is enough to make my complexion smooth and even. I brush on some blush to highlight my cheekbones, then take my time with the eyeliner because it's the easiest thing to mess up. I make my eyelids and brow line smoky with eyeshadow and brush on some mascara in "noir" which sounds so much more chic than "black." I go with my new plum lipstick since I haven't had the chance to try it out yet. I put on the yellow wig and try to brush and fluff the cheap synthetic "hair."

At first when I look at the full effect in the mirror, I can only see what's wrong with it. The wig is awful. If I had a bra, I could stuff it, but as it is, I'm flat as an ironing board and so couldn't be more unlike Dolly in that department.

But after I stop seeing what isn't there, I start seeing what is: I've gotten better at makeup, and my face looks—even though I feel a little conceited saying it—pretty. The kimono is no substitute for a real gown, but it does look like something Dolly might wear in the dressing room, and the satin feels so much better against my skin than the cheap, stiff fabric of my Walmart clothes.

I feel the best I've felt all day.

Why? I don't know. I don't think it's a sex thing, exactly, though I feel like I look sexy. And it's not that I want to be a girl all the time. It's more like I have this beautiful little yellow canary inside me that I have to keep locked in a covered cage all day when I'm around other people, and this is the only time of day I can uncover the cage, unlock the door, and let her sing and fly free.

Most of the time, she sings in Dolly's voice. I stand in front of the mirror, moving my lips to the words of "Jolene." I don't just flap my lips either; I move them and my tongue so each syllable looks like I'm the one doing the singing. I keep an open, pleasant look on my face like Dolly wears when she sings.

I don't move my body too much, but that's okay because country divas don't tend to dance. They may pace or tap a foot or make an occasional dramatic hand gesture, but they don't dance like pop stars do. The only country divas I can think of who ever danced much are Tanya Tucker and Shania Twain. Nanny says it's because they're both whores, but I think that's a little too harsh.

I "perform" my way through Side A, then flip the record. It's hard to explain how good I feel in front of the mirror in my makeup, feeling like I'm inside Dolly's songs, inside her spirit. Somehow when I'm pretending to be Dolly I feel most like I'm being me even though this probably doesn't make any sense. It's the one time of day when I'm 100% doing what I want to be doing.

When the last song on Side B fades out, I hear the phone in the kitchen ringing. I usually don't leave my room during Dolly Dress-Up Hour, but I run to answer it.

"Hello?" I say, smoothing my kimono where it's gapping.

"Kody, is that you?" It's Mommy. Her voice sounds scratchy and far away, like she's calling from another country instead of the same holler.

"What other guy would be answering the phone at Nanny's house? It ain't like she's got a secret boyfriend."

"I've been calling and calling. Where have you been?"

"I've been right here. I just had my music turned up loud. I'm sorry—"

"Kody, I'm sick. Real sick."

I switch to emergency mode. "Do you need to go to the hospital?"

"No. No hospitals."

If she went to the hospital they'd drug test her.

The selfish part of me wants to stay here and do Dolly, but I hear my conscience saying, "Mommy, do you want me to come out there and check on you?"

"Uh-huh."

I look down at my yellow kimono. No way I'm walking up the holler in it. "I was just about to get in the shower right quick. Give me fifteen minutes, and I'll be there. Will you be okay for that long?"

She doesn't answer, which worries me a little. Finally, she says, "I think so."

I jump into the shower long enough to wash off the makeup. I put on a clean change of boy clothes and put all my Dolly things back into their box and slide the box under my bed. I write a little note to Nanny so she'll know where I am and leave it on the kitchen counter.

I walk down the holler with Loretta and Tammy trailing behind me. I walk past the field of Dolly-loving cows and past an old, abandoned church I've always thought was spooky. It used to be white but has faded to a dirty gray. There are a couple of nice houses—one belongs to the family who owns the cows—but the deeper you get into the holler, the sorrier looking it gets. There are old trailers with car parts scattered in the front yard and cages of fighting roosters in the back. One trailer has a mean dog chained to a tree. I'd be mean if I was chained to a tree all the time, too. Loretta and Tammy bark at him because they know that no matter how mad he gets, his chain's too short to reach them.

Back when Mommy's trailer belonged to Nanny, it looked as nice as a trailer can look. Nanny planted flowers around it, and it had a nice porch Uncle Jay built for it. Now it looks beat up and run down, and instead of a porch there's just concrete blocks stacked up to serve as steps to the door.

I knock, and when there's no answer I just push the door open. The smell of cigarettes, rotting food, and stale beer hits my nose and goes straight to my gut. Some of the beer smell comes from the carpet which is stained and matted from spills and which never gets vacuumed. The coffee table is cluttered with empty beer and soda cans and an overflowing ashtray.

Mommy is laying on the old green couch that belonged to Nanny in better days. She doesn't even seem to notice me.

"Hey, Mommy," I say.

"Kody," she says, barely above a whisper. "You came."

"I did." She's taking up the whole couch and there's no place else to sit so I stand. "So is this sick like a stomach bug or a cold, or are you just dopesick?"

Mommy rubs her eyes. "I ain't had my medicine in a couple of days, but when I get some, I'll feel better."

"Dopesick then," I say. "Listen, I'm gonna start out by getting you a glass of water. You can never go wrong with a glass of water."

The kitchen is a nightmare. A half-empty package of moldy bologna sits next to a bunch more empty beer and soda cans. The sink is piled with crusty dishes, and the garbage can is overflowing and swarming with flies. I find a box of paper cups in a cabinet and grab one since at least I know it's clean. I fill the cup with tap water and take it to Mommy. She drinks in tiny, birdlike sips.

I reach in my pocket and pull out a tube of Chapstick. "Here, use this."

"You've taken to carrying lipstick?"

"It ain't lipstick," I say, hoping I got all the plum shade off my lips in the shower. "It's lip balm for your chapped lips."

She takes it, rubs it over her mouth, and tries to hand it back to me.

"Keep it and use it. I've got more at the house. Now when was the last time you had something to eat?"

Mommy knits her brow like I've just asked her a hard question. "Yesterday maybe?"

I feel sorry for her and mad at her at the same time. "You've got to eat every day, Mommy. I'm gonna fix you something."

"I don't think I can eat nothing, Kody."

"Well, you're gonna try to."

I go back to the nasty kitchen and find a can of Campbell's soup Nanny must've got the last time she bought Mommy groceries. There's a saucepan crusted with old Spaghetti-O's in the sink. I scrub it and rinse it and get the soup heating on the stove.

Mommy wasn't always like this. She was in a bad wreck when I was real little. I was in the wreck too, but I was in my safety seat and came out without a scratch. Mommy had to have stitches in her forehead, and she hurt her neck and shoulder real bad. That was how she started using the pain pills. They really were medicine back then.

I stir the soup and wash a bowl and a spoon. The kitchen table's too messy to eat off of, so I take the bowl to Mommy in the living room. "Chicken noodle soup," I say in this fake cheerful voice I get sometimes when I'm taking care of Mommy. "Best thing for a sick person."

"Thank you, baby." She grabs my arm as I try to hand her the bowl. "I'm proud of you, you know that? You're such a good boy."

"Thank you, Mommy." I wonder if she'd think I was a good boy if she knew I'd been prancing around in a lady's kimono and makeup when she called me. Not that Mommy's in any position to judge anybody. "Try to eat some soup now, okay?"

She holds the bowl in her lap and brings the spoon to her mouth with a shaky hand. As soon as she swallows, she gags.

I tense up, afraid she's going to vomit. There's nothing I hate worse than cleaning up vomit.

But instead, she takes a deep breath, looks down at the bowl, and says, "I don't think I can do this." It's like I've given her an impossible task, like moving a mountain.

"Here." I take the bowl. "Let's try this a different way." I take the bowl into the kitchen, wash a stained coffee mug, and pour the soup into it. "Here," I say. "Just sip the broth. Go real slow."

She holds the mug in both hands and takes a tiny sip. "Better," she says.

"Good," I say. "Try to drink all the broth even if you can't eat the noodles. You wanna watch TV?"

She nods.

I grab the remote from between the empty beer cans and turn on the TV. I flip past talk shows and infomercials and find a rerun of *The Andy Griffith Show*. The town in the show,

Mayberry, North Carolina, is a happy place. Everybody has a job who wants one. There's Floyd the barber and Helen Crump the teacher and Gomer Pyle who runs the gas station. Even bumbling Barney Fife gets to be the deputy sheriff, even though he probably shouldn't be. The only addict in Mayberry is Otis, the town drunk who locks himself in jail to sleep it off when he's had a few too many. Andy's son, Opie, doesn't have a mom, but he gets lots of love and lessons from his daddy and his Aunt Bea. There are no problems in Mayberry that can't be solved in thirty minutes (including commercial breaks) with Sheriff Andy's homespun wisdom.

Mommy has finished the broth and lights a cigarette. Her phone rings, and she lunges for it. "Yeah?" she says. "When? How much?"

We're a long way from Mayberry.

Chapter 3

ON WEDNESDAYS, NANNY COMES HOME AN hour early and we go downtown to the public library. It's something we've done every week since I was little. Nanny always checks out any new inspirational romance and craft books they've got. Me, I've read and reread all the country diva autobiographies—Loretta Lynn's *Coal Miner's Daughter,* Tanya Tucker's *Nickel Dreams,* and especially Dolly's *My Life and Other Unfinished Business.* I've read that one at least a dozen times. I've checked it out so much that the librarian always says, "This one again?"

The other thing I love about going to the library is getting to use the computers. You only get to use them thirty minutes at a time, but I know how to make the most of my minutes, checking different social media for news stories about Dolly and looking up ideas for sewing or craft projects me and Nanny could do together. I guess I use the internet like an old lady, but I do what makes me happy.

And for the record, the actual old lady in the family doesn't use the internet at all. She says she doesn't want the government spying on her more than it already does. I say if the government wants to know about my searches for needlepoint patterns and Dolly Parton news, they're welcome to them.

Once we get to the Morgan County Library, I leave Nanny to browse the inspirational romances. Honestly, I can't think of a more boring kind of book—she's particularly stuck on a series about Amish people, who aren't exactly famous for their wild passion—but each to their own.

I go to the computer station and log on for my weekly half hour of living in the modern world. Googling Dolly doesn't pull up any interesting new results, so I hop over to Facebook. There probably won't be much doing there either. My list of friends is pitifully short: L.J., Uncle Jay and Aunt Tiff, about half a dozen people from church, and a few of my old elementary school teachers. Usually it doesn't get much more exciting than Mrs. Harris from fourth grade posting an "easy and yummy" recipe for hash brown casserole.

When I log on, I notice it says I have a message, which hardly ever happens. It'll probably be one of those messages people send out to everybody on their list, something like "Pass this hug to all your friends, or you will die painfully and soon."

When I check the message it comes with a friend request from somebody I've never heard of. I accept the request and open the message:

Hi, Dakotah,

I know this is weird, but I need to ask you a question. Is your mom named Amanda Prewitt? I'm asking because I think I might be your sister. Sorry to bother you but do write me back if you can.

Macey Stewart

I put both hands over my mouth to trap whatever sound might come out. I feel like the whole world has shifted, like when I stand up there won't be solid ground under my feet anymore.

Of course it's not true. It must be some other Dakotah
Prewitt she's looking for. She knew my mother's name is
Amanda, but surely there are other Dakotah Prewitts with
moms named Amanda. The year Mommy was born, Amanda
was the most popular baby name in the country. I tell myself
all this, but my hand is still shaking when I click on Macey
Stewart's name to pull up her page.

The first thing I have to say about her is that she's beautiful—
glossy black hair and hazel eyes with just enough mascara to
make them pop. The picture is just her head and shoulders but
she looks to be petite. If I was a girl, I'd be very happy if I looked
like Macey Stewart.

But here's the second thing about her. She's not white. So
she's definitely not my sister.

This isn't something to be proud of, but Morgan County,
Kentucky, is about as white as the inside of a mayonnaise jar.
There are students of different races and from different
countries who go to Randall College and live on campus, but
when you're talking about the real population, there are just
four Black families in Morgan, and they live in town and
send their kids to the city schools. Morgan County High
School has an all-white population.

I guess what I'm trying to get at is that having this girl who
is also Black say she's my sister is kind of a shock on top of a
shock. How could it be true?

I look at her profile. She's two years younger than me and a
freshman at Central High School in Knoxville, where she's on
the dance team. She has two pretty cats she likes to post pictures
of. She likes something called anime. She seems nice enough.

I figure I might as well go ahead and clear up the misunderstanding. My time on the computer is almost up, so I

type, *Hi. Yes, my mom is named Amanda Prewitt but I don't think I'm who you're looking for. Good luck.*

I just manage to send it and log off. For a minute I sit there stupidly staring at the screen that says my session has expired.

In the car Nanny's in a good mood because she managed to score not one but two romances with women in bonnets on the cover, but I'm a million miles away. I think about telling Nanny about the Facebook message but decide against it. It can't be true, but it would still get Nanny thinking about Mommy's poor choices which she spends too much time doing anyway.

"Kody?"

"Huh?" I'm startled, like if a teacher called on me when I'd just dozed off in class.

"I was asking," Nanny says, "if you want to pick up a pizza to take home for supper."

"Sure, okay."

"Are you feeling all right?"

Usually I'm super excited when Nanny offers to spring for pizza. I'd better snap out of it or she'll start grilling me about what's wrong. "I'm fine, Nanny. Just tired. A pizza would be great."

Back at the house we get paper plates and plastic cups of Pepsi and eat our pepperoni pizza on the couch watching a rerun of *The Golden Girls.* The pizza is good and gooey, and the show is Nanny's and my favorite, but even when Blanche says something trampy, then Rose says something stupid, my mind wanders back to the mystery of Macey.

I try to put the pictures I saw of her together in my mind— her looking natural outdoors in her profile picture, her looking glam in dramatic makeup and a sparkly leotard in her school's gym. Her complexion isn't dark, just a shade past tan. I wonder if she could have one Black parent and one white parent.

And if she did, could the white parent be Mommy?

But Mommy has never lived outside of Morgan. Where would she find a Black guy to run around with? And Macey's fifteen. Mommy was still with the man who passes as my father fifteen years ago. And how come Macey is all the way in Knoxville? None of it makes any sense.

When the credits are rolling to the tune of "Thank You for Being a Friend," Nanny says, "I can't believe what they got by with saying on television."

"It's because they were old ladies," I say. "When they said it, it was cute."

Nanny smiles. "So if I said dirty stuff would it be cute?"

"You're not old enough yet. Give it ten more years." It's unthinkable that anything less than G-rated would ever come out of Nanny's mouth. When she's frustrated, instead of cussing, she says, "Oh, foot."

"What do you reckon Pastor would say if I started talking thataway?"

"He would wash your mouth out with soap."

"You wanna work on our quilt for a while?"

"Sure." Sewing soothes me, and this weird message has me all confused and nervous. It will feel good to concentrate on stitching straight lines, on making all the pieces fit together.

* * *

ON THE SCHOOL BUS, I WAIT until we're close enough to town to get a signal and take out my crappy little phone. Getting to Facebook is slow and clunky and frustrating, but I finally manage to log in and click on my messages. I read:

Ok, I think I'm your sister. Well, half-sister. My dad was Calvin Stewart. He died when I was a baby and his sister adopted me. I'd like to know more about my mom—and you, too. Can I call you?

It's hard to message back with the bus barreling over pot-holes, but I finally manage to write

606/531-1537. Call M-F between 4 p.m. and 6 p.m. ONLY.

* * *

"ARE YOU OKAY, SWEETIE?" L.J. ASKS me in homeroom. She's wearing a t-shirt that says *Up, Dressed, and Blessed.* One of these days I'm going to have to ask her where she buys these things.

"Yeah, just tired. And worried about Mommy. You know." This isn't technically a lie. I'm always worried about Mommy. Right now, though, I'm also worried that Mommy might have given birth to and given away a sister I didn't know I had.

L.J. reaches out and touches my arm. "I pray for her every single night."

"I know you do. I appreciate it."

"Hey, listen," L.J. says, brightening. "I was wondering if you want to come over Saturday night and help make stuff for the youth group bake sale. Momma got stuff to make brownies and chocolate chip cookies and Rice Krispies Treats. We can sample some of what we make." She grins. "You know, just to make sure it's good enough to sell."

This is absolutely as naughty as L.J. gets. Eating a couple of the brownies she's making for the church bake sale.

"Sounds fun," I say. "And fattening. I'll ask Nanny."

"If you was a girl we could bake and have a sleepover," L.J. says. "But I don't reckon it'd be right since you're a boy."

"Well, I don't see anything wrong with it, but I'm guessing your daddy might."

L.J. giggles. "Yeah, he would. There's no 'might' to it." L.J. wears a silver purity ring her daddy gave her as a pledge that she'll stay pure until marriage.

Not that I'd be any danger to L.J.'s purity. I could sleep in the bed right next to her, and she'd be safer than if she was cuddled up next to a housecat. I love L.J., but not the way a regular boy loves a girl.

Of course, if L.J.'s daddy thought too hard about the ways I'm not a regular boy, he might not want me hanging out around his daughter either.

The day crawls by, and I try to pay attention in class, but most of the time I'm thinking, will she call today? Tomorrow? Next week? What will she say? What will I say? I'm a nervous wreck thinking about it. Even though it pains me, I decide I'd better not do my Dolly Dress-Up Hour until I've had my phone call with Macey. I don't want to get all Dollied up, then have to hurry to get off the phone and shower before Nanny gets home.

One secret at a time.

Back at the house, I don't know what to do with myself. I stare at the phone like I can shoot lasers out of my eyes that will make it ring. I can't put on Dolly because then I might not be able to hear the phone. I can't do needlepoint because my hands are shaking too hard. I think about turning on the TV, but the show choices at 4 p.m. are pretty grim and I don't think there's anything that could hold my attention. And so I sit on the couch with my spine straight and my hands in my lap like I'm in a pew at church.

When the phone does ring, it's kind of like a jack in the box. When you turn the crank, you know it's only a matter of time until the puppet jumps out, but when it happens, it scares the living daylights out of you anyway.

I don't want to answer on the first ring. It feels too desperate, so I wait until the third even though it just about kills me. With my luck, it'll be a telemarketer and I will have gotten myself all wound up over nothing.

I take a deep breath, then say, "Hello?"

"May I speak to Dakotah, please?" The voice is crisp and light. The pace is unhurried Southern, but the accent isn't twangy like mine.

"This is he." Because she lives in a city, I'm trying to sound proper so she doesn't think I'm a total hillbilly, even if I am.

"Dakotah, this is Macey." She sounds happy to be talking to me.

"I know," I say. "You can call me Kody."

"I don't guess we need to be all formal since we're brother and sister," she says.

"Are you sure we really are? I mean, I ain't calling you a liar or nothing,"—so much for sounding proper—"I'm just still pretty shocked is all."

"Yeah, me too. Auntie Diane's told me stories about my dad my whole life. But when I asked about my mom, she'd say she didn't know her well, or she'd say, 'Besides, aren't I your mom now?' like she was hurt I was even asking. And Auntie is my mom in all the most important ways. But I'm still curious, you know?"

"Mommy's story's not a very pretty one to tell," I say.

"Auntie said she has problems with drugs."

"Oh, she don't have problems with drugs—she loves them!" I'm relieved to hear Macey laugh at my bad joke. "But she has problems with every other part of her life because she loves drugs so much. She can't hold a job, can't pay her bills, can't raise her kids." A thought occurs to me. "Hey, you know I—I mean, we—we've got a little brother, right?"

"No! Auntie didn't say anything about him, but she may not know herself. How old is he?"

"Caleb is nine. Mommy got pregnant with him during one of my dad's in-between jail sentences. Caleb's sweet as can be, but Mommy was using when she got pregnant with him. He had to stay in the hospital a real long time after he was born, and he's always getting in trouble in school because he can't sit still and pay attention."

"That sounds like me when I was little," Macey says. "Wow. Two brothers."

"Wow. One sister," I say, and she laughs. She has a pretty, bubbly laugh.

"So Kody, what are you like? I mean, what kind of things do you like?"

"Well, I love Dolly Parton."

"Well, here in East Tennessee, just about everybody's a Dolly fan. And Dollywood's just up the road in Pigeon Forge. Have you ever been?"

"No. I've always wanted to."

It's an understatement to say I've always wanted to go to Dollywood. Seeing it is my biggest dream, maybe my only dream. Most people I know who have been there talk about the big roller coasters, but for me, it's not about the rides. It's about Dolly. Dollywood is Dolly's vision. It has a replica of her childhood home, a museum of her memorabilia, performers and craftspeople, and her music playing everywhere. All kinds of people come from all over the world to see it, and all of them are welcome because Dolly accepts everybody. I feel like Dollywood is a little like how the world would be if Dolly was in charge. And wouldn't the world be better if she was?

But even though Dolly's theme park is just two and a half hours down the road, it's expensive—two weeks' worth of groceries just to pay for the tickets, and then we'd also have to pay for the gas to get there and back and the food we'd eat on the trip.

We've gotten pretty close to going a couple of times. The first time a belt broke in Nanny's car, and we had to use the money we'd saved for Dollywood to get the car fixed. The second time Mommy got busted for a DUI and possession and we had to use our saved money to pay her bail. That was on my birthday, and I have to admit that a little voice from the worst, ugliest place in my heart kept saying, *Let her stay in jail so you can go to Dollywood.* But we bailed her out, of course.

"Dollywood's pretty fun," Macey says. "There are some good rides. I like the roller coasters. Besides Dolly Parton, what else do you like, Kody?"

It's a simple question, but it's a hard one, too. I don't really know what I like. I mean, I know some things, but I've barely been out of the county so there are lots of things I haven't experienced yet. "Well, I like needlework. Sewing and needlepoint and crochet. Nanny and me are working on piecing a quilt in the evenings."

"That's super old-fashioned . . . like pioneer days! I think it's cool, though."

"Yeah, I guess being raised by Nanny has made me like some older stuff . . . not that she was around in pioneer days!"

Macey laughs.

"Oh, and I like animals," I say. "Nanny and me rescue dogs people have dumped on the side of the road. Right now we've got four."

"Four's a lot! We've got a dog and two cats, though, so I can't judge."

"We'd rescue cats off the side of the road, too, but they're too hard to catch. We leave food for them, though. So . . . I guess that's what I like." Funny, I never knew I was such a boring person until I started talking about myself. "How about you? What do you like?"

"Hmm . . . I like dance, and I like cats. Oh, and also coffee."

"You don't make your cats drink coffee, do you?"

Macey laughs again. "No."

"Good. Cats and caffeine don't mix."

We're quiet for what feels like a while even though it's probably only a couple of seconds, then Macey says, "I want to meet you, Kody."

My stomach does a flip-flop. "I want to meet you, too."

"I can't drive yet. Can you?"

"I can, but I don't have my own car."

"Hmm. Do you think you could borrow your nanny's car and drive to Knoxville one Saturday?"

She might as well have said, "Do you think you could sprout wings and fly to Knoxville?"

The complications are overwhelming. I haven't figured out when I want to tell Nanny I know about Macey because obviously if Nanny had wanted me to know about her, she would've told me by now. And then there's the fact that Nanny won't let me borrow her car to go further than five miles down the road. So what do I ask her? *Hey, Nanny, can I drive your car to another state for a secret meeting with somebody I can't tell you about?*

Somehow, I think she might get a little suspicious.

I don't know what else to say at this point, so I just say, "I'll see what I can do."

"That would be awesome!" Macey says.

I guess to make this work I'll have come up with a lie to tell Nanny, and I'm a terrible liar. I get so flustered and over-heated it's like my pants are going to literally catch fire.

"Listen, I've got to go to my jazz class in a few minutes," Macey says. "Let's talk again soon, okay?"

"Any weekday but Wednesday between four and six," I say. I reckon I can turn Dolly down low enough that I can hear the phone ring.

"Okay. And Kody?"

"Yeah?"

"I like you."

I feel my mouth spread into a grin. "I like you, too."

"Bye."

People don't say that to each other much—*I like you*. Maybe they should.

Chapter 4

BEFORE MACEY FELL INTO MY LIFE, I only had two secrets
from Nanny. One is Dolly Parton Dress-Up Hour. The other,
which is kind of related to the first, is that I like boys. I mean,
don't get me wrong, I love women. They're strong and smart
and beautiful, and when I think of my heroes, they're all
women, from Dolly Parton to Wonder Woman to Nanny.

But when I think of somebody *that way*, it's always a boy. A
hypothetical boy. Maybe one I've seen on TV or in a magazine, but most often it's just one I've dreamed up in my head.

None of the deer hunting, underage drinking, ATV
riding boys at Morgan County High are my type, and I'm
sure as shooting not theirs either. Since there are no boys
in the present, just thoughts of a future boy, I figure
there's no reason to tell Nanny about myself yet. She'd just
cry and pray and worry, and Lord knows she's already got
plenty to pray and worry about.

If I find a real boy before Nanny dies of old age—Lord,
if I find a real boy before *I* die of old age!—then I'll tell
her, and I hope that even if she doesn't understand, she'll
still love me. Surely it won't be that much of a surprise. Do
you really expect your grandson who quilts with you and

watches *The Golden Girls* with you every night to marry a woman and have a passel of babies?

* * *

TALKING TO MACEY STIRRED UP ALL kinds of things in my mind—and pushed things I usually try not to think about right up to the surface. My brain feels like scrambled eggs. But driving helps settle my mind, and right now I'm about to drive over to L.J.'s to help her bake for the youth group sale.

"You call me if you're gonna be home later than eleven," Nanny says.

"I will."

"Lord, I'm gonna be so lonesome without you here I'm not gonna know what to do with myself."

Nanny and me depend on each other a lot. Maybe too much. But both of us lost my mommy to drugs, so that's just kind of what happened. We filled up that empty space with each other.

"You'll be fine," I say. "You can have a girl's night in. You can take a bubble bath and eat macaroni and cheese right out of the pan and watch some sappy movie on the Hallmark Channel."

Nanny smiles. "That don't sound half bad, actually."

The radio in Nanny's car is always tuned to the local gospel station that plays what I call Jumpin' Jesus music. I switch it over to the classic country station that comes in from Lexington. It's a little staticky, but I can still hear George and Tammy singing about how now that they live in a fancy two-story house, they're not in love anymore.

It seems like a lot of country songs are like this—they basically say you can either be dirt poor but in love or rich but lonely and heartbroken. I hope life isn't really like this. I mean, I'd choose love over money, of course, but it's hard because me and Nanny are always on the edge of being broke. By the end of the month, we're living off store-brand macaroni and cheese and Aunt Jemima pancake mix. Sure, I want love someday, but I also don't want the kind of worry that comes from being broke all the time.

L.J. and her family live in a little yellow house out in Amblyn. Amblyn isn't a town, really—just "a wide place in the road," Nanny calls it, with a post office and a gas station with a food mart. In Kentucky every little pig path like Amblyn has a name, even if it doesn't seem big enough to deserve one.

I knock on the door, and L.J. opens it, smiling. Her t-shirt today says *Blessed, Not Stressed.* "Hey, hon," she says, and I follow her inside. Her daddy is sitting in a recliner in the living room watching UK basketball. His gaze never leaves the screen. I don't believe L.J.'s daddy has said more than twenty words to me during all the years me and L.J. have been friends. I think this means he doesn't like me, but L.J. says he's just a quiet person.

L.J. talks enough to make up for anybody's quiet. "Momma had to take Dustin to his ball game, but she got us some sandwich stuff so we won't just be eating cookies and brownies all night." She grins. "But you know what? I'm still gonna eat cookies and brownies all night. I'll just eat me a sandwich first."

On the kitchen table is an extra-large loaf of white bread and a plate stacked high with bologna, pickle loaf, and American cheese singles. There's also a jar of Duke's mayonnaise, a squeeze bottle of yellow mustard, a family-size bag of potato chips, and a plastic tub of onion dip. It's enough to feed both the ball teams L.J.'s daddy is watching in the living room.

"Your momma went a little overboard, didn't she? How much does she think we can eat?"

"I'll make Daddy a sandwich, and Dustin'll be hungry when he gets home." Dustin is her little brother who's in middle school. "He's having some kind of crazy growth spurt right now and you can't keep him full. Daddy says trying to keep him fed is like throwing sand down a rat hole." L.J. reaches in a cabinet and pulls out a cast iron skillet. "I was thinking I might fry my baloney. You want yours fried too?"

"Sure. Thanks." I know bologna is awful—it's probably made of snouts and eyeballs—but there's something about frying it up so it's all greasy and black around the edges that I can't resist. It's in my hillbilly DNA.

I watch as L.J. drops four bologna slices in the pan and cuts a slit in each of them with the spatula so they won't curl up too much as they fry.

"You don't have to cook for me," I say.

"This ain't hardly cooking." She flips the meat slices. "Hey, I like to put a piece of cheese on top of the bologna while it's still in the pan and let it get all melty, kind of like a grilled cheese."

"Fancy."

"You wanna try it?"

"Sure."

She grabs four cheese singles off the plate and puts one on each slice of bologna. After the cheese melts, she puts two slices of bread on two paper plates and tops the bread with double decker bologna and cheese. "You want mayo?"

"Mustard."

She looks surprised. "I just learned something about you."

"That I like mustard on my fried baloney sandwiches?"

"Uh-huh."

"Well, that's some pretty top-secret information. I hope you don't use it against me."

L.J. laughs. "Well, I reckon you'll have to stay on my good side from now on just in case." She opens the fridge, which is covered in Jesus magnets and church bulletins. "We've got Pepsi, Mountain Dew, and cherry Kool-Aid."

"Kool-Aid, please."

We sit at the kitchen table with our warm fried bologna and crunchy chips to drag through creamy onion dip. Delicious.

"Kool-Aid always makes me think of Bible school," L.J. says, taking a sip.

"Me, too. They'd always give us those little paper cups filled with Kool-Aid that wasn't even cold along with two of the cheapest kind of cookies they sell at Walmart."

L.J. laughs. "But we always ate them."

"Of course we did. We were little kids. A cookie is a cookie."

"Hey, do you remember that really mean kid that was always at Bible school? He always complained he'd already heard all the stories and done all the crafts, and it turned out it was true because his parents sent him to every Bible school in the county just to get rid of him for a few hours."

"And I don't blame them! He was a nightmare. He bloodied my nose that one time." He also called me a sissy, but I don't want to talk about that.

"Yeah, and I held him down and sat on him till one of the teachers came. He wasn't no bigger than a minute."

"That was awesome. You were like a seven-year-old Wonder Woman."

L.J. and me have all these memories we share from the time we were old enough to start remembering. We're like brother and sister that way.

But then there's Macey, a blood sister I don't have any memories with at all. It's strange to think about.

"You okay?" L.J. asks. "You had a funny look on your face for a minute."

"Just remembering that bloody nose," I lie. "That kid didn't learn to punch like that in Vacation Bible School, that's for sure. He'll probably end up being one of those MMA fighters, and I'll be the one who gave him his start."

"I bet he ended up in Juvie," L.J. says.

"Well, that's probably more likely."

L.J. gets up to clear our plates. "Hey, I thought we'd start the brownies first, and then we can work on the Rice Krispies Treats on the stove while the brownies are in the oven."

And then we're breaking eggs and stirring ingredients and making a mess and laughing. Just like I'd hoped, having busy hands helps calm my mind down.

"Wanna put on some music?" L.J. asks. She's pouring the brownie batter into a baking pan.

"Sure," I say even though her taste in music and mine are way different. But I'm the weird one, I know that. Most high school kids consider songs that came out two years ago too old to listen to, and here I am, listening to music that came out years before my mommy was born.

The music L.J. puts on is the kind that sounds like pop music but is really about Jesus. If you don't listen to the words too carefully, the songs sound like love songs but then they'll say something like "You are my salvation" and you'll remember that the "you" in the song is supposed to be Jesus. Sometimes I wonder if the Christian pop bands tried to make it in regular music and couldn't, so they just changed their lyrics a little to be about Jesus instead of some girl. It might be mean of me to think that, but the music business is tough and people will do whatever they have to do to get a break.

L.J. is really rocking out to Jesus pop, not really dancing because dancing is vulgar, so she's just moving her lips to the music and kind of swaying. I wonder if she ever does this in front of her bedroom mirror like me doing Dolly. She sets a big pot on the eye of the stove. "You wanna stir the Rice Krispies Treats?" she asks.

"Sure."

She smiles. "Good. The stuff gets so thick and sticky my arm always gets tired stirring it. It's good to have somebody strong to do it."

I dump the jumbo bag of marshmallows into the pan, but not before I grab one for me to eat and one for L.J. "Yeah, it's good to have a man around the house to do your manly chores," I say. "Chopping firewood, home repairs, stirring Rice Krispies Treats."

L.J. laughs and measures out the Rice Krispies. "You're silly."

As the marshmallows melt and the mixture thickens, I begin to wonder if L.J. needs to find somebody with a manlier arm—a cowboy or lumberjack, maybe. "Lord, L.J., I'm afraid I'm ruining your pan."

"It's not burning. It'll be okay. Wait," she says. "We've got to do this. It's the best part." She grabs two big spoons and drags them through the hot cereal and marshmallow goo.

She hands me one and says, "Blow on it first so you don't burn your mouth."

It's like I can look into the future and see what a good mother L.J. will be. "Yes, Mom," I say. I blow on the spoon and then get a mouthful of the warm, crispy goo. "Yum."

"It really is the best part, isn't it?"

"It'd be the best part of just about anything."

"I reckon I'll get started on the chocolate chip cookies," L.J. says. "Your job is to keep me from eating all the raw dough."

I switch stirring arms since my right arm is about to fall off. "I might have to stop you by eating some of the dough myself. You know, I remember seeing on TV one time that the person who invented chocolate chip cookies was trying to make regular chocolate cookies but the chocolate didn't melt right."

L.J. smiles. "Happy little accidents."

"Bob Ross," I say, grinning back.

L.J. and Nanny and me all love Bob Ross, the painter who had a TV show on PBS in the eighties that still gets rerun. Bob Ross had a crazy white-guy Afro and was the most relaxed person you've ever seen. He always talked about "happy little accidents" when he'd mess something up but it turned out good anyway. Mommy watched Bob Ross with me and Nanny once and said he was high on weed.

But I think she was wrong. Bob Ross was high on life.

After all the goodies are baked and cooled and wrapped up to sell and all the dishes are washed, I say, "Well, I'd better head home. I told Nanny I'd be back by eleven."

"I'll walk you to the door," L.J. says.

After the hundreds of times I've visited her house, I know good and well where the door is, but L.J. would never dream of letting me walk to it by myself. Her politeness is one of the things I like about her.

At the door I say, "Thanks for having me over," and give her a hug. L.J. is a good hugger—not the kind of person who does the lean-forward-and-back-pat kind of thing. A few seconds into the hug, L.J.'s dad starts coughing in this loud, fake way, like he's impersonating a cat hacking up a hairball.

L.J. pulls away from me and whispers, "Daddy thinks our hug went on for too long."

"Oh, okay," I say, feeling confused. "Well, 'night."

Driving home, I wonder, does L.J.'s daddy really think that a boy who just spent three hours in the kitchen baking and giggling with his daughter could be a danger to her purity? It's weird what people notice. And what they don't.

* * *

NANNY AND ME ALWAYS EAT A cooked breakfast on Sunday. Part of the reason is that she actually has time to fix it unlike on weekdays when we usually just have a quick bowl of cereal. The other reason is that we know we're gonna be in church a long time, so we have to fuel up. This morning it's scrambled eggs and sausage and biscuits (out of a can but still pretty good) and orange juice for me, coffee for Nanny. Nanny would let me drink coffee if I wanted to but it's so bitter drinking it feels like a punishment.

"What time was you supposed to work the bake sale table?" Nanny asks, buttering a biscuit.

"Nine till nine forty-five, right before Sunday school."

"We're all right on time, then. I just need to fix my hair. We can let the breakfast dishes wait till we get back. They ain't going nowhere."

Sunday is also the only day Nanny and me get dressed up (Dolly Parton Dress-Up Hour doesn't count). For me, all that means is I put on my one pair of khakis and what Walmart sells that passes for a polo shirt. I've got three of these, so I can pick between navy, yellow, and white. Excitement.

Church is the only time Nanny wears a dress instead of a track suit. Her dresses always come down almost to her ankles because she thinks women should dress modestly in church. Today she's wearing her light-blue floral print dress with a dark-blue cardigan. The only thing that bothers me about her outfit is her shoes. They're blue flats that match her cardigan, but they look cheap. You can get by with buying clothes at Walmart and still look pretty okay, but cheap shoes always look cheap.

I don't know what I'll do for a living when I'm an adult, but I want to do something that pays me enough to buy brand-name shoes.

Even with the tacky shoes, though, Nanny cleans up good and is still a pretty lady. Her hair is a nice honey blonde, and unlike a lot of ladies her age, she doesn't carry too much extra weight. One time I asked her why she doesn't ever go on any dates since Papaw's been gone for such a long time, and she told me I was being foolish, that "all that" was over for her.

* * *

"Now which ones did you'uns make?" Mrs. Hatmaker, who works with Nanny at the uniform factory, is standing over the bake sale table in the church fellowship hall.

"The brownies and the Rice Krispies Treats and the chocolate chip cookies," L.J. says. She's also dressed up. Church is the one place she ditches the inspirational t-shirts for a sweater and skirt.

"Well, I'd better take two of each of them, then, since I know they'll be good."

"Thank you," L.J. and I both say.

"Now them cupcakes," Mrs. Hatmaker says, her lip curled, "is store-bought."

"Well, people do what they can, ma'am," L.J. says. "Not everybody has time to bake."

Mrs. Hatmaker hands me a few dollar bills. "Well, I reckon it's all right as long as you don't try to pass it off like you made 'em yourself." She leans forward and half whispers, "There's a certain person in the ladies' missionary group who brought Little Debbie's Swiss Cake Rolls to a meeting and said they was an old family recipe. She thought because she took them out of the wrappers and cut them up pretty we wouldn't know the difference."

After Mrs. Hatmaker has left, L.J. and me have fun talking about the Great Little Debbie Swiss Cake Roll Scandal.

* * *

THE TEEN SUNDAY SCHOOL CLASS IS real small because our church is mostly old people. There's L.J. and me and three other kids: Brianna, a thin, pale girl who's so shy it's almost painful to watch her; Tyler, a big farm boy who's always got mud or worse on his cowboy boots; and Colton, a big, tall kid who's on the Morgan County High School football team and basketball team. Tyler and Colton don't hang with each other much at school, but they're big buddies at church. They're not mean to me because it's church and we're brothers in Christ and all that, but they don't have much to say to me either.

I stick close to L.J., and we try to bring Brianna into our conversations as often as we can, but I think she wishes we wouldn't. When she answers one of our questions with a simple yes or no, she speaks so softly we have to lean in to hear her, and then our being physically closer to her seems to make her even more anxious.

Brother Mike, who's in his early twenties and has a grin like a thousand-watt lightbulb, grabs a folding chair, turns it around, and straddles it. He always sits like this, and even L.J., who never says anything bad about anybody, thinks it's weird. "Hey, little brothers and sisters," Brother Mike says. "Is there anything on your hearts that you want to share this morning?" He puts his hand over his own heart. "Anything weighing it down like lead or lifting it up like a balloon?"

Colton says, "We've got the big game against Morgan City this week, so I reckon that's kind of weighing on me."

"That is a big game," Brother Mike says. "Well, we'll pray that you and your teammates feel your best and play your best this week. We won't pray for you to win, though, because it ain't fair to ask the Lord to pick sides. Thank you for sharing, Colton." He flashes Colton his big grin.

We sit in awkward silence for a couple of minutes until Tyler finally says, "We had twin calves born last night, and both of them's doing good, so I reckon I'm grateful for that."

"We should always thank the Lord for new life and for the wonder of His creation," Brother Mike says. "Thank you, Tyler. Anybody else?"

Everybody knows good and well that we could sit here till the Rapture and Brianna wouldn't say anything, so it's up to L.J. and me. Finally, L.J. says, "Kody came over to my house last night to help me make stuff for the bake sale and we had a real good time and I'm thankful to the Lord for giving me a friend like Kody."

"Aww, L.J., I'm thankful for you, too," I say, giving her a little side hug.

"Thanks, Lexy Jo and Kody," Brother Mike says. "Now let's have a few moments of silent prayer so you can talk to the Lord about what's on your heart that you might not have wanted to talk about out loud." He looks right at Brianna as he says this, and her face turns tomato red.

I close my eyes and bow my head. I am thankful to have L.J. as a friend, but what's really on my heart is something that, like Brianna, I'm afraid to say out loud, so I try to talk to God in my head.

Dear Lord, thank you for bringing Macey into my life because I guess you were the one that led her to me. I want to get to know her and be a real brother to her, but right now I feel like I have to keep her a secret until I understand things better. And to get to meet her I'm going to have to lie to Nanny. There's a lot I don't tell Nanny, but there's a difference between just not telling somebody something and flat-out lying. Please forgive me for any lies I tell so I can meet Macey. I promise to make things right as soon as I can.

I hear people shifting in their seats. I open my eyes to see that everybody else is done praying, and all eyes are on me. "Um . . . amen?" I say.

Chapter 5

When I walk home from the bus stop, Mommy is in the front yard, throwing a Frisbee for Dolly, Loretta, and Tammy, who are racing each other to get it. George Jones stays on the porch.

Mommy's laughing, loose-limbed, and happy. She's high.

Well, what the h-e-double-hockey-sticks am I supposed to do? Not only is she interrupting my precious Dolly Dress-Up Hour, but Macey could call, and I can't talk to her with Mommy here.

She sees me, and her mouth spreads into a huge grin. "There's my big handsome boy!"

She runs over to hug me. She's barefoot, and her feet are dirty. It's not a warm day. Plus, I guess she walked the gravel road from her trailer to here barefoot. I guess as high as she is, it would've felt like walking on clouds.

The hug goes on a long time, and she leans on me so heavy I kind of have to brace myself.

"I thought I'd meet you when you got home from school," she says. "That's what mamas do, right? They're there when you get home from school, and they give you milk and cookies." Her expression darkens. "Oh, shit, I don't have no milk and cookies."

"Come on in. I bet we can find some," I say, taking her arm and leading her to the door. In my mind, I kiss Dolly Dress-Up Hour goodbye.

Mommy sits at the kitchen table, and I get out the milk and two glasses and a package of Oreos. I notice Mommy and me eat our Oreos the same way. We dip them in milk and hold them there till they're in danger of falling apart and then eat them all milky and soggy. It's like we have to drown them before we can eat them.

"God, I've not had Oreos in so long," Mommy says. "They're so good."

"I know. I try not to keep them in the house too much because I know I'll eat them, but Nanny bought these because they was on sale."

"You know what we ought to do after we have our after-school snack?" Mommy slaps the table. "We ought to go see Caleb."

"Well, Nanny's still at work with the car so we don't have a way to get there," I say. "Besides, he's probably at basketball practice or some other kind of practice."

Mommy grins. The Oreos have blackened her teeth. "He's such a little jock."

"At least you got one kid who is. If you throw a ball at me, I duck."

Mommy laughs. "Yeah, but you got the brains in the family."

"I get by," I say. I don't know why Mommy wants to cast me as some great genius just because I'm bad at sports. Probably because she's high.

The phone rings. I jump, but then I pretend to ignore it. What I want to do is shove Mommy out the door and then pick up the phone.

"Are you gonna get that?" Mommy says. She's eating too many Oreos. She must be hungry. I wonder if I should take the cookies away from her and make her a sandwich or something.

"No, probably just a telemarketer. If it's a real person, they'll leave a message." Unless it's Macey, who knows not to.

"It's probably a girl calling for you. Some poor girl whose heart you broke."

It's a weird thing to say. Unlike Nanny, Mommy has always known I'm not the straightest arrow in the quiver. "Mommy, you know I don't date girls."

"I do know," Mommy says. "And that's why you break their hearts. Because you're sweet and funny and smart and handsome, but they can't have you. That's how it always is with girls and gay boys like you." She shakes her head and laughs. "Lord, Nanny would shit a brick if she knew you was gay."

I feel a prickle of fear. "Which is why you can't tell her," I say. I honestly don't know what Nanny would do if she found out, but I do know that whatever it was, I wouldn't like it.

"I won't tell her," Mommy says, taking out a cigarette. "I've been keeping secrets from your nanny a lot longer than you have."

And from me, too. I think of Macey. How can you not tell your kids they have a sister? I know it was her that called just now, and it's driving me crazy I couldn't talk to her. "Wanna watch TV?" I ask because suddenly I can't sit here and look at Mommy anymore.

We watch a rerun of a show I liked as a kid, about a girl who has her own web show, and it's still pretty funny. The girl lives in a modern-looking apartment in the city, with red brick walls, and I wonder if that's what Macey's life is like.

Nanny comes in looking tired and carrying a plastic grocery bag. When she sees Mommy, a cloud of worry passes over her face. "Oh, hey. I didn't know you was coming over."

"I don't need an invitation to come over and see my big, good-looking son, do I?" Mommy says.

"You know you can come over any time you want to," Nanny says. "You want to stay for supper? I picked up stuff to make chili dogs."

"No, I already ate too many of them Oreos." Mommy reaches over and ruffles my hair. "Me and my boy had us an after-school snack. I wish Caleb could've been here, too. I feel like I ain't seen him in ever."

"Well, you know how busy he stays with his ball games," Nanny says, standing at the counter between the living room and the kitchen. She takes a package of hot dogs, a bag of buns, and a can of chili out of the plastic sack. "I'll get Jay on the phone directly and see if you can visit Caleb this weekend."

"That'd be great." Mommy gets up and hugs Nanny, who hugs her back but looks uncomfortable. Nanny has the most loving heart in the world, but she's not a huggy-kissy kind of person. It probably doesn't help that Mommy could use a shower, so her hugs smell like sweaty armpits.

After Mommy leaves, I help Nanny fix supper. There's not much to it, but I know she appreciates the gesture.

"You know," she says, dumping the chili out of the can and into a saucepan on the stove, "when your mommy's in a good mood like that, the first thing I think is well, good, she's happy. But then I remember she's happy because she's high."

* * *

ON THE WAY TO SCHOOL, AS soon as the bus is close enough to town that I can get a signal, I take out my sad little phone and text Macey.

> Me: Hey. Texting you from the school bus
>
> Macey: I'm on the bus too LOL
>
> Me: Did you call me yesterday?
>
> Macey: yes
>
> Me: I couldn't answer because my mom was there
>
> Macey: You mean OUR mom?
>
> Me: Weird but yeah
>
> Macey: Are you going to be able to come to Knoxville Sat.?
>
> Me: I'll try. I have to get the car.
>
> I hesitate on the next part because I don't want to sound like as much of a rube as I am, but I finally text: I'm a little nervous about driving in the city.
>
> Macey: There's a Starbucks the first exit into town. Why don't we meet there so you won't have to drive in city traffic?
>
> Me: ok
>
> Macey: 1:30?
>
> Me: If I can't make it, I'll let you know
>
> Macey: ok so excited!
>
> Me: me too bye

I go through the school day with a ball of nervousness in my stomach that feels as heavy as a bowling ball. It must be noticeable because L.J. asks more than once if I'm okay. I say it's just my usual worries about Mommy, but of course what I'm really worried about is what kind of story I can cook up to get Nanny to let me borrow the car on Saturday.

Nanny and me have just finished our supper of beans and cornbread, and we're sitting on the couch with the quilt we're piecing spread between us. Needlework with Nanny is always a peaceful time, so I figure it might be a good opportunity to ask about the car.

I take a deep breath. "Nanny, is there any way I could borrow the car on Saturday?"

She looks up from her sewing. "What for?"

I had hoped she wouldn't ask but knew that was unlikely. I look down at my quilting so I don't have to make eye contact. "There's a praise music group playing at a church over in Middletown, and L.J. wants to go see them real bad. Her mommy and daddy can't take her, so I thought I might could."

Nanny frowns. "All the way in Middletown?"

"Yes, ma'am." My heart is pounding so hard I'm sure Nanny can hear it.

"Is it of a night?"

"No, ma'am. It's in the afternoon. One o'clock."

Nanny sighs. "Well, I reckon it'll be all right if you're not driving in the dark. Jay and Tiff are bringing Caleb over here on Saturday to eat pizza and watch a movie with your mommy and me, so I won't need the car then." She looks at me hard. "But I want you back home before dark, you hear me?"

"Yes, ma'am."

It was easier than I thought. Now all I have to be nervous about is driving all the way to Knoxville and meeting Macey. Which is plenty.

Chapter 6

MY BELLY FEELS LIKE IT'S FULL of squirming snakes when I drive onto the ramp to get on the interstate. I've only driven on the interstate a couple of times, like for ten minutes when I was taking Drivers Ed with Coach Braden, who always seemed so scared, I figured he must have been forced to teach the class as some kind of punishment.

The eighteen wheelers are what scare me the most. They're so huge I keep imagining them squashing Nanny's little Ford Focus like a bug under a giant shoe.

Breathe, I tell myself. Just drive the speed limit and keep it between the lines. I put on the *Dolly's Greatest Hits* CD Nanny keeps for me in the car, and Dolly's voice soothes me. If she clawed herself from poverty to fame, then the least I can do is have the courage to drive to Knoxville on the interstate.

After a few songs and a few miles, I start to appreciate that the interstate is easier driving in some ways than the curvy country roads I'm used to. The lanes are wide and clearly marked, and there are no curves so sharp you have to put your foot on the brakes. After a few more songs and a few more miles, I'm feeling pretty comfortable.

When I cross the state line into Tennessee, I feel a little tingle of excitement. It's Dolly's home state for one thing, but it's also the fact that if I'm driving to another state myself, I must be having an adventure.

I've only been in Tennessee once before, to go with Nanny to take my great grandmother to a doctor's appointment. I was so little I can barely remember it. The only thing I do remember is that when the appointment was over, we stopped at McDonald's, and I got a Happy Meal. That was my one trip outside of Kentucky as a seasoned world traveler.

Dolly's Greatest Hits has played through three times by the time I get to the first Knoxville exit. The Starbucks is right where Macey said it would be. Once I pull into a parking space, my mind fills with everything that could go wrong with this meeting. What if she hates me? Talking on the phone is different than talking face to face. What if I embarrass myself because I don't know how to act in a place like this? Every question that pops into my mind starts and ends with something bad, and for a second I think about starting the car and booking it back to Kentucky.

But then I think about how Dolly was younger than me when she came to Knoxville to audition for *Cas Walker's Farm and Home Hour* TV show. She must've been scared, too, but she knew she couldn't pass up the opportunity.

Meeting Macey is an opportunity.

I check my hair in the rearview mirror, then get out of the car. Freshman year in English we had to write a descriptive essay that used all of our senses. Starbucks would be a good topic for an essay like that because as soon as I walk in, my senses are activated. There's the smell of the coffee, dark and earthy, and the whooshing sounds of all the fancy coffee machines that temporarily drown out the soft pop music that's playing. There's the colors, too, soothing browns and greens, and a display of baked goods much fancier than what L.J. and me made for the youth group bake sale.

Before I can take anything else in, a pair of arms wraps around me, and I'm smelling floral-scented shampoo. I hug back.

We pull out of the hug, and there's Macey, grinning all over herself. "You're Kody, right?" she says, then laughs.

"Who's Kody?" I say, then smile so she'll know I'm kidding.

She laughs more, then grabs my hand and holds it. "I should've asked before I hugged, but I'm just so excited."

"Me, too." As I say it, I realize a lot of my nerves were just excitement. I mean, since when have I been truly excited about something? I feel it so seldom I don't even recognize it.

But I'm feeling it now.

Macey is one of the prettiest girls I've ever seen in person. Her hair is black and curly and past her shoulders. It seems to float around her head like a cloud. Her complexion is perfect—unlike me, I bet she's never had a pimple in her life—and her eyes are hazel with green flecks and long, dark lashes. She isn't dressed up. She's just wearing jeans my nanny would say are too tight, a t-shirt that says Central High School Dance Team, and canvas slip-on shoes. But she still looks beautiful.

She pulls me by my hand. "Let's get our drinks so we can sit down and talk." She doesn't even look at the menu board, just tells the woman at the counter, "I'll have a Grande mocha with an extra pump of chocolate, please." She nudges me. "What do you want, Kody? My treat."

The menu board might as well be written in Russian for all the sense I can make of it, so I say, "I'll just have a tea."

"Tall or Grande?" the cashier asks.

"Uh . . . tall?"

"Iced or hot?"

"Hot."

The woman fires questions at me like a cop on a TV show interrogating a suspect. "Black or green?" she asks.

"Uh . . . black," I say, and then I feel my face heat up because both Macey and the cashier are Black, and saying "black" in front of them makes me afraid I might sound racist.

I really need to get out of the holler more.

There are two cozy armchairs in a corner, and Macey and me settle there with our drinks. She tucks her legs underneath her and looks as comfortable as if she was in her own house.

"Thanks for driving all this way," she says. "I haven't told Auntie I'm talking to you yet, but even if I did, I don't know if she'd be willing to drive to where you live. She says Kentucky's too full of bad memories about what happened to my dad." She reaches over and squeezes my hand. "I will tell her about you, though. I just need to wait for the right time. Besides, I'm terrible at keeping secrets." She takes a drink from her fancy coffee which leaves a cream mustache on her lip.

"Secrets are hard," I say. I should know.

"I don't know if Auntie's been keeping you a secret from me," Macey says. "She may not even know you exist. When I've asked her questions about where I came from, I guess she's told me what she thought I could handle depending on what age I was. Like, when I was little and I'd ask about my dad, she'd just say he died in an accident. She didn't say what kind, so I just assumed it was a car accident." She sips her coffee. "When I got old enough that we were getting anti-drug lectures in school, she told me what kind of accident it was."

"An overdose," I say.

She nods. "It's weird because he didn't seem like the druggy type. He grew up here and played high school football. He wanted more than anything to play for the University of Tennessee, just like every other high school football player in this state. He didn't get recruited by UT, but he got a full athletic scholarship to Randall College. It wasn't what he was hoping for, but at least he'd get to play ball and go to college for free."

I try to imagine my mess of a mother dating a college football player. Why would he date her when he could have any college girl he wanted?

"It's weird to think about him getting together with Mommy," I say. "I don't think she's ever set foot on a college campus."

"Yeah, well, I don't think that's where they met. See, my dad got hurt playing ball and had to have knee surgery. They gave him Oxycontin for the pain, and Auntie says things just went down from there. After he couldn't get it from doctors anymore, he started getting it from sketchy places."

"Which is where he met my mom." My tea is still too hot to drink, so I just hold the cup to have something to do with my hands. "That makes a lot more sense. It's not exactly one of those romances on the Hallmark Channel, is it?"

Macey smiles. "No. But you know what? I've got one picture of them together, and they actually look happy. It's probably because they're high, but it at least looks like they like each other." Macey digs through her purse and pulls out an old photograph.

I can see where Macey got her good looks. Her dad is gorgeous—tall and muscular, but with a sweet little boyish smile. In the picture he's sitting in a recliner, and Mommy's perched on the recliner's arm, leaning into him and smiling. It's strange to see Mommy without so many years of using behind her. She's a healthier weight, and her eyes aren't as sunken and empty. She has on a cute top, and her hair is clean. The photo could pass for a picture of a cute young couple on a date. Even though they're probably both high. Even though Mommy is cheating on my dad with Macey's dad.

"Wow," I say, handing the photo back. I can't make all the words that are racing through my head come out of my mouth.

"Weird, right?" Macey says, studying the photo. "I want to meet her."

"It'll make you sad."

Macey nods. "I know. I mean, I'm not thinking that I'll meet her and all of a sudden, she'll give up drugs and decide to be a real mom to me like in some stupid movie. But I'd like to talk to her. I'd like to hear any memories she might have of my dad."

"Some days she don't have memories of what she was doing five minutes ago," I say, then I realize I must sound terrible. "I mean, I love her, but she's a mess."

"I know. Auntie doesn't want me to meet her. She says I should just think of her as my mom, and I do. She's a great mom, but I guess I'd just like to see where I came from, you know?"

"So you can be thankful you got away?"

Macey grins. "Maybe so, yeah."

I finally take a sip of my tea. It's so strong you could trot a mouse across it. "Well, one thing that'll be good is you can meet Nanny. You know, there's been times when Mommy's dropped off the radar and not had any contact with Nanny and me. I figure that's what happened when she was pregnant with you. Nanny's gonna have a fit when she realizes she has a granddaughter, especially one as pretty and nice as you."

It's only when I finish talking that I see Macey is looking at me like I've been speaking a foreign language. I know I sound like a hillbilly, but hillbilly is a form of English, isn't it?

"Kody," she says finally, "your nanny knows she has a granddaughter."

"Wait . . . what?" Now I'm the one who's confused.

She reaches across the table and puts her hand on top of mine. "Your nanny knows I exist. She was there when I was born."

Suddenly I can't think straight. "That can't be right—"

Macey is looking me right in the eye. "Auntie says she would've fought for custody of me if she'd had to, but she didn't. Your nanny didn't want me. She didn't want to raise me, and she didn't want any kind of relationship with me."

There must be some misunderstanding. Maybe Macey's auntie and Nanny had a hard time communicating with each other. "But why wouldn't she at least want to have a relationship with you? Birthday cards, a phone call every once in a while—that kind of thing?"

"Kody." Macey's tone is firm, serious. She looks down where her hand is still holding mine. "What's the difference between your hand and mine?"

I'm not sure I'm ready to go where she's trying to take me. "Yours has got nail polish on it. I love that glittery teal, by the way."

Macey smiles a little. "Thanks. But you know what I'm saying, don't you?"

"I know what you're saying, but I think there must've been some kind of miscommunication. Nanny's a good Christian. She loves everybody."

I search my brain for evidence that Nanny is a racist. It's hard because we live in a county that's about 95% white, so I've not really gotten the chance to see her interact with people of other races. Our church is all white. The TV shows she watches are about white people, and the gospel music she listens to is by white people. But none of that means anything, does it?

"Okay," Macey says. "I probably shouldn't speculate about why she did what she did. But she does know I'm a person who exists. And she never told you about me."

My eyes are starting to get all misty. I don't want to cry in front of Macey, not the very first time we've met each other.

"I didn't mean to upset you," Macey says.

"You didn't. It's just a lot to take in, you know?"

"It is a LOT." Macey smiles. "But you know what the most important thing is?"

I shake my head. I don't feel like I know anything anymore.

"The most important thing is that we found each other and we like each other." She crinkles her nose. "Or at least I like you. You might drive all the way back to Kentucky thinking, I hate that girl."

"No!" I say loud enough that some businessman drinking coffee turns around and looks at me. I cover my mouth, embarrassed. "I like you, too," I say softly. "I think you're awesome."

"I think you're awesome, too," Macey says. "I think we should make a pact with each other."

Not for the first time in this conversation, I feel stupid. "I don't know what a pact is."

"Oh, it's like a promise. I think that since we've had so many secrets kept from us, we should make a promise never to keep secrets from each other. I'm talking total transparency."

Does this mean I have to tell her about Dolly Dress Up Hour? Maybe I only have to tell her if she asks me, and really, what are the chances she's going to say, *Kody, I just found myself wondering . . . do you ever put on makeup and a cheap wig and women's lingerie and prance around your room lip synching to Dolly Parton?*

"Total transparency," I repeat, imagining Macey being able to see through my skin to my bones and organs, my beating heart.

Macey holds up a pinkie. "Pinkie promise?"

I smile. I haven't made a pinkie promise since me and L.J. were in elementary school. "A pinkie promise . . . that's pretty serious."

"I was thinking we'd swear a blood oath, but the sharpest object I have is this plastic coffee stirrer."

Since I haven't made the promise yet, I choose not to tell her that I've got my papaw's old pocketknife in my jeans. Besides, I'm pretty sure bleeding on the table would get us kicked out of Starbucks. I hold up my pinkie, and we hook our little fingers together.

"Pinkie promise," Macey says. "No secrets between brother and sister."

"Pinkie promise," I say, and even though it's a playground promise, it feels powerful. Maybe it's just hearing her say "brother and sister" like that and knowing it means us.

"Now," Macey says, holding up her phone. "We have to take some pictures. Our first meeting must be documented."

She gets up and approaches a young guy with a blonde beard and long hair in a bun. I wonder what Nanny would do if I grew my hair and wore it like that. Come after me with scissors, I reckon.

"Excuse me," Macey says to the guy. "Would you mind taking our picture?"

"Sure." The guy takes her phone. "Are you guys on a date or something?"

Macey and me both get the giggles. Finally, she says, "No, actually, we're brother and sister and just met each other for the first time."

The guy's eyes get big. "Wow," he says. "That's pretty amazing."

"It is very amazing," Macey says, pulling me out of my seat. She squeezes up against me and puts her arm around me. I put my arm around her tiny waist. I'm usually shy about touching people but being close to Macey feels natural. The guy doesn't have to tell us to smile because we're already smiling. For the second picture, Macey stands on tiptoe and kisses my cheek.

"Adorable," the guy says, handing Macey her phone.

After we thank the guy, we sit down and talk another half hour, just about fun stuff. Macey shows me a picture of herself in her new dance team costume, which is gold and sparkly and shows a lot of leg. Nanny would say it's immodest, but I think she looks perfect. Her makeup is as sparkly as her leotard, and she's smiling, arms stretched wide, like she owns the world. I wonder what it would be like to look that way, feel that way.

"Macey, you're beautiful," I say, handing the phone back to her.

She rolls her eyes. "There's a lot of glitter and makeup there. Smoke and mirrors."

But she's wrong. She's beautiful, too, sitting there bare-faced in her jeans and t-shirt. "Well, Nanny always says, 'If you ain't got it, you can't paint it on.' And girl, you got it."

Macey laughs. "You want to see what a really beautiful girl looks like? Here."

She hands me her phone again. This time it's a photo of a long-haired orange and white cat, splayed for the camera like a pinup model. "She's beautiful, too," I say. "The difference between her and you is that she's beautiful and she *knows* it."

"You've got that right," Macey says, laughing as she takes her phone back. I like how easily I can make her laugh. "Do you have any pics on your phone?"

"Lord, no. I've got the saddest old phone in the world. It doesn't take very good pictures."

Macey shakes her head. "Kody, we've got to drag you into the modern world."

"Please, drag away," I say. And right then I see how Macey and me fit together. She needs me to show her where she came from, and I need her to show me where I can go.

Chapter 7

CALEB ALWAYS COMES TO CHURCH WITH us on the Sundays we go visit Daddy in jail. It's a periodic duty, and I reckon I dread it the way girls dread their periods.

I don't hate my daddy, but he's mostly been in jail since I was a little kid. He went in first for DUI and possession when I was just a toddler. After he got out that time, he was in and out of my life for a while. But when Caleb was still real little, our daddy got arrested for armed robbery. He was sentenced to fifteen years that time, so Caleb can't remember seeing his daddy outside of jail.

When we walk into the church sanctuary, L.J. is already sitting in a pew with her parents and Dustin. She waves and pats the empty place beside her.

"Can we go sit with L.J. and them?" I whisper to Nanny, and she nods.

When I sit next to L.J. she gives my hand a little squeeze. "How you doing, sweetie?"

I shrug. "All right, I guess. It's a Prison Sunday, and you know that always makes me nervous."

"I think it'd make me nervous, too," L.J. says. "But just think how happy it'll make your daddy to see you."

I manage a little smile. But to tell the truth, I don't think Daddy's that happy to see me. I don't think he knows what to make of a boy like me who doesn't care about cars or sports or girls (well, not about girls, *that* way). He always seems glad to see Caleb, though, and calls him Daddy's Little Man.

"She's getting so big." Nanny is talking to Janice Pickens who's sitting in the row in front of us holding her blue-eyed toddler granddaughter who she's raising because her daughter's too high on pills to take care of a baby. Next to her are Naomi and Hank Dixon, who are sitting with their two grandchildren they're raising between them. In our little church alone, there are a dozen kids who are being raised by their grandparents. I guess this is what it means to be part of an epidemic, like those slick, polished people on the news call it.

The preacher's wife starts banging away on the piano, and we stand and sing about being washed in the blood of the Lamb. I've never liked this one much. I know it's about Jesus and washing away your sins, but I don't like the pictures it puts in my head. Sitting in a bathtub full of blood. Dead baby lambs. Horror movie stuff.

Pastor Martin is wound up today. "Have you noticed, brothers and sisters," he says, starting to pace, "that once we took prayer OUT of schools, we got guns IN our schools?"

Several people say "Amen."

"Children can no longer look up at the walls in their classrooms and see The Ten Commandments," Pastor Martin says, prowling back and forth. "They cannot see 'Thou Shalt Not Kill' right there in front of them. They cannot pray for help and guidance throughout their day." He holds up his big black Bible. "Well, I say THIS is the most important book to have in school or anyplace else!"

More amens.

"And," he says—his face is starting to take on a sweaty sheen—"if we put God back IN our schools, we'll get the guns OUT of the schools!"

Lots of amens and hallelujahs, including one from L.J.

I wonder if Pastor Martin is right. Would anybody who's crazy enough to shoot up a school be talked out of it because he saw the words "Thou Shalt Not Kill" on the wall? It seems to me that making it harder for crazy people to buy guns might do more good, but around here that's a very unpopular opinion. Eastern Kentuckians love their guns, and if you talk about taking away some people's guns, they think you want to take everybody's guns, and what would they do during deer season?

I also don't get the idea that there's no prayer allowed in school because isn't praying silently something you can do any time you want to?

Nobody can stop you if they don't know you're doing it. I even pray in school sometimes, but usually it's something like *Lord don't let me fail this test.*

Like always, my mind has focused on one thing the preacher said and then wandered off so far I don't even hear the rest of the service. As we're heading out to the parking lot, Nanny says, "Who's ready for Dairy Queen?"

"I am!" Caleb shouts, raising his hand like he knows an answer in school.

Driving through the Dairy Queen is a traditional part of Prison Sunday. I just get a little hamburger and a small Coke because I'm too nervous to want to eat much of anything.

Caleb orders a double cheeseburger and large fries, plus an Oreo Blizzard.

Once we're on the road, Caleb starts in on his Blizzard. "You gotta eat your ice cream before your food so it won't melt," he says.

"Yeah," I say. "You eat your dessert for an appetizer."

"What's an appetizer?" Caleb asks, licking ice cream off his plastic spoon.

"Well, in fancy restaurants it's the food they bring out first, like a little snack you eat till your main food comes."

"How do you know about fancy restaurants?" Caleb says.

"I don't," I say, nibbling my burger. "Just what I've seen on TV, like if one of the Golden Girls goes out on a dinner date. Or like a commercial for Olive Garden or Red Lobster."

"Lobster is a funny word," Caleb says. "Hey, Nanny, did you ever eat a lobster?"

"Mercy, no!" she says. She's eating French fries from the Dairy Queen bag while she drives. "Them things ain't nothing but giant crawdads!"

Caleb and me laugh. I look out the window. The sun is shining, the mountains are pretty, and the grass is green. It's a beautiful day for a drive. I just wish we was going someplace else.

It takes a little more than an hour to get to Green Mountain State Correctional Facility. Visitor day is always crowded with people like us. Once Nanny is parked in the visitor lot she says, "Now give me a minute to get situated." She gets out a Walmart bag for me to give to Daddy—I don't have to look inside to know it's socks and under-wear—and a tote bag of her own stuff. Nanny refuses to speak to Daddy, so while we visit him, she sits in a corner and crochets or reads one of her Christian romance novels.

"Nanny, why don't Mommy come with us to visit Daddy?"

Caleb asks this every time we go, and Nanny always gives the same answer she does this time, "Honey, they broke up before she had you, and she said she didn't want to see him no more."

"How come they broke up?" Caleb asks.

"That's grownup stuff, not for you to worry about," Nanny says as she swings the car door open. "She had her reasons."

Mommy says Daddy hit her, which is probably true. And now I know Mommy cheated on Daddy. Hitting and cheating—I guess those are grownup reasons, but they don't sound too grownup to me.

Green Mountain Correctional Facility is about half an hour off the interstate exit. I guess the idea is to keep the bad people as far away from society as possible. The building is big and gray, as square and blocky as something a little kid would build out of Legos. There's a guard tower with a view of the whole property and a tall fence, angled to make it hard to climb, and topped with twisted barbed wire like a crown of thorns. The guard at the gate where we stop is a chunky white guy with a buzz cut and a head shaped like a potato. "You'uns here for visitors' day?" he asks.

"Yessir," Nanny says. The guard is young enough to be her son, but since he has a uniform on, he's "sir."

"I need to see your ID," the guard says.

Nanny hands him her license, and he squints at it. "Who is it you was coming to see?" he asks.

"Robert James Prewitt," she says.

He flips through some pages on a clipboard, then nods. "Go in the door marked Visitors' Entrance. You'uns have a good day now." He says these last words like he just sold us some ice cream at Dairy Queen.

The guard at the visitors' entrance is a pretty Black woman with her hair in long braids. "I need you to sign in for me," she says, "and ma'am, I need to look inside your bags."

We know the drill because we do this every time we visit. Nanny hands her bags over to be searched. I try to pay attention to how Nanny looks at this guard, how she talks to her, to see if what Macey says about Nanny having a problem with Black people is true.

I so desperately want it not to be true.

But Nanny doesn't give me anything to work with. She's silent as the guard digs through her tote bag, and when she hands it back to her, she takes it without a word.

After we go through the metal detector another guard escorts us to the visitors' area. The walls are dingy white concrete block, and the air smells stale. The room is full of tables kind of like a school cafeteria, except at these tables orange jumpsuited men sit with their wives or girlfriends and children. There are lots of tears from the wives and girlfriends. Babies drink their bottles, and toddlers play with brightly colored plastic toys that have been played with by countless other prisoners' children. I hope somebody at least sprays them down with bleach water every once in a while.

The kids are too little to know what a sad place they're in. A lot of the inmates are Black or brown; others are white people who you can tell are poor because of their bad teeth and pasty complexions. I wonder how many of the prisoners are in here for drug-related offenses. I would bet most of them.

One time when I talked to L.J. about visiting Daddy in prison, she said, "Aren't you scared being around all those bad people?"

I told her I felt sad, not scared.

I hadn't thought about it enough to put into words when L.J. asked me, but when I come here, I don't feel like I'm surrounded by bad people. I feel like I'm surrounded by poor people who did something dumb or desperate to try to make their lives feel less hopeless. But then they got caught. They're poor people who wouldn't have gotten into such bad trouble if they hadn't been poor, who wouldn't have felt the need to commit the crime they did (if they even did it) in the first place.

Nanny finds a corner where she can crochet but still keep an eye on Caleb and me. The guard takes Caleb and me to a table and tells us to wait there. In a few minutes, another guard brings Daddy out. Daddy is tall and gangly like me. His hair is buzzed close, which make his cheekbones and gray eyes more prominent. He's pale because he's kept away from the sun. We're allowed to hug him, but Daddy isn't a hugger, which is fine by me. He just sits down across from us at the table and says, "Hey."

I mumble hey back, but Caleb sounds all hyper and excited and says, "Hey, Daddy! Go Vols, am I right?"

Daddy smiles. It's a running joke between him and Caleb. Daddy always says the orange prison jumpsuits are a special punishment for Kentucky Wildcats fans because they're the team color of the Tennessee Volunteers.

"Nanny brought you socks and underwear," I say, handing over the Walmart bag.

"She gives me socks and underwear every time you come here," Daddy says. "What does she think I do—eat 'em?"

Caleb laughs.

"What you been up to, Little Man?" Daddy asks Caleb.

And Caleb is off and running on one of his long, rapid-fire ADHD speeches about junior basketball and Little League and 4H Club. I know I'm not going to get a word in for a while, so I catch Daddy's eye and point to the Pepsi machine in the corner. He nods.

While Caleb talks, I go to buy Daddy a Pepsi, grateful to have something to do. Since I have some extra change in my pocket, I buy him a pack of peanut M&M's from the snack machine, too. Inmates don't get soda and candy, so a lot of visitors buy their incarcerated family members treats from the vending machines. It's awful, but it kind of reminds me of buying those little ice cream cones full of feed for the animals in the petting zoo.

I take Daddy the Pepsi and candy. He nods his thanks, then pops open the can and takes a long drink. "Damn, that's good," he says. "So, what you been up to, Kody?"

I want to say, well, I've been getting to know the sister I never knew I had from back when Mommy was cheating on you with a guy who dreamed of playing football for the University of Tennessee. But instead, I shrug and say, "Not much. School. Church. Piecing a quilt with Nanny."

I know saying that last thing was a mistake because of the look that comes on his face. "She teaching you how to sew lace on your drawers, too?" he says, which makes Caleb laugh.

"That's our next project," I say. It's kind of sassy, but ultimately how much can he judge me when at the end of this visit, I'm free to go and he's not?

He shakes his head, then tears open his bag of M&M's. He offers some to Caleb and me. Caleb takes a couple, but I don't. Daddy eats his M&M's slow, sucking off the candy shell before he bites into them. It's the same way I eat M&M's, so that's exactly one thing Daddy and me have in common. Finally, he says, "How's your mommy?"

"About the same," I say.

Daddy nods grimly. "She's lucky she ain't ended up in jail, too. Or maybe she ain't so lucky. At least jail got me clean. I'm gonna stay that way once I'm out of here, too. And the first thing I'm gonna do once I get out is take Caleb fishing."

"That's right, Daddy," Caleb says, grinning.

I picture Daddy and Caleb walking together with their fishing poles like Andy and Opie in the opening credits of *The Andy Griffith Show*. Except that by the time Daddy gets out of jail Caleb will almost be a full-grown man. But still, I hope that it'll be like that, that Daddy can make good on his promise. But it's one thing to stay clean in jail when you're watched all the time and drugs are hard to get. It's another thing to stay clean when you're free and back in your hometown where pills and heroin are as easy to come by as a Pepsi and a pack of M&M's. Back when Mommy got out of jail, she was using again within twenty-four hours.

The guard comes to get Daddy after exactly thirty minutes. Daddy says, "Thanks for coming to see me, boys," and lets the guard lead him away.

"Thirty minutes is too short," Caleb complains, as he always does, when the visit is over.

I know it's terrible, but my thirty minutes with Daddy feels longer than thirty minutes anywhere else, and that includes my horrible Algebra II class that I have a D in. I think that's about the grade I'd give Daddy's and my relationship, too. Like with algebra, I'd like to understand Daddy, but I just can't.

Caleb dozes off on the way home, so Nanny and me don't talk much. She puts on the Dolly CD softly, which I know she does to calm my nerves. Nanny is so good to me that I can't believe what Macey says is true. I love Macey, and I'm not calling her a liar. I just think there's been a misunderstanding somewhere along the line.

After we've dropped Caleb off at Uncle Jay and Tiff's, Nanny says, "Why don't we stop at the Walmart and pick up your mommy a few groceries? We can grab something easy to fix for supper, too."

"Sure," I say. I know walking around Walmart is Nanny's way of calming her nerves after Prison Sunday. Some people drink and smoke. Some people meditate. Nanny goes to church and Walmart.

I walk alongside Nanny as she pushes her cart down the grocery aisles and help pick out food for Mommy: milk and bread, bologna and cheese, cornflakes and bananas and orange juice. Nanny doesn't buy Mommy much that requires cooking. She's terrified that Mommy will be so high she'll forget she left the stove on and burn the trailer down.

When I see that taco kits are on sale—the kind where they give you the crunchy shells and seasoning and you just add the meat and toppings—I say, "Can we have tacos for supper? I'll fix 'em."

Nanny smiles. "Honey, if you'll fix 'em, I'll eat 'em."

I grab a pound of hamburger, some shredded cheese, and a head of lettuce. I know Nanny didn't grow up eating tacos, so this meal is a little exotic for her, but I don't understand how a person can be happy their whole lives eating the same thing over and over again.

Once we get home and feed the dogs, I get out a pan and start browning the hamburger, humming "9 to 5" under my breath.

"Maybe we should call your mommy and see if she wants to come eat and pick up her groceries," Nanny says.

"Okay," I say.

I must not sound too enthusiastic because Nanny says, "I know. You don't ask for the parents you get, and we can't know why the Lord gave you the ones he did. Maybe because he knew you was strong enough to handle it."

I'm tempted to say, "Gee, thanks, God," but I know Nanny would think I was being blasphemous, so I just say, "Maybe so. I don't feel that strong, though."

"But you are," Nanny says. "I figure if we have your mommy over for supper after we've visited your daddy, we'll go to bed tonight knowing we did the right thing." She picks up the phone, and after Mommy finally answers, she says, "We picked you up some groceries at the Walmart, and Kody's fixed supper. You want to come over and eat?" After a minute, she says, "We'll see you directly, then," and hangs up.

I shake the seasoning packet into the ground beef. "Which Mommy are we getting, High Mommy or Sick Mommy?"

"The sick one, I think. She sounded pretty puny."

It is Sick Mommy. When I let her in, her eyes have dark circles under them, and she's twitchy, like ants are crawling under her clothes. "Hey, baby," she says. She hugs me, and I can feel her ribs.

"Supper's almost ready," I say.

Mommy sits at the kitchen table, and I pour her some Pepsi. She lights a cigarette. Nanny doesn't like her smoking in the house, but she doesn't say anything.

"We went to see Daddy today," I say, sliding the cookie sheet of taco shells into the oven.

"Is he still an asshole?" Mommy says.

"Amanda! You know I don't allow cussing in my house." That's Nanny.

"I just kinda think of 'asshole' as his name," Mommy says, ashing her cigarette into her empty Pepsi can.

"Then you shouldn't have to ask if he still is one," Nanny says, which strikes me as a good point.

"Okay." I feel like it might be a good idea to turn everybody's attention to food. "The taco bar is open!" I've lined everything up on the counter in the right order: shells, meat, lettuce, chopped tomatoes, cheese.

Mommy puts her head on the table like an elementary school kid during Quiet Time. "I don't think I can eat anything, baby. I hurt all over."

A lot of the time Nanny and me will coax her, say things like, "You'd feel better if you ate something," but I look at Nanny and see in her eyes that she's too tired to make the effort. Nanny must see the same thing when she looks at me because we just go ahead and make our tacos and sit down at the table to eat, ignoring Mommy while we crunch away.

After supper we go into the living room and put on *The Golden Girls*. I sit on the couch, and Mommy lays down with her head on my lap. I don't know what to do with my hands. By the time the show's off, Mommy is snoring lightly. "I need to get up and do my homework," I half-whisper to Nanny.

"Just slide out from under her," Nanny says.

I lie on my bed and answer some history questions, then work on some algebra problems I'm sure I get wrong. When I'm done, I take a shower. It feels like I'm washing away the experience of the prison, of Mommy being such a mess. When I come back into the living room, she's still on the couch, moaning in her sleep like something's hurting her. I take the afghan Nanny and me crocheted last winter and drape it over her. In my room, I put on Side 1 of *Coat of Many Colors* real soft and snuggle down under the covers.

"Coat of Many Colors" is one of my favorite songs. It's about how Dolly grew up poor and her mama made her a multicolored coat from rags. She tells Dolly about Joseph's coat of many colors in the Bible, and Dolly is proud to wear her homemade coat to school. But when she gets there, the kids make fun of her for being different and poor. I think it's one of the truest songs ever written. Every time I hear it, tears spring to my eyes and I think, *Dolly gets it.*

When I wake up around three, I go into the living room to check on Mommy. The afghan is wadded up on the couch, but she's gone. I check the fridge and see that she at least remembered to take her sack of groceries with her.

A couple of winters ago, this stray tabby cat started coming around. She'd show up on the porch and meow, and I'd run to the fridge and pour her a saucer of milk. I wanted her to stay and be my cat, but she never did. She'd just show up, take what she needed, and leave.

Mommy's the same way. I love her, but she'll never really be mine.

Chapter 8

IN U.S. HISTORY CLASS WE'RE TALKING about Henry Ford and the Model T and how people having cars and the freedom to travel changed life in America. This gets a bunch of boys in the class talking about their favorite makes of cars. Some of them even started talking about NASCAR, which is totally not the point.

But it does get me thinking. If I had a car of my own, I wouldn't have to borrow Nanny's. It would be easier to go see Macey, and I could drive to school instead of taking the bus. Ever since Macey said what she did about Nanny, I've been thinking about how close Nanny and me are, almost like we're the same person, with our needlework and our *Golden Girls* reruns. I love Nanny and quilting and Betty White, but maybe I should spend some of my free time like I'm not a sixty-three-year-old woman.

In the cafeteria at lunch, I unwrap my usual PB and J and wait for L.J. to finish praying over her chicken nuggets. "I want to buy a car," I say.

"What with?" L.J. tears open a ketchup packet.

"Exactly," I say. "I need to make some money."

L.J. takes a bite of nugget and chews. "I do all right baby-sitting. I bet you could, too."

"I probably could. I like kids." I think about all the grand-parents at church raising their grandkids. I bet a lot of them could do with a night off every once in a while.

"And since you're a boy, you could mow grass and do other yard work and odd jobs," L.J. says.

I don't know what being a boy has to do with it, but I could do all those things. "That's a weird expression—odd jobs."

"I think it means odd like random," L.J. says. "Like odds and ends."

"Yeah, but wouldn't it be funny if it meant odd like weird? Like if somebody said, 'I want you to dress my chickens up like all my favorite country divas.' That would be an odd job, wouldn't it?"

L.J. laughs. "I reckon it would."

"Or, 'I want you to teach my dog how to recite the Declaration of Independence.'"

"Odd and impossible," L.J. says, laughing.

"'I want you to paint my house . . . plaid.'"

L.J. is laughing really hard now. "Seems to me," she says when she catches her breath, "that you're the one who's odd."

Guilty as charged.

* * *

MACEY CALLS ALMOST AS SOON AS I get home.

"Hey, bro," she says.

"Hey, sis, what's up?"

"Well . . ." she says, and I can hear the smile in her voice. "Quite a bit. I told Auntie I've been talking to you."

My stomach feels prickly. "And?"

"And she said she wished I had felt comfortable telling her sooner, but other than that, she was totally cool with it. Kind of excited, actually. She wants to meet you this Saturday if you can."

"I don't know if I can get away with taking Nanny's car for that long. I want to real bad, though."

"Here's what Auntie suggested," Macey says. "There's a state park—Grove Lake—about halfway between Knoxville and Morgan. Auntie thought we could meet there around one o'clock and have a picnic. It's supposed to be unseasonably warm on Saturday. We'll bring lunch, and you just bring you."

"I'll see what I can do."

* * *

I GUESS LYING IS LIKE ANYTHING else. The more you do it, the better you get at it. I told Nanny that on Saturday L.J. wanted me to drive her over to Crown Bible College for a tour. Nanny gave me permission, but she did say, "Can't that girl's parents drive her anywhere?"

I wonder if it makes me more of a sinner because my lie involved a Bible college.

Grove Lake State Park is in a valley between mountains. The lake is big and flocked with ducks and Canadian geese. We're supposed to meet in the picnic shelter area. One shelter, decorated with balloons, is being used for a little girl's birthday party. Another houses a large family having a cookout. Before I can find the right place, Macey comes running out and throws her arms around me. "There you are!" she says.

"Here I am."

We hug for a long time, then Macey pulls back holding both my hands, and says, "Let me look at you."

We stand there holding hands, looking at each other. At first, I check out Macey's outfit, a cute pink top with jeans and glittery pink canvas slip-on shoes. But then I look at her face. The first time I saw her, all I could think about was how pretty she is, but today I'm looking at her as my sister and seeing if I can see any of myself in her features.

We both have Mommy's pointy chin and sharp forehead. But overall, Macey turned out way better than I did in the looks department.

She lets go of one of my hands but leads me by the other. "Come on," she says. "You need to meet Auntie."

We go to a shelter where a petite woman with a cute short haircut is riffling through the contents of a cooler. When we get close, she looks up and smiles. Her complexion is a couple of shades darker than Macey's, but they have the same wide set eyes. "Kody!" she says and comes out from behind the table for a hug.

It's a good hug, the kind that makes you feel secure but not smothered. When we pull apart, I say, "Nice to meet you, Mrs.—Lord, I don't know what to call you!"

She's still smiling. "You can call me Auntie Diane. That's what Macey calls me."

"Well, if you're comfortable with that. I mean, you and me aren't blood relatives—"

"Macey's my family, you're her family, so you're my family, too," Auntie Diane says. "Now I don't know about y'all, but I'm hungry. Why don't we get this picnic unpacked?" She looks at me. "You're a teenage boy, so I figure you're always hungry."

"Pretty much," I say, feeling a little shy.

Auntie Diane goes back to the cooler. "I remember when Calvin—Macey's daddy—was your age he ate so much our Mama used to say he had a hollow leg. He could especially put it away during football season." She pulls a stack of wrapped sandwiches out of the cooler. "Now Macey and I didn't know what you liked to eat, so we made all kinds of sandwiches: egg salad, chicken salad, pimento cheese. You're not one of those kids who won't eat meat or dairy, are you?"

"No, ma'am. I'll eat anything you put in front of me."

It's a good picnic. The sandwiches are tasty, and the bread's cut in fancy crustless triangles. There's a bowl of chilled grapes and a fresh bag of potato chips and a bottle of cold lemonade. "Thank you for putting all this together," I say.

"It was my pleasure," Auntie Diane says. "Cooking soothes me. I'm an ER nurse, so my job can get really stressful. Sometimes when I come home I have to cook something just to calm myself down."

"Sometimes she'll make blueberry muffins at one o'clock in the morning," Macey says.

"Well, I didn't hear you complaining when you woke up for breakfast," Auntie Diane says.

I like listening to the easy way the two of them talk to each other. Anybody who didn't know would just assume they were mother and daughter. "I'm not complaining either," I say. "This is the best pimento cheese I've ever had."

"My mamaw's recipe," Auntie Diane says. She looks at me. "So I like to cook and Macey likes to dance. What do you like, Kody?"

I don't think anybody's ever asked me what I like before. It's a personal question, but it's a nice question, too. It's nice to think that somebody cares about what you like.

"Well, I like to sew and crochet and knit," I say. "And I like Dolly Parton a whole lot."

Auntie Diane smiles. "How can you not like Dolly? I like her and I can't stand country music. She uses her fame to do a lot of good. And I like that she's not ashamed of where she comes from and doesn't think anybody else should be either."

"I like that, too," I say. I feel good, sitting here in the sunshine with my sister and my auntie, talking about what we like.

"You know who I like?" Macey says. "I like Kody."

"Aww, I like you, too," I say, leaning into her for a half hug. She rests her head on my shoulder for a few seconds.

Auntie Diane's expression gets more serious. "So, Kody, how's your mama doing?"

It's her right to ask, of course, but part of me doesn't want to talk about Mommy, doesn't want to rain on our picnic. "Not good. I mean, she's an addict—"

"Substance abuse disorder," Auntie Diane says.

"I beg your pardon?" I say.

"Substance abuse disorder." Auntie Diane pops a grape into her mouth. "That's what healthcare professionals are calling it now instead of addiction. It sounds less judgmental. I don't know if changing what we call it will help the problem, but we're trying it. We're trying everything we can think of."

I nod. "It can't hurt," I say. But to tell the truth I don't see how changing what you call something is going to make that big a difference.

"You know, Kody, it's amazing your mama's still alive after using all these years. Calvin had just been using a year and a half when he died. It was like one minute he was on the football field, the next minute he was hurt, and by the third minute he was dead."

"I'm sorry." I look over at Macey to see if this talk is upsetting her, but she doesn't look sad. This story is one she's probably heard many times before. "Mommy's had some close calls. She's ended up in jail a few times, in the hospital a few times, and gone through detox there. "

"Has she ever gone through a rehab program?" Auntie Diane asks.

I think about the rehab programs the Hollywood stars get sent to, the kind Nanny reads about in the tabloids. They're like fancy hotels with personal chefs and massages and yoga classes. "We don't have money for rehab. For a while Nanny took her to this therapy center in Morgan. It had some name from the Bible."

Auntie Diane nods. "Faith-based. Those programs work sometimes. But if you're hurting real bad, it's hard not to choose a pill or a shot that will make you feel good right now over a heaven that won't make you feel good until you're dead." Auntie Diane looks over at Macey. "Macey wants to meet your mama." I notice she says your mama, not her mama. "But I think it would make her sad."

"I know it would make me sad, but I still want to meet her," Macey says.

I nod. "I think she should get to meet her if she wants to."

Auntie Diane looks at me for a moment. She's one of those people who can make you feel like she's looking right through you. "You're right. I guess to make that happen, you'll have to talk to your mama and tell her you've been in touch with Macey."

It's hard to find a time to talk to Mommy about anything serious. She's either high, sick, or unconscious. "I'll talk to her the next time she has a good day or what passes for one. I don't know when that'll be."

"Okay," Auntie Diane says. "You talk to your mama when she's capable of conversation. And then we'll figure out a time to drive up there." She shakes her head. "I've got to tell you looking like I do, I don't much care for going to that part of Kentucky. When Calvin moved there, I told him they would kill him. And they did."

What Auntie Diane is saying doesn't make any sense. Drugs, not racism, were what killed Macey's dad. "I don't—"

"Understand? Of course you don't, honey. But you've probably at least noticed that the demographic of where you live is overwhelmingly white."

"Well, sure," I say, "but I always just figured it was because Black people didn't want to live there."

Auntie Diane smiles. "Exactly. And lions don't want to live in the Antarctic. Because for them it's a hostile environment."

Macey grabs my hand suddenly. "Auntie Diane, is it okay if Kody and me go for a walk?" Maybe Macey senses that I'm overwhelmed, that Auntie Diane has thrown more ideas at me than I can make sense of right now.

"Sure. Y'all didn't come here to listen to me lecture. Meet me back here in an hour. We can't keep Kody out too late."

Macey and me walk towards the lake, holding hands. Next to the water, two old papaws are fishing. I nod to greet them, but they look away. As soon as we get to the bank, an army of white ducks waddles up and surrounds us, quacking.

Macey reaches down to pet one. "I love ducks," she says. "They're so dumb and happy-looking."

I hadn't thought about it, but it's true. "I like how they're graceful in the water but move all weird on land."

A half dozen Canadian geese are lurking behind the ducks. Macey tries to move closer to one, but it gives her the evil eye and hisses. "Ducks are sweet, but these guys are jerks," she says.

"Takes all kinds," I say. "People. Waterfowl." We start walking, and Macey takes my hand again. "I like your auntie. Our auntie," I correct myself. "She's smart."

"She's the smartest person I know," Macey says.

I weigh my words carefully. The last thing I want to do is make Macey mad or hurt her feelings. "Do you agree with what she said . . . about where I'm from being prejudiced?"

"Well, I've never been to Morgan, Kody, so I don't really know for sure. But there's prejudice everywhere. Like did you see the way those old guys fishing looked at us? They gave us the total stinkeye."

I smile. I've never heard "stinkeye" before, and I like it.

"It's because we were holding hands," Macey says, "so they thought we were boyfriend and girlfriend."

"Do you think so? Do you think they would've like it better if they'd known we were brother and sister?"

Macey laughs. "Probably not. "

We walk past some evergreen trees. "You know," I say. "I thought those old coots was frowning at us because of the way I walk."

Macey looks at me. "How do you walk?"

"Well, you know, kind of girly."

"Huh," Macey says. "Well, it could've been that. It's not like we can read their narrow little minds." She's quiet for a couple of seconds. "Wow. There are so many reasons to be a jerk. Because you don't like somebody's skin color. Because you don't like the way somebody walks."

"Because you're a Canadian goose," I say.

We both laugh, and then, before I even know what's about to come out of my own mouth, I say, "Macey, you know I'm gay, right?"

"I thought you might be," she says, like I've not told her anything more surprising than my favorite color. "I think I might be bi, but I'm not sure. Last year I had a boyfriend for six months until we broke up, but sometimes I get crushes on girls."

I don't know what shocks me more, what she says or how casually she says it. "Does your auntie know?"

"Sure. She's cool. She's got a gay cousin who's like her best friend."

My eyes are tearing up a little, but it's because I'm happy. "You're the first person I've told."

Macey gives me a big hug. "Aww, thank you. I'm glad it was me."

"I'm glad it was you, too."

When we break out of the hug, Macey says, "Hey, there's a playground. Let's go swing!" She breaks into a run. She runs like a gazelle, and I run like one of the ducks down by the lake. A girly duck. By the time I reach her, she's already swinging high, her legs stretched out. I squeeze myself into the swing next to her and push off.

"I think this is the first time I've been in a swing since grade school," I say, trying to push myself up to her level.

"It still feels great, doesn't it?" Macey says.

"It sure does." It feels like flying.

"Well, look at you!" Auntie Diane calls from the walking trail.

"We didn't have a childhood together," Macey hollers at her. "So we're having one now."

"It's never too late," Auntie Diane says.

"Hey, Auntie," Macey says, dragging her feet on the ground to stop the swing. "Will you take some pictures of Kody and me?"

Auntie Diane takes out her phone, and all of a sudden, it's a photo shoot. I pose behind Macey on the swing like I'm about to push her. We climb the jungle gym and pose sitting on top of it together. We slide down the slide one after another and pose at the bottom. We all laugh a lot. I feel so comfortable and free that it's almost like Dolly Dress-Up Hour. Except it's even better because I'm not alone.

Chapter 9

AT CHURCH, JUST BEFORE SUNDAY SCHOOL, I tack a handwritten sign on the bulletin board that says:

YARDWORK

BABYSITTING

ODD JOBS (The odder, the better!)

Call Kody 539-2792

L.J. looks at the sign and laughs. "The odder, the better?"

"Hey," I say. "That's my life motto."

Walking from the Sunday school room to the church service, I hear a voice say, "Hey, Kody!" It's Mrs. Jenkins, an old lady who always wears her silver hair in an elaborate updo. When it's down, it must hang to her waist.

"Good morning, Mrs. Jenkins."

"I saw your sign, and I was wondering—me and Ed have got an anniversary on Friday. Our fortieth. I know you young people stay busy on the weekends, and I don't want to mess up your social life. But if you're free to babysit so me and Ed could go out to eat, that would be a real treat for us."

I choose not to tell her that my busy Friday nights usually involve watching *The Golden Girls* with Nanny. "I'd be happy to do that for you," I say.

Mrs. Jenkins' whole face lights up. "Well, God bless you, Kody. That's just wonderful. It's been so long since we've got to go out, just the two of us. How much do you charge?"

I realize I haven't even thought about how much to charge—haven't thought past the basic idea that if I do work for people, they'll give me money. "Is ten dollars an hour all right with you?"

"It's a deal," Mrs. Jenkins says, smiling.

After church, Alvin Simmons from the farm supply store drapes his arm around my shoulder and says, "Hey, buddy. I saw your sign. I hurt my back and the doctor says no lifting for two weeks. You reckon you could help me haul some firewood?"

"Sure." I'm already counting the money I haven't made yet.

"How much would you charge?"

I have no idea, so I say, "Twenty?"

"That'll work. The sooner, the better, though. My wife's losing her patience."

"I can do it this afternoon if you want me to."

"Well, it's the Lord's day, but if you don't think He'll mind, I won't either."

* * *

I START OFF THE SCHOOL WEEK with twenty dollars in my pocket. I'm saving it, not spending it, but it's so weird for me to have money of my own that I just like carrying it around. On the school bus, as soon as we're close enough to town to get a signal, I check my phone. There's a text from Macey:

Here are the pics from this weekend. It was great seeing you.

I text back "You too" and save the pictures in my photo album. I've never even kept photos on my phone before. I look through them—Macey and me on the swings, on the slide, on the jungle gym—and smile at how goofy and happy we look.

At lunch I take the twenty out of my pocket and show it to L.J. "Check this out. I am now twenty dollars closer to owning a car." I put the bill back in my pocket. "I know that's almost nothing, but it's a start. I earned it hauling firewood yesterday."

"You're a working man now," L.J. says, forking up some runny mashed potatoes that are sitting beside an unidentifiable disk of meat.

"That's me," I say. "Look at these manly calloused hands." I stretch out my hands which are actually soft from Nanny's Jergens lotion. "And I've got a babysitting job on Friday night."

"So you'll be changing diapers with your manly calloused hands."

"That's right," I say in a fake baritone. "I'll change the baby's diapers, then I'll chop down a tree and use the wood to make a crib." I pull up an image on my phone of Paul Bunyan, gigantic and bearded and wearing what looks like the world's largest plaid flannel shirt, wielding a mighty axe. "See, this is me," I say.

L.J. laughs. "You could be twins."

I set down my phone and pick up my PB and J. "Separated at birth," I say.

* * *

I DON'T NOTICE IT'S MISSING UNTIL right after biology. I hurry to the main office. The school secretary is on the computer doing whatever school secretaries do.

"Has anybody turned in a phone?" I ask.

"Sure haven't, hon," she says without looking away from the screen. "You should probably check back before the end of the day though."

During study hall I usually go to the library, but today I'm too upset to concentrate on studying. Even cheap phones are expensive to replace, and I don't know when we'll be able to afford a new one . . . or if Nanny will even let me have a new one after I've been careless enough to lose the first one. Not having a phone means no texts from Macey during the school day, no pictures of her and me. The only way we'll be able to talk is on the landline phone when Nanny's at work.

I feel a hand on my shoulder. I look up to see L.J. holding my phone. Relief floods over me. "Oh, L.J., you're my guardian angel!" I want to shout it, but I whisper since I'm in the library.

"You left it on the table in the lunchroom," she says.

I stand up to take the phone and to hug her. She doesn't hug back, which is weird. "L.J., are you okay?" I ask.

She looks like she's trying not to cry. "Can I talk to you for just a minute?" she says.

I follow her into one of the little side rooms that are supposed to be for study groups. She closes the door behind us.

"Okay, Kody." Her voice is trembling. "I did a bad thing, and I'm gonna tell you about it, but then there's something I want you to tell me."

"Okay." I have no idea where this is going, but I don't think it's going to be a very fun destination.

She takes a deep, shaky breath and grasps the edge of the table like she needs it for support. "I looked at your phone. I shouldn't have done it, but the devil tempted me, and I wasn't strong enough to resist."

At first, I wonder how she could have done it since you have to have a password to see stuff on my phone. But then I remember my password is DOLLY. As well as L.J. knows me, it would be the first thing she'd try. "It's okay," I say. "I forgive you."

L.J. nods. "Okay, but when I looked, I saw something. You don't have to tell me about it if you don't want to. I know I shouldn't have been snooping in your business."

My belly is tied up in knots. Is there something on my phone that would let L.J. know I'm gay? I can't think of anything, but the way she's looking at me, something must've freaked her out. "What did you see?"

L.J. runs her fingers under her eyes. "Who's the girl, Kody?"

"What girl?" I have no idea what she's talking about.

"The skinny little colored girl in the pictures on your phone, the one that's kissing on you in some restaurant and hugging on you at a playground. I know she don't go to this school. Who is she?"

I sink down into a chair. I know I should've told L.J. about Macey by now, but I thought I should tell Nanny before I told anybody else. L.J.'s my best friend. I should've started with her. "Lord, L.J., it's a long story—"

"Don't bring the Lord into this."

"You're right. I'm sorry."

"Just tell me her name and how long you've been dating her."

You know how cartoon characters can do a double take so hard it'd probably cause whiplash in real life? That's what I do. "Wait, what?"

And just like that, L.J. is melting down. Her face crumples, and tears leak from her eyes. "You know what? You don't even have to tell me her name. It's just that you'd see her behind my back and not say anything . . . I mean, is she even a Christian?"

In the Bible it talks about scales falling from Saul's eyes so he could finally see the truth. I had no idea I'd been looking at L.J. through scales myself. "L.J., did you think you and me was . . . dating?"

She sighs like she's exasperated. "No, I'm not stupid. I knew we wasn't dating yet. You know my daddy won't allow me to date and that purity's real important to me." She holds up her hand with the silver ring her father gave her. Her hand is shaking. "But I always thought down the road, when we were done with school, when we were ready, it'd be you and me."

Now I'm crying, too. How could I have never noticed that the way L.J. loves me is different from the way I love her? "Oh, L.J., I do love you—I really do—but it ain't never gonna be that way between you and me."

Her eyes are wide and hurt-looking. "Why? Because of this other girl? I mean, okay, she's skinnier than me and prettier than me, but pretty only gets you so far. Kody, she ain't even—"

"No." I cut her off before she can say "white." "L.J., it's not because of any girl at all." I take a deep breath. I've got to say it. It's the only way to stop her pain and confusion. "L.J., I'm gay. I never told you because I figured you already kinda knew. I should've said something sooner. I'm sorry.""

L.J. takes a step backwards. "You mean you want to marry . . . a boy?"

"Years from now. If I meet the right one, yeah."

She looks at me like I'm somebody she's never met. "But that's not the way the Lord created us. He made Adam and

Eve to be man and wife. To go against that is going against God's will."

I know L.J. believes this and probably everybody in church believes it, too. And maybe they're right. Maybe I am going against God's will. But I don't think so. "L.J., God made me, and you know me. I'm not a bad person. I'm good to my Nanny and my little brother. I try to help Mommy all I can. I've been a good friend to you all these years. God made me with these feelings, L.J., and He must've done it on purpose. I mean, I don't think he ever makes somebody, then says, 'Whoops!'"

L.J. shakes her head. "Don't you understand, Kody? God ain't the one making you feel those feelings." She closes her eyes for a moment, maybe to try to calm herself down. "I can't believe I gave you my heart all these years, and I couldn't see that the devil had yours." She stands up. "I've got to go."

"L.J.—"

"I'll pray for you, Kody." She runs out of the room.

I have to sit for a minute. I realize I never even got the chance to tell L.J. that Macey's my sister, but maybe it's best. I already threw too much information at her.

Memories of L.J. and me play in my mind like scenes from a movie. The time in kindergarten when we were finger painting and painted red dots on each other's noses and couldn't stop giggling. The time we were in the church nativity pageant and played Mary and Joseph. The time the youth group went bowling and I was so bad at it I accidentally rolled the ball over L.J.'s foot.

Had she been in love with me all those times, with me just thinking of her as my best friend, the sister I never had? And now that I have a real sister, do I have to lose L.J.'s friendship?

* * *

TODAY I NEED DOLLY DRESS-UP HOUR real bad. As soon as I get home, I go straight to my room and get out my makeup and wig and silky robe from under the bed. I strip off my boy clothes, put on the robe, sit down in front of my dresser, and start to paint. I bet L.J. would really think I'm in Satan's service if she saw this.

I smooth on some foundation first to even out my skin tone, then I brush some blush on over my cheekbones. I do an okay job with the eyeliner, but I always feel like I do better on the right eye than the left one. Then the eye-shadow. Back in the seventies, Dolly was a big fan of this light blue eyeshadow that was almost turquoise. That shade's hard to come by these days, so I go with a soft lavender, then darken my too-short eyelashes with mascara. Someday I'm going to have to learn how to put on false eyelashes.

Lips are last. I have two shades to choose from, a candy pink and a red. Today, the redder, the better.

There's only one song that's right for today. I put on "I Will Always Love You," and as I stand in front of the mirror and move my red lips to Dolly's words, tears run from my eyes, streaking my mascara into black stripes down my cheeks. It's the song Dolly wrote when she outgrew her mentor Porter Waggoner and decided to pursue a solo career. It's about leaving somebody even though it breaks your heart because it's what you have to do to become the person you need to be.

No matter what happens, I will always love L.J. Just not the way she wants me to.

I play "I Will Always Love You" three times until I'm a blubbering mess and my face looks like a fresh painting that got left out in the rain. I put away my Dolly things, grab a t-shirt and some sweatpants, and head for the shower.

The shower is a good place to cry. The tears mix with the water so you can't tell which is which and it all gets sucked down the drain.

Nanny comes home a few minutes later than usual. I'm flipping through channels on the TV, not really paying any attention to anything because my mind's on L.J.

Nanny sits down in her recliner, takes off her shoes, and sighs. "I couldn't get your mommy on the phone this afternoon, which got me to worrying. I stopped by her trailer, you know, just to check—"

"Is she okay?" Checking on Mommy really means checking that she's not dead.

"I let myself in when she didn't answer. She ain't home. The place looks like a tornado hit it, but that's nothing new."

"She's probably staying over with a friend," I say.

"Such friends as she's got," Nanny says. She looks even tireder than usual. "Well, I'd better figure out what to do about supper."

I can tell she doesn't feel like cooking. "You know what sounds good? A grilled cheese sandwich." It does sound good, but I mainly say it because it's so easy it barely qualifies as cooking.

Nanny smiles. "That does sound right good. And I think I've got a can of tomato soup I can heat up."

"I'll help."

"Well, there ain't much to help with, but I appreciate the company."

Sitting at the table, dipping our grilled cheese sandwiches into our mugs of tomato soup, I feel so comfortable I hear myself saying, "Something happened with L.J. at school today."

As soon as I say it, I realize what a corner I've painted myself into: I have to tell Nanny what happened without mentioning (a) Macey, or (b) being gay.

"Is she all right?" Nanny asks.

"I don't know. I think I might have hurt her feelings."

"I have a hard time believing that," Nanny says. "I've never seen a boy as careful with people's feelings as you are."

"I try to be careful. But L.J., she saw—" How to explain the situation without telling an outright lie? "—she saw I'd been talking to this other girl, and she got all jealous and weird. L.J. likes me, Nanny—like, likes me, likes me. Did you ever pick up on that, seeing us together?"

Nanny chews her grilled cheese thoughtfully. "I always thought you was more like brother and sister."

"Exactly!" I say, relieved. "But apparently she's been planning our wedding for when we're grownups. I told her I loved her but not that way. She cried, and then she got mad at me."

"She won't stay mad," Nanny says.

"You don't think so?" I want to believe Nanny so bad, but there's a big piece of the puzzle I haven't given her: that I'm gay and so as far as L.J. is concerned I might as well have horns and a pitchfork.

"Not as close as you are," Nanny says. "She might stay mad a little while, but then she'll miss you too bad to stay away."

"I almost wish I could be her boyfriend just so she wouldn't be sad," I say. "But it wouldn't be fair to her."

"No, it wouldn't," Nanny says, getting up to clear the dishes. "It wouldn't be honest—to her or to you. You can't make yourself feel something you don't feel."

"That's exactly it," I say. Even without having the whole picture, I feel like Nanny understands.

Chapter 10

MOMMY'S BEEN GONE FOR THREE DAYS. Nanny checks her trailer every morning before she goes to work and every evening when she comes home. I call Mommy's cell number from school every day at lunch and then again before I get on the bus. I leave different versions of the same message over and over: Nanny and me are worried. Call us. Text me to let me know you're all right. Where in the Sam Hill are you anyway?

No response. Nanny called the police to make sure Mommy wasn't in jail. She says if she doesn't show up in the next twenty-four hours, she's going to call the police again and report her as a missing person.

It's funny the way Nanny and me go on about our daily business even though we don't know where Mommy is. But she's done this before. One time she went off to Lexington with some dealer she was kind of dating. She came back home with a black eye and a busted lip. Another time she crashed for a few days at the old Falls Road Motel, which used to be a place for tourists, but now it's a rent-by-the-week flophouse for drunks and junkies and meth heads.

It's like in one way Nanny and me don't know where Mommy is, but in another way we do. The answer to the question "Where is Mommy?" is always "Where the drugs are."

L.J. is ignoring me. When she passes me in the hall at school she stares straight ahead. She's taken up with Brianna, that girl from our Sunday school class who never says anything. I wonder if L.J.'s told her that I'm a godless homosexual, if they pray that I'll be cured.

I don't even go into the cafeteria at lunchtime because I don't want to be reminded that I'm not welcome to sit with her. Instead I gobble down my PB and J in the stairwell like I'm some kind of troll that lives under the stairs. Then I go to the library where it's at least peaceful. Sometimes, when I'm lucky, I can even use the computers.

Today I'm lucky. I get on Facebook and like a bunch of new pictures Macey's posted: a group picture of her with her dance team, a picture of her cats giving each other a bath, one of her and Auntie Diane at a pizza restaurant holding up big slices and smiling. I see that Auntie Diane is on Facebook, too, and I send her a friend request. She accepts immediately. My number of Facebook friends is climbing into the high single digits!

Seeing Auntie Diane's face makes me think of our conversation at the park about the ways we have tried to help Mommy. I search "drug treatment" and "Morgan Kentucky." The first things that pop up are ads for rehabs in Lexington and Louisville that probably cost more than what Nanny makes in a year. But further down on the page, there's a link to a Narcotics Anonymous group that meets at the United Methodist Church downtown. Nanny thinks the Methodists are heathens because they sprinkle instead of dunking when they baptize, and in

Nanny's opinion, if you're not dunked like a doughnut, you're basically sitting in hell's waiting room.

But even if the Methodists are sinful sprinklers, I decide I'm getting Mommy to those meetings. When she comes back. If she comes back.

* * *

MACEY CALLS ALMOST AS SOON AS I'm home. "I saw you liked my photos," she says.

"I did." I get some juice from the fridge and settle down at the kitchen table to talk. "I love those sparkly blue costumes your dance team was wearing. I can't imagine what it feels like to wear something so glamorous." My stomach does a flip-flop. I feel like I'm just inches away from telling her about Dolly Dress Up Hour.

"Itchy is how it feels," she says. "Sparkly things are always itchy. It's the dancing I love. I don't care that much about the costumes and makeup. Hey, have you talked to our mom about me yet?"

"Our mom" sounds so strange when she says it.

"Not yet," I say. "She's been . . . gone."

"Like out of her mind gone or out of town gone?"

"Definitely the first, maybe the second. She's not home, not answering her phone."

"I'm worried."

It's kind of sweet, how fresh and new this worry is to her, the same worry I've been carrying around for as long as I can remember. "Well, if you're gonna have any relationship with Mommy, that's the feeling you're gonna have the most." I know I must sound harsh, but it's the truth. "She does this every few months. Disappears for a

few days. She's always come back though. If she doesn't
show up in a couple of days, we'll call the police—see if
they can shake her out of wherever she's hiding."

"Okay," Macey says. She sounds scared.

"And I'll tell her about you as soon as she's in a condition
to listen. Hey, you started some drama here without even
knowing about it." I tell her about L.J. seeing the pictures
and thinking Macey and me were girlfriend and boyfriend.

"Wait," Macey says. "She's your best friend and she doesn't
know you're gay?"

"I told you. You're the first person I ever told."

"I get that you never told her, but didn't she just kind
of *know*?"

I laugh. "Is it that obvious?"

"Kinda, yeah."

"Well, not to L.J. In her mind, her and me was practically engaged."

"Poor, deluded girl," Macey says.

"Yeah. I guess to her—and well, to a lot of people around
here—I can't be gay because I'm good to my nanny and go
to church every Sunday. They look at me and see what they
want to see."

"Well, when I look at you, I see you, Kody, and I think
you're pretty great."

I wish I could reach through the phone and hug her.

After supper, Nanny and me have our half hour of quilting
and *The Golden Girls*. When the credits are rolling to the
tune of "Thank You for Being a Friend," I say, "You know,
there's a Narcotics Anonymous group that meets on Tuesday
nights at the Methodist church."

"Methodists," Nanny says darkly. "They sprinkle, you know."

"I know," I say, trying not to roll my eyes.

"Don't know why you'd be trying to save on the church's water bill when you're giving somebody a new life in Christ." She ties off the perfect line of stitches she just finished.

"Well, the N.A. group isn't run by the Methodists. The Methodists just let them meet there."

"And what does it cost to go?"

"It's free."

Nanny's quiet for a few seconds. "You reckon we could get her to go?"

"Well, the way I see it, the only reason she's got a roof over her head or food to eat is you. It seems like she kinda has to do what you say."

Nanny laughs a good long time. "You'd think that'd be the way it worked, wouldn't you? Just wait till you have young'uns, Kody. You'll see."

* * *

IN THE MIDDLE OF THE NIGHT, there's a banging at the door. The dogs are outside barking like crazy. I drag myself out of bed and run into Nanny in the hall. She's in her long old-lady nightgown, and her hair is smooshed down from sleep. "It's the police," she says. "She's dead." She sounds surprisingly calm, like this is what she's been waiting for.

"We don't know that." I don't tell her that this was also my first thought. "Let me see who it is."

Mommy is not dead. She's standing in the doorway, looking like holy hell, dressed in a stained white spaghetti-strap top, Daisy Dukes, and flip-flops, even though it's not much more than thirty degrees outside. Her skin is pale, and her arms are dotted with small scabs. A year ago, when

I begged her, she promised me that even though she was using, she'd never shoot up again because it scared me. "There's my handsome boy!" she says, smiling. "You was blowing my phone up so bad I thought I'd stop by to tell you I'm okay. Shit, did I wake you up? What time is it?"

"Two-thirty," Nanny says, "but come on in. Why in the Sam Hill didn't you call me back? The phone works two ways, you know."

Mommy takes my hand and leads me to sit on the couch with her. "My phone didn't. It ran out of juice. I was able to charge it some just now in my friend's car when he brought me home. That's how I got your messages."

"You didn't think about us being worried?" Nanny says. It's hard to read the look on her face. I know she's glad Mommy's not dead, but the way Mommy's shown up doesn't exactly make a person feel that much relief. It's like she's not dead . . . yet.

"Mother, I am thirty-five years old. I don't have to report to you or anybody else. You can't put me on curfew like Kody." She looks over at me and catches me looking at the tiny scabs on her arms. "Cat scratches," she says. "The friends I was staying with . . . they have cats."

"Cat scratches don't look like that," I say. I have this thing about needles. I get woozy when I have to get blood drawn, and I never donate when there's a blood drive because I know I'll pass right out. Unless it's the kind of needle you sew with, I don't want to be near it. I know it's bad when Mommy crushes up pills and snorts them, but the thought of her injecting drugs makes me sick to my stomach. It's so desperate, pushing in the needle, pumping the poison into your vein, like you don't care about anybody or anything but the high, not even yourself.

"Amanda," Nanny says, her voice heavy with exhaustion. "You may be thirty-five years old, but you don't take care of yourself. You've got that trailer because I gave it to you, and I pay the rent on the lot it sits on. I pay your light bill, I buy your groceries—"

"So what do you want me to do, Mother? Get down on my knees and thank you?"

"No," Nanny says. "I want you to try to do better, and you don't. You don't try, and you've got two kids—"

Three, I think, but I know better than to say anything. This moment is the definition of Not a Good Time.

"How is anybody supposed to do better living in this place?" Mommy says.

In a way, Mommy has a point. Most of the mines are closed down, and all the factories except the little one where Nanny works have moved off to Mexico. There aren't really any opportunities here, but people stay because their people are here, because it's where they're from.

On the other hand, for Mommy to do better, the bar is set pretty low.

"Well, maybe instead of getting on your knees and thanking me, you could get on your knees and pray to the Lord to help you get off that junk and find a path in life," Nanny says.

Mommy rolls her eyes. "Here we go—"

I squeeze Mommy's hand. "Mommy, there's a Narcotics Anonymous group that meets on Tuesday nights at the Methodist church—"

"It's always got to be a church with you people. I guess it figures that letting your nanny raise you, you'd turn out to be a Bible-banger, too."

"It's not a church group, Mommy. They just meet in the church. They're like A.A. but for drug—" I stop myself and remembered the name Auntie Diane used "—for people with substance abuse disorder. They talk about a higher power but it can be anything you want that isn't drugs."

"Huh," Mommy says. "You want me to do this?"

"I do, and Caleb does, too," I say. I haven't talked to Caleb about N.A., but I know he'd be all for anything that might make Mommy better. "You've got quite a few years left to be a real mom to him if you want to."

Mommy's eyes glitter with tears. "He's my baby."

I nod.

"If I go to these meetings, will you drive me there instead of her?" She jerks her head in Nanny's direction. "I don't need her judging me."

Nanny clamps her lips in a tight line and doesn't say anything.

"Nanny, can I have the car on Tuesday nights to take Mommy to her meetings?"

Nanny nods.

"Okay." I take Mommy's cold, bony hand. "We're gonna do this, okay?"

Mommy nods. Tears spill from her eyes. "I'll try," she says. "I promise I'll try."

Chapter 11

THE LITTLE TOWHEADED BOY IS HIDING behind his mamaw's skirt. "Jaden's a little bashful," Mrs. Jenkins says, "but he'll warm up to you."

"Hi, Jaden," I say.

He peeks out from behind his mamaw but doesn't say anything. His little hands are clutching Mrs. Jenkins' skirt like he's a baby monkey hanging on to its mama. She unpeels his fingers and turns to face him. "Now me and your papaw are gonna be gone for a couple of hours, but Kody here is gonna stay and play with you. He's gonna fix you pizza for supper, and you'uns can watch a movie."

Jaden's big blue eyes get even bigger, and his bottom lip sticks out. I just have enough time to think *uh-oh* before he screams "No!" so loud everybody in the state of Kentucky probably heard it.

"Now Jaden, we talked about this," Mrs. Jenkins says. She's gotten all dolled up by church lady standards, in a nice blouse and a mid-calf-length floral print skirt. Her silver hair is in a fancy updo. "I told you it was me and Papaw's anniversary."

"No!" Jaden screams. "No 'versary! No go!"

"Charles, you about ready?" Mrs. Jenkins calls, sounding a little desperate.

"Sure am," Mr. Jenkins says, as he comes into the living room. He's the church gentleman version of dolled up, I guess, in a short-sleeved dress shirt and clip-on tie. Bless his heart. At least he's made an effort. "Now Jaden, you be a good boy for Kody while we're gone."

"No!" Jaden screams.

Great, I think. Mr. and Mrs. Jenkins get out of the house so fast you'd think they'd just robbed it and heard the police coming.

Jaden looks at me with cold, narrowed eyes. "I hate you," he says.

"Well, that's starting things out on the right foot," I say. "You don't hate me. You're not supposed to hate anybody. And it's not like I'm a stranger. You know me from church."

"You're a poo poo head," he says.

"Well, I'm the poo poo head who's fixing your supper. Maybe you ought to be nice to me because I'm old enough to use the oven. You about ready for me to cook that pizza?"

He doesn't say no, so I figure that's the best I'm going to do. He follows me into the kitchen and stares at me while I take the pizza out of the freezer.

I set the pizza down on the kitchen table and turn on the oven. When I turn around, Jaden is holding the plastic-wrapped frozen pizza. "Frisbee!" he yells and hurls it right at me.

It hits me square in the ribcage. The kid's got a good arm, and the blow hurts more than you'd think. "Hey," I say, "that's not okay, buddy. We don't throw food at people." I don't know why I'm saying *we* don't. One of us clearly does.

"Throw! Food!" Jaden yells, then giggles. There's a bowl of apples on the kitchen table, and he lobs one at me. I dodge, and it hits a cow-shaped saltshaker on the counter. It falls to the floor and breaks, leaving an anthill of salt on the floor.

"See, that's why we don't throw things," I say, with that *we* again. "You broke your mamaw's nice cow saltshaker."

"I kill cow?" Jaden says, giggling.

"Yeah, and you'll have to tell your mamaw you're real sorry," I say, putting the pizza in the oven. I try to think of something to keep him occupied while the pizza cooks. "Why don't you show me your room?"

"Okay." It's the first thing he's agreed to. Little kids always want to show you their rooms for some reason.

One wall in Jaden's room is hung with pictures of big-eyed children kneeling in prayer. I'm guessing his mamaw picked these out. His bedspread has a race car on it, though, and there's a plastic racetrack on the floor with a bunch of those little metal cars I remember Caleb loving when he was little. "You like cars, huh?" I say.

"Yeah. I make 'em CRASH!"

"You do, huh? Show me."

Jaden squats on the floor and sets up the little cars on the tracks so they have multiple head-on collisions. When this kid is old enough to drive, I'm staying off the road.

The oven timer goes off, and Jaden yells, "Pizza!" and abandons the highway disaster he's created.

In the kitchen, I pour him a sippy cup of apple juice and put a piece of pizza on a plastic plate with a cartoon puppy on it. Nothing breakable for this kid. I get him settled at the table.

I get myself some water from the tap—there's cans of Pepsi in the fridge, but I don't know if I should take one—and grab a piece of pizza for myself.

I sit down across from Jaden and he says, "MY pizza! No pizza, you!"

"Look, bud," I say. "I've got to eat something to have the strength to keep up with you. You eat what's on your plate, and if you want more, I'll get you more. There's plenty."

He chomps through his pizza glaring at me with angry eyes.

"You want another piece?"

He nods. I get I for him, but he loses interest halfway through, maybe because he's full, maybe because he can't stand to sit still any longer.

"How about you pick out a movie for us to watch?" I say.

He runs to the living room and comes back with a DVD from a series about vegetables that act out Bible stories. I remember liking these when I was little, too, but when I think about it now, it's a super weird idea. I mean, I guess one day the show's creator just woke up and said, "Hey, I know! Christian vegetables!"

Thank the Lord, the Christian vegetables hold his attention and calm him down. Once the show is over, he says, "One more! One more!"

I don't know the rules for TV in this house, but if it keeps me from being pelted with pizza and apples, I'm all for it. If Jaden wears me out this bad, I wonder what it must be like for his grandparents who, like my nanny, thought their days of raising kids were over.

Jaden is getting sleepy by the time the second show is over, but he still yells, "One more!"

"Maybe you should put on your pajamas and brush your teeth first," I say.

"No brush teef!" he yells.

"Then no more TV," I say calmly.

He stares at me for a second like I'm the meanest person that ever lived, then finally turns his back on me and goes to his room, hopefully to put on his pajamas. In a few minutes I hear water running in the bathroom.

Jaden comes into the living room in his light blue pajamas. Little kids always look cute in their pajamas, even if you're pretty sure they have a 666 hidden somewhere in their scalp. It's just been two hours with this kid, and I'm plum wore out, as Nanny would say.

Thankfully, the door opens. Mr. and Mrs. Jenkins are smiling and obviously in a great mood. Probably it's not because of their anniversary so much as because they got to spend some time away from the hell spawn.

Jaden runs to his mamaw and hugs her around the legs. "Was you a good boy for Kody?" she asks.

"I was sooo good," Jaden says, looking over at me like he's daring me to challenge him.

"All right, well, go on to your room," Mrs. Jenkins says. "Papaw will check under your bed for monsters, and I'll come read you a story."

After Jaden leaves, Mrs. Jenkins whispers, "How was he really?"

"He's got a lot of energy," I say, which doesn't really answer the question.

Mrs. Jenkins nods. "His mommy was on dope the whole time she was pregnant. The doctor says that's why he won't mind nobody."

"My mommy was using when she was pregnant with Caleb," I say. "He bounces off the walls, too." What I don't say is that Caleb's never been mean-spirited. He just needs to be run a lot like a dog that's real playful, which is why sports are great for him.

Mrs. Jenkins shakes her head. "It's some world we live in, ain't it? It's a good thing we've got our heavenly reward to look forward to. Well"—she holds out two bills to me—"we appreciate you."

It's two twenties. "This is too much."

"No, it ain't. Jaden's a handful."

"Well, thank you. And if you ever need me to babysit some other time, just call me or give me a holler at church."

Mrs. Jenkins' eyes widen like I've just said something shocking. "You mean that?"

I carefully put my money in my wallet. "Sure."

Mrs. Jenkins breaks out in a big grin. "Well, Kody, you're a blessing. We ain't never had nobody babysit Jaden who was willing to do it a second time."

* * *

MOMMY SHOWS UP AT THE DOOR looking halfway respectable. Her hair is clean and brushed, and she has on decent-looking jeans and a pink sweater. She's even remembered to put on shoes.

"You look pretty," I say. I figure my job in this situation is to give her as much confidence as possible.

"I'm a nervous wreck," she says. "I'm doing this for you and Caleb, you know."

"Do it for me, too!" Nanny hollers from the living room. "My old nerves is shot, and I can't be worrying about you all the time."

"Okay," Mommy says, but she rolls her eyes.

I jingle Nanny's car keys. "You ready to go?"

She nods. "Ready as I'll ever be."

When we get in the car, Mommy doesn't reach for the seat belt.

"Put on your seat belt, Mommy."

"Oh, I hate them things. They smoosh my boobies."

"Well, they'll just have to be smooshed, then, because I ain't leaving this driveway till you buckle up."

It's a familiar pattern when I'm with Mommy. She says things a kid would say, and I find myself saying things a parent would say.

She sighs but fastens her seatbelt. "Your nanny would kill me for smoking in her car, but if I'm gonna do this, I've got to have a cigarette."

"Crack the window." I'm not crazy about Mommy smoking in the car either, but you've got to pick your battles.

"So tell me some high school gossip," Mommy says, blowing a double lungful of smoke out the window. "You and L.J. patched things up yet?"

"No. She still won't even look at me. I can mostly manage to avoid her at school, but Sunday school and church are the worst. It's not big enough there to hide."

"And your nanny's more likely to let you skip school than she is church."

"That's for sure," I say. "In Sunday school L.J. sits with this real quiet girl and they both ignore me. Who does that leave me to talk to? The football players?"

"You know," Mommy says, "sometimes I wonder if your nanny hadn't shoved so much church down my throat growing up if I would've turned out different. I had to rebel."

"There are other ways of rebelling besides ruining your health," I say as we're driving into town. "Like Dolly—she left the mountains to go to Nashville and get famous."

Mommy laughs. "Yeah, but she's talented, and I'm not good at much of anything. I take that back. I'm good at doing a bunch of drugs and not dying."

"Yeah," I say. "So far."

I pull into the Methodist church parking lot.

"Kody?" Mommy says. There's a tremble in her voice.

"Yeah?"

"What if I can't do this?"

"You can do it," I say even though I have no idea whether she can or can't. I take her hand and give it a squeeze.

"You're coming in with me, right?"

"This meeting is closed. It's got to just be you."

Mommy swallows hard. "Will you walk me to the door?"

"Sure." I take her hand and walk with her to the church's big double doors, like I'm a mother walking her scared child to her first day of kindergarten.

The big doors close behind her, and, for the next hour anyway, what happens to her is out of my hands. I brought homework with me, so I go across the street to the little city park to sit on a bench and work on it. Maybe homework will be less like torture if I do it in the fresh air.

I settle on a bench and try to focus on a history packet about immigration. All through it are stories about how mean people were to immigrants—how they wouldn't hire them for jobs or even let them come inside their stores. I wonder why people work so hard to find reasons to hate other people. Does L.J. hate me now that she knows I'm gay? Or is she just hurt because I broke her heart?

Right when it's getting too dark for me to keep working outside, a man sits down on the bench opposite me. He's maybe around forty and is dressed in an off-brand polo shirt and khakis. He's a little thick around the middle. He looks like somebody's dad.

He sits there quietly for a couple of minutes, staring straight ahead, then he mutters, "How much?"

He hasn't turned his head so I'm not even sure he's talking to me.

A few seconds later, he repeats, "How much?"

All of a sudden, I understand. "Do you think I'm selling drugs?"

"No, but what you do with my money once you get it is your business. Come on, everybody knows what it means if you're still hanging around this park once it starts getting dark. I'm not picky, so just tell me what you're offering, your hand, that hot little mouth, or—"

"Sir!" I jump up from the bench like it's red hot. "I was sitting on the bench so I could do my homework while my mom's in a meeting at the church."

The man looks horrified, like he might cry. "Oh, I'm sorry! I'm truly sorry. Look, you don't want to hang around here at night. People . . . might get the wrong idea."

I run as fast as I can to the church. I don't stop until I'm inside the lobby, where I sink into a folding chair, panting. I know there are places in town and truck stops out by the interstate where women sell themselves for drug money. I wonder if Mommy's ever been one of those women, but I stop my mind when it goes down that road.

But a man soliciting a boy right in downtown Morgan! And for me to be mistaken for somebody who would do things for money with a stranger, especially when I've never done so much as go on a date with another boy.

There's a water cooler in the lobby, and I drink down two of the weird little paper cones of water and start to feel calmer. I think about the man on the bench. He looked like somebody with a regular job, like an insurance agent or a bank employee, somebody with a house and a wife and maybe a couple of kids. Approaching me the way he did was wrong, but I still feel sorry for him. He seemed so lonely, so desperate, and the look on his face when I told him I wasn't what he was after was the look of somebody who in his whole life has never been understood.

It doesn't make what he did right, but I still know how he feels.

The N.A. meeting must be over because I hear people coming up the stairs from the church basement. I head back to the car so I don't make anybody feel self-conscious.

When Mommy comes to the car, her eyes are red and she's holding a wad of Kleenex in one hand and a stack of pamphlets in the other. When she slides into the passenger seat, she says, "Well . . . that was something."

"Was it good?" I feel stupid as soon as I say it because it sounds like I'm asking about a movie she just saw or something. "I mean, do you think it'll help you?"

She sniffs. "It might. Being around other people who are going through the same thing. It's sad listening to people's stories and hearing about everything they've lost. The jobs, the people, the time." She reaches over and squeezes my hand. "I'm gonna do this, Kody."

"Good," I say, starting the car. "Let me know what I can do to help." I decide not to say anything about the man on the park bench. Her mind should stay on getting clean.

"I don't think I can stand to quit all at once. I'll have to taper off. But when the time comes when I quit for real, will you stay with me?"

"Of course I will."

"I've only detoxed once before and that was when I was in jail that time for shoplifting. It won't be pretty, Kody."

"I didn't think it would be."

"It'd be better if I could do it in the hospital, but no money, no insurance, you know?"

"I know. But I'll be there. I'll take care of you."

Mommy smiles a little. "Will you hold my hair while I puke?"

"You know I will."

"Hey, look!" Mommy says, pointing to a squat orange concrete block building. "It's the Root Beer Stand! I used to hang out there all the time in high school."

I try to picture Mommy at my age, doing something as wholesome as hanging out at a drive-in. "You want a root beer?"

"You got money?"

"I'm loaded," I say, pulling into the parking lot. "On account of babysitting the Jenkins' demon grandbaby."

Mommy laughs.

The carhops at the Root Beer Stand are all in their fifties but have been working there since they were teenagers. They all still wear the cut-off short shorts and halter tops they wore in their younger days. "What can I get you?" our carhop asks. Her eyeshadow is blue and frosty.

"Two root beers, and Mommy, would you share some onion rings with me?"

Mommy nods.

"One large order of onion rings."

"Their onion rings are the best," Mommy says after the carhop has left.

"They are, and the root beer's perfect for washing down all that salt and grease." It's kind of weird being out with Mommy in a place where a regular mother and son might go.

"It's nice being out with you," Mommy says. "I want there to be more times like this with you and me and Caleb, too. Maybe we can start going to some of his ball games."

"Maybe," I say, even though I can't think of anything more boring than sitting through a ball game. "I'll bring my knitting." I picture myself sitting in the stands with my needles clicking. "Lord, can you imagine how embarrassed Caleb would be?"

Mommy laughs. "He is a manly little thing, ain't he? He loves his guns and balls—" she giggles. "That didn't sound right, did it?"

"No, but all the things guys like make it sound like you're talking about their privates."

"They do, don't they? It's funny how two kids so different could come from the same parents, but you know I love you both the same, right?"

I'm about to get a little emotional so I'm grateful when the carhop comes with our root beers and onion rings. They go together so well, the salty and sweet, the hot and the cold. This is the first time in so long that Mommy and me have been happy and comfortable together, and I hear myself saying, "Mommy, I need to tell you something."

"Oh my God, you're gay!" she says with a fake shocked expression.

"I never had to tell you that," I say, smiling. "Listen, I met somebody on Facebook—"

"You have a boyfriend?"

Of course that's what it sounded like. "No, there was a person who friended me on Facebook, somebody I didn't even know existed—"

Mommy's hands fly to her mouth. Her eyes are wide.

"You know what I'm gonna say, don't you?"

Mommy's eyes are full of tears. "My little girl. I didn't even get to name her."

"Macey. Her name is Macey." I take out my phone and pull up a picture of her in her sparkly dance costume.

Mommy takes the phone and looks at it, tears running down her cheeks. "She's so beautiful. And a dancer, huh? I'm not surprised. Her daddy was such an athlete."

Now my eyes are getting teary, too. "Why didn't you or Nanny tell me I had a sister?"

Mommy looks out the car window and is quiet for a minute. "Because I had to give her up. I didn't want to, but I had to. And talking about it hurt so much that I just didn't. I numbed the pain with pills instead." She wipes her eyes. "So you know her? How is she?"

"She's good. She lives in Knoxville, and she's a real nice person. Her aunt's nice, too."

"Diane," Mommy says. "Calvin's sister."

"Tell me about Calvin," I say. What I really want to know is why Macey has a different daddy than Caleb and me, but I don't know how to ask it without sounding mean.

Mommy lights a cigarette. "Well, see, there was a stretch where me and your daddy wasn't living together. He was using anything he could get his hands on and drinking real bad, too. He got rough with me a few times, and I was afraid he might get rough with you, too, and you still just a baby. I was holding down a job back then—at the Burger Boy. Nanny wouldn't let me stay with her since I was using, so you stayed with her, and I got me a room at a motel I rented by the week. I met Calvin at the Burger Boy one night. He'd started using after he got hurt playing football, but Kody, he was the nicest, sweetest guy. It was never serious between us—we just hooked up a few times—" She stops short. "That's probably more information than you wanted to know."

"It's okay. Since there was a baby, I kind of figured sex was involved." Having a parent who's an addict means you always have more information about them than you're comfortable with.

"So after a few weeks your daddy came crawling back, with all kinds of apologies and a full bottle of Oxys. I moved back in with him. And then when I noticed I'd missed my time I figured the baby must be his. I think I convinced myself of that because I was so scared of what would happen if it wasn't. Your daddy was out somewhere partying when I went into labor, so he wasn't at the hospital when she was born. But when he finally dragged in and saw her skin and her hair, he slapped my face and called me a whore and said, 'Get rid of it.' It. Like she was a thing, not a person." Mommy has given up on wiping her tears. "And God, she was such a beautiful baby."

So far everything in Mommy's story has been about the way I imagined it. It's the missing piece I'm worried about, the question I'm not sure I want the answer to. "What about Nanny? Where was she at?"

"She was at home taking care of you while I was in labor," Mommy says. "But when she came to the hospital, she took one look at the baby and said, 'Lord, girl, what have you done?' I told her what your daddy'd done, and she said 'Well, he ought not to have hit you, but he's right that you can't raise this baby.' She said people were already talking about my problems and how I'd had a child out of wedlock and gave it to her to raise. What would they say if there was another child, this one colored? 'Colored' was your nanny's word, not mine."

The onion rings in my stomach are threatening an uprising. "So . . . do you think Nanny's a racist?"

"Duh," Mommy says. "It was the way she was raised. Just like about every white person around here. They never get out of these hills, so they never learn any different." I must look as upset as I am because Mommy reaches out and takes my hand. "But listen, don't be too hard on her. She drives me crazy, but she loves you with her whole heart and always has."

"But would she still love me if I was Black?"

Mommy sighs. "No. Probably not."

We sit for a minute, just holding hands before Mommy starts talking again. "Calvin was in rehab when Macey was born. Diane had gotten him a bed at the hospital where she worked in Knoxville. He couldn't take phone calls so I called Diane, and soon there were lawyers and papers and she was taking legal guardianship of the baby. I could tell Diane loved Macey as soon as she saw her, so I told myself I was doing the right thing." She sniffs hard. "But you know what? It was love at first sight when I saw her, too."

"She wants to meet you," I say.

"She does? I thought she'd hate me."

"She doesn't hate you. She wants to get to know you."

Mommy nods. "Okay, that's good. But not yet. Let's give it a few weeks. Give me time to get clean. I don't want her to see me like I am now."

"Got it," I say. "And just so you know, I've not said one word to Nanny about her yet."

"Good." Mommy leans back in her seat. "Can you take me home now? Today has been . . . a lot."

It has. For both of us, I guess. I feel like I've been living in a dark room with a big black curtain covering the only window. Now somebody's ripped off the curtain. The sunlight is streaming through the bare window, and now I can see what I've been surrounded by my whole life. It's so bright it hurts.

Chapter 12

NANNY AND ME DECIDED THAT MOMMY should detox at our house. It's not as good as a hospital or rehab, but at least it's clean, and, unlike her trailer, it's not a place where she's sat around doing drugs with her druggy friends. We also figured that Friday would be a good time to start because that way me and Nanny can be with her all weekend. As soon as I get home from school, I call her. "You can come over whenever you want to," I say. No Dolly Dress-Up Hour for me today.

"I'll be right over," she says. "I ain't had nothing but half an Oxy last night so I could sleep. That was my last one, Kody, I swear to God."

Mommy shows up twenty minutes later with a paper sack with God knows what in it. "Are you ready for the worst sleepover ever?" she says. She looks pale and sweaty and queasy, like somebody with a bad stomach virus.

"I'm ready," I say.

She reaches into the paper sack. "I brought pajamas and a toothbrush and . . ." She pulls out a clear plastic bag with four white pills in it. "I scored these last weekend. They're the last I got. I want you to get rid of them for me."

I take the baggie, but I don't like even touching it. The
pills are small and white and don't look much different than
aspirin. Maybe that's why some people try them who wouldn't
do other drugs. They don't look like cocaine or heroin or
even marijuana. Doctors prescribe them. They're medicine.
"Let's get rid of them together," I say.

I take her hand and we go down the hall to the bathroom.
I open the baggie and shake the pills into the toilet.

"Just like Goldy," Mommy says.

"What?"

"Your goldfish when you was little. When it died, we
flushed it down the toilet. Your Nanny told you the pipes
would take it to fish heaven."

I must've been about four. I have only vague memories of
a pretty orange fish swimming in a clear glass bowl. "You
want to do the honors?" I ask.

Mommy nods. She reaches over and flushes the toilet.
The pills circle the drain, then disappear. "Okay," Mommy
says. "Okay."

"Good," I say. "How about I fix us something to drink and
we watch some TV?"

Mommy nods. "I need to go outside and smoke a cigarette first."

While Mommy feeds her legal addiction, I go into the
kitchen and mix up a pitcher of cherry Kool-Aid. I fill two
tall glasses with ice.

Mommy comes back in, pale and sweaty, and I hand her a
cold glass. She lifts it, and I think she's going to drink from
it, but instead she presses it to her forehead.

We settle on the couch, and I flip through the channels. I
turn past daytime talk shows about people's family problems

because we've got enough problems of our own. It's too early for a *Golden Girls* rerun, but I do find an *Andy Griffith* on the rerun channel for old people that always advertises catheters and back braces. "Sheriff Andy okay with you?"

Mommy nods. She grabs my hand, and we sit there holding hands and sipping Kool-Aid, watching the gentle, down-home humor of daily life in Mayberry, North Carolina.

"Your papaw loved this show," Mommy says. "He said Mayberry was just like Morgan."

"Not anymore," I say.

"No," she says. "Not anymore."

"Mayberry wouldn't be like that anymore either," I say. "All the stores downtown would be closed, even Floyd's Barber Shop and Gomer's gas station, and everybody would just do all their business at the Walmart."

"The Darlins would be cooking meth," Mommy says.

I laugh. The Darlins are a huge hillbilly moonshining family that lives on the outskirts of Mayberry. Mommy is exactly right.

"The jail cell would be full of addicts, not just drunk old Otis," I say.

A strange look has come over Mommy's face. She says, "Kody, I—" and then a stream of bright red vomit shoots out of her like she's a human volcano. The color scares me at first because I'm afraid it's blood, but then I look down at my own glass of cherry Kool-Aid. The vomit's all over the coffee table, all over Nanny's crafting magazines, all over the beige carpet Nanny keeps spotlessly clean.

"I'm sorry," Mommy says. "I—" She clamps her hand over her mouth, jumps up, and runs down the hall.

I follow her. She's kneeling in front of the toilet, retching.

"This is the part where I hold your hair," I say. I gather up her hair like I'm putting it in a ponytail to keep it out of her face.

"There's nothing else to bring up," she says, gasping. "But I can't stop retching."

"Try taking deep breaths," I say.

She sits on the bathroom floor, and I sit down beside her. Together we breathe. In and out, in and out. We sit there a long time. Anybody who saw us sitting on the bathroom floor staring into each other's eyes and breathing would think we were as crazy as bessbugs . . . like we were members of some religious cult or something.

After a while, I say, "Better?"

She nods. "A little."

"There's mouthwash in the medicine cabinet. You want some?"

She nods.

I open the medicine cabinet. There's a prescription bottle of pills on the shelf next to the mouthwash, and I can feel Mommy staring at it. I grab the bottle and read the label. "This is some leftover antibiotics from when Nanny had that sinus infection," I say. "So don't get too excited." I shake the bottle so the pills rattle around and put it back on the shelf.

"God, that sound," Mommy says. "It makes me want to get high so bad."

"I'm sorry. I didn't mean to make it worse."

I remember reading in psychology about how Pavlov conditioned dogs to start drooling when a bell rang because they associated the bell with food. I guess the sound of pills shaking in a bottle is like that for Mommy.

"It's okay." She gives a sad little smile. "To tell you the truth, everything makes me want to get high."

I take out the mouthwash and pour some in one of the paper cups Nanny always keeps in the bathroom. I hand it to her. She swishes the mouthwash around, then spits it into the toilet and flushes.

"Okay," she says. "Ready to get out of the bathroom."

In the living room, she lies down on the couch. *The Andy Griffith Show* is over, and now *Matlock* is on, starring a much older Andy Griffith. It feels like he aged all those years just while Mommy and me were in the bathroom.

"I feel so weak," Mommy says.

"Throwing up will do that to you," I say. I've gotten out three different kinds of spray cleaner and am attacking the puke on the carpet and coffee table. The challenge is not puking myself. The red stain is lifting out of the carpet which is good. I'm afraid Nanny's magazines are a lost cause, though.

"Yeah, but it's more than that," Mommy says. "I mean I'm a weak person to let myself get in this situation."

"No, you're not," I say, scrubbing the carpet. I remember what Auntie Diane said. "Addiction is a disease. You caught a disease, that's all."

"Yeah, but disease always strikes the weakest members of the herd," Mommy says.

I put down my cleaning rag and sit on the edge of the couch. "Sounds like you've been watching too much Animal Planet," I say. I take her hand. "You're not weak, Mommy. You're strong. Look at what you're doing here. You're going on twenty-four hours clean."

Mommy has tears in her eyes. "That ain't much."

"What is it they say in N.A.?"

"One day at a time," she says. She's really crying now, and I get up to grab some Kleenex. Tears are better than puke, I reckon.

When I bring her the Kleenex, she says, "I love you, Kody."

"I love you, too, Mommy."

She blows her nose. "I love Caleb, too, but he's too little to see me like this. It'd upset him."

"Probably so." Caleb has seen Mommy do plenty of upsetting things, like begging in the street for money, but I figure now isn't the time to bring this up.

"Kody, could you cover me up with that afghan? Your nanny keeps it too damn cold in here."

I cover Mommy up with the afghan Nanny and me crocheted last fall. It's real pretty—Nanny let me pick out the yarn, and I chose all jewel tones: emerald, garnet, sapphire.

I pick up Nanny's magazines and throw them in the wastebasket.

"Sorry about those," Mommy says.

"It's okay. At least you didn't puke on the family Bible." It's on the other end of the coffee table and is as big as a dictionary. "You did get a little on this Jesus figurine, though," I say, wiping the vomit off Jesus.

"Sorry, Jesus," Mommy says.

"I'm sure he forgives you," I say, and we both laugh a little.

I sit down on the recliner so Mommy can stretch out on the couch. After a minute or two, Mommy says, "Tell me about her."

"About who?"

"About my little girl. About Macey." Mommy is still crying, but she's shaking, too. It's probably more from the withdrawal than from the cold, but I take the afghan that's draped over the back of the recliner—a pastel one that Nanny made—and throw it over her, too.

"She's great," I say. "Sweet and funny and smart, and there's something about her that's so . . . open, I guess you could call it."

"Did you tell her you're gay?"

"I did. And she didn't bat one long, beautiful eyelash."

"That's how it ought to be," Mommy says. She does a long, slow blink that makes me think she might doze off. I change the channel from *Matlock* to the evening news from Lexington. The newscasters have flawless hair and speak in fake concerned voices as they report on busts of pill mills and show mug shots of a couple of obvious addicts who got arrested in a poorly planned bank robbery. Then comes sports and a light story they feed you to try to cheer you up after they've been breaking your heart for half an hour. This one's about some guy who rescued an orphaned baby fox and raised it, and now he takes it to elementary schools to teach kids about nature. The fox looks miserable being petted by all those kids, like all it's thinking about is escaping to the woods and never getting any closer to humans than stealing chickens from their henhouse.

"Trapped," Mommy says.

I turn to her. "What?"

"Trapped. That fox feels trapped."

"I think so, too," I say. "A fox don't want to be petted like a poodle." When I look in Mommy's eyes, they're wild and scared like the fox's.

Nanny comes in from work. "How's it going?" she asks. I can tell she's trying to sound cheerful and encouraging.

"I feel like hell," Mommy says from where she's lying on the couch.

To my surprise, Nanny lets the cussing slide. "Well, I'll tell you what. I made us a big pot of potato soup last night. I just need to heat it up and make some cornbread. Maybe eating a bite will make you feel better."

Nanny's potato soup is the official Sick Person Food in our family. It's bland and comforting, and you can eat it when you can't eat anything else.

"I don't think I can eat anything," Mommy says.

"Well, you need your strength, so you've got to try," Nanny says. She's already in the kitchen, taking the soup out of the fridge and turning on the stove.

"Try, try, try," Mommy says in a sing-song. "Don't you ever get tired of trying, Mama?"

"Of course I do," Nanny says. "Every day. But that's when I pray and the Lord gives me strength."

"Jesus and potato soup," Mommy says.

"That's right." Nanny takes the buttermilk out of the fridge. "And I know when I die it'll all be worth it."

"Your nanny thinks she's gonna get her some cotton candy in the sky," Mommy says, almost whispering.

"Something like that," I say.

"But what if it ain't real?" Mommy says. "What if when you die, you're just worm food? Seems to me you'd better get your candy while you're alive just to be on the safe side."

"Mommy, I don't think you're really talking about candy," I say. People don't cry and shake and puke because they can't have a Snickers bar.

"I'm just talking about feeling good," Mommy says, her eyes half closed. "I'm talking about it because I sure don't feel good right now." She sits up suddenly and throws off the afghans. "Lord, I don't know why I wanted all them covers. I'm burning up now." Her face is glazed with sweat.

We sit down at the kitchen table for our soup and corn-bread. Mommy doesn't even pick up her spoon.

"Eat a little, honey," Nanny says.

Mommy looks at the soup like the thought of it sickens her. "I can't."

"Don't make me play 'here comes the airplane' like I did when you was little," Nanny says.

"You might as well," Mommy says. "You already treat me like a child."

"Just eat three bites," Nanny says.

Mommy rolls her eyes but picks up her spoon and dips it into the soup. After she swallows a spoonful, she says "uh-oh," jumps up from the table, and runs.

"She can't keep nothing down," I tell Nanny. "She puked up Kool-Aid this afternoon."

"If we ain't careful she's gonna get so dehydrated she ends up in the hospital," Nanny says. "And we can't afford no hospital."

"Shoot," I say, remembering suddenly. "I've got to go hold her hair. That's part of the deal."

Nanny looks at me the way she does when she's sizing up a cut of meat in the grocery store. "You're a good boy, Kody. Listen, after I get the dishwasher loaded, I'm gonna run to Walmart's and get some Gatorade. We'll see if she can keep that down."

Mommy is sitting on the floor beside the toilet, crying. "I can't do this, Kody. I can't be sick like this all the time."

I offer her my hands and pull her up. "But you won't stay sick like this. After all the poison is out of your system, you'll feel good again. Regular good."

Mommy looks at me with fear in her eyes. "I don't remember what that feels like."

I'm not surprised. For over ten years, Mommy's life has been a cycle of high, then sick, then high again. "Well, you'll like it," I say because I can't think of anything else.

Mommy is leaning heavily on me as we walk down the hall. "Is that how you feel all the time?" she asks. "Regular good?"

"Pretty much, yeah," I lie. The truth is a lot of the time I'm a nervous wreck. I worry about the present—about how I've lost L.J., about whether or not I failed the algebra test I took today, about Macey and Caleb and Nanny and Mommy, all the people I love. I worry about the future because I don't think I have much of one in this dried-up mountain town where there are no jobs and nobody who's boyfriend material. But how could I leave Nanny and Mommy? They need me.

I decide I'd better not say any of this to Mommy. For right now she needs to believe that being off drugs will solve all her problems. Sometimes you've just got to let people believe what they need to believe.

She lays back down on the couch, still crying softly, and I say, "Covers on or off?"

"Off. I'm still roasting alive."

It's time for *The Golden Girls*. I sit at the end of the couch with Mommy's feet in my lap as the theme song starts to play. It's weird to be watching *The Golden Girls* with Mommy instead of Nanny. "Nanny ran to the Walmart to get you some Gatorade. You know she loves you because she's missing *The Golden Girls* to do it."

"She never says it," Mommy says.

"Never says what?"

"She never says 'I love you.'"

I'm sure I've heard those words come out of Nanny's mouth before, but I'm not sure when. "No, she don't say it

much. But she shows it in other ways. Like what she does
for you."

"It'd still be nice to hear it, though," Mommy says.

"Well, you can hear it from me. I love you, Mommy."

"I love you, too, Kody." She cries harder. "God, it just hurts
so bad."

"What hurts?"

"Me. All of me."

* * *

NANNY COMES IN WITH A PLASTIC Walmart bag. "I talked
to the pharmacist, and she showed me all this stuff you give
to little kids when they're dehydrated from being sick.
There's a drink, but there's popsicles and lollipops, too,
which she said would help settle your stomach."

"Give me a lollipop," Mommy says, sitting up.

The lollipop is in the shape of a teddy bear, which strikes
me as funny for some reason. "Now you have candy,
Mommy," I say.

"I do," Mommy says. "It's just not the candy I want."

Nanny puts a hand on her shoulder. "Kody, why don't you
take a break and go listen to some music or something? Me
and Amanda might settle down here and see if we can find
us a sappy movie to watch."

I don't realize how tired I am until Nanny offers me a
break. I go to my room, put on Dolly singing "Love Is Like a
Butterfly," and close my eyes. Something about her sweet,
clear voice always soothes me. When I do Dolly Dress-Up
Hour, I feel like I am Dolly. But laying here now, just listening
to her voice, I feel almost like she's my mother—not a mother
I take care of, but a mother who takes care of me.

* * *

TODAY IS THE ONLY SUNDAY OF my life I've been allowed
to stay home without running a high fever. But Nanny said
she had to go to church, and Mommy said she was in no
shape to go, which is true. Mommy can't be left alone, so
here I am, at home on Sunday morning like a heathen.

In some ways being a heathen is a relief. Sitting in the
Sunday school classroom while L.J. ignores me makes my
heart hurt.

Mommy is sitting at the kitchen table sipping on a glass of
Gatorade. She actually slept a little last night, and she looks a
little better. Not great or anything, but now she looks sick
instead of dead, so that's an improvement.

"You don't know what to do with yourself not being at
church, do you?" she says.

"Not really." I look up at the ceiling. "I'm still not sure a
big lightning bolt isn't gonna strike me dead where I stand."

"It'll get me first," Mommy says. "The church where N.A.
meets is the only church I've been in since I got too old for
Nanny to make me go." She gets up from the table and puts
her glass in the sink. "I'll tell you what. Them chicken and
dumplings on the stove sure smell good. I don't know if I can
eat any of them, but I do like smelling them."

"Well, it's a good sign that food smells good to you,
anyway." This afternoon Jay and Tiff and Caleb are coming
over for Sunday dinner. Nanny's already fixed chicken and
dumplings and some of the green beans we put up this
summer. She'll make the cornbread and fix the iced tea when
she gets home from church, and Tiff is bringing dessert
which I hope is something chocolate.

"I hope so," Mommy says. "This is so hard."

"I know, but you're going on seventy-two hours clean, which is great."

"I wish I felt great."

"Me, too," I say. Since Friday afternoon, Mommy's been stuck in this house, puking and sweating and shaking. An idea pops into my head. "You wanna go for a walk?"

Her eyes light up a little. "You reckon we could?"

"Sure. This ain't a jail. As long as we're back before Nanny gets home from church, it should be fine."

"As long as the service at that damn church lasts, we could probably walk to Florida and back," Mommy says.

As soon as we're on the porch, the dogs go crazy, wagging and barking. "Come on, let's go for a walk," I say, and they run ahead of Mommy and me, romping like the happy idiots they are.

It's a pretty day, bright and not too cold. Mommy lights a cigarette, and we walk together alongside the little creek that runs through the holler.

"It's almost spring," I say, looking up at the buds that have started to form on the tree branches.

"Yeah," Mommy says. "I like spring." She picks up a pebble and tosses it in the creek, where it hits with a plop. Loretta goes in after it and looks confused when she can't find it. "So do you believe in all that stuff?"

"What stuff?" Loretta has jumped out of the creek and is making a big show of shaking off the water.

"Church stuff," Mommy says, taking a long drag off her cigarette. "All that Bible stuff your nanny force-feeds you the same way she did me."

I'm surprised by the question. "I believe most of it," I say. "I mean, I like Jesus."

Mommy laughs. "You *like* him? Somehow I don't think that's enough to satisfy your nanny."

It is kind of funny that I said "like." If somebody asked me how I feel about Dolly, I'd say I love her. "I guess what I mean is that I like what it says he did in the Bible, the way he treated the people that other people thought they were too good for. But some of the other stuff, I don't know." I've never said something like this out loud, and I'm waiting for a lightning bolt to strike me. It doesn't, so I keep talking. "Like Paul said some awful things about women, and then the Old Testament—God's just so angry most of the time."

Mommy laughs. "He is one pissed off dude."

I laugh, too. "Like when He tells Abraham to kill his son just to prove his faith, and then he tortures poor Job for the same reason. And don't even get me started on Sodom and Gomorrah."

"I didn't think that'd be your favorite Bible story," Mommy says.

"And you're right." We watch the dogs splash around in the creek, getting all wet and muddy. I like how dogs don't worry about anything; they just have fun. "But I couldn't say any of that to Nanny. With her, you have to believe every single word is the literal word of God. It's all or nothing."

"Well, then I choose nothing," Mommy says.

"I don't know what I choose yet," I say. Around here it seems like people are drawn to one extreme or another. You either go to church every time the door's open and believe that all pleasure is a sin, or you live only for pleasure and get high on Oxys or meth and chase the next high until you OD or die in a car wreck. I want something different, but I don't know what.

I do know that when I talk to Macey, it makes me think there might be some place in the middle where I could carve out a life for myself. Macey gives me hope.

* * *

ONCE NANNY GETS HOME FROM CHURCH, she changes into a track suit and gets started making the batter for the cornbread.

"Can I help?" Mommy asks her, sounding like a kid who wants to be mommy's little helper in the kitchen.

Nanny looks surprised. "Sure. Why don't you help Kody set the table?'

Mommy says, "Kody, how about you get the plates and I'll get the silverware? I don't want to handle nothing I can break."

I can see why Mommy worried about breakage. As we set the table, her hands are shaking so bad it's hard for her to set down the forks and knives and line them up beside the plates. I'm about to say, "Here, let me do it," and take over, but I stop myself. If Mommy's going to stay off dope, she's going to have to do things on her own, even when they're hard.

Jay and Tiff come in still wearing their church clothes. I can hear Caleb on the porch playing with the dogs. When I see Tiff, she's usually just got on jeans shorts and a t-shirt and has her hair yanked up in a messy bun. Today, though, her makeup's done nice, and her hair is styled and down past her shoulders. She's wearing a short denim dress and wedge-heeled sandals. She looks pretty enough to be a country star, and I tell her so.

"Thank you, Kody," she says. "I'm glad somebody around here appreciates the effort a gal goes to." She nudges Jay in the ribs. "This one sure don't."

"Hey, is there anything wrong with saying you're naturally beautiful?" Jay says.

"No, but there ain't nothing wrong with appreciating me putting on a fresh coat of paint neither," Tiff says. She hands me the rectangular pan she's carrying. "I made a dirt cake. I know you and Caleb like them."

"Thanks! I'll put it in the fridge." Dirt cake is really chocolate pudding with smashed-up Oreos on it to look like dirt. Tiff puts gummy worms in it to make it more realistic. I always give Caleb my gummy worms and eat the pudding and Oreos.

When Caleb comes in, his church clothes are a mess. His shirttail is hanging out, and the knees of his khakis are muddy.

"There's my baby!" Mommy says from where she's sitting on the couch. "Come over here and give me some sugar!"

Caleb runs over and throws his arms around Mommy and plants a kiss on her cheek. That's when I see Jay and Tiff see her.

I don't know when the two of them last saw Mommy, but apparently she looks worse than whenever that was. I've been looking at her all weekend—covering her when she's cold, uncovering her when she's hot, cleaning up her puke—so there's nothing shocking about her appearance to me.

But when I look at her from the point of view of somebody who hasn't seen her for a while, she does look bad—too thin, too pale, with bad teeth and dark half-moons under the eyes of a wild thing caught in a trap.

The kitchen table is too small for all six of us, so me and Jay set up a card table and some folding chairs. We help ourselves to the chicken and dumplings, green beans, and cornbread on the stove. Nanny fills glasses from a big, sweating pitcher of iced tea.

"Isn't this nice? Everybody all together," Nanny says, once we've all settled. "Jay, would you say the blessing?"

"Yes, ma'am."

I bow my head and close my eyes and brace myself because I know it's going to be a long one.

"Dear Lord," Jay begins. "We are thankful for this food to the nourishment of our bodies and to the good Christian women who prepared it for us. We pray for my sister Amanda who is trying to leave a life of sin behind her and follow you on a new road to salvation. We pray for our deliverance from those in the government who want to take away our right to bear arms and our right to freely worship—"

As Jay drones on, my mind starts to wander. Did God really give people the right to bear arms? Guns weren't around back in Jesus's time, so the Bible doesn't say anything about them.

I don't really mean to do it, but I open my eyes for just a second. Everybody else has their eyes closed and their heads bowed except for Mommy who's looking right at me. She glances over at Jay and rolls her eyes. Then she looks at me and sticks out her tongue.

I have to bite my lip to stifle a giggle.

Finally, Jay says, "In Jesus' name we pray, Amen," and we have God's permission to dig into our now lukewarm Sunday dinner.

"Nanny's chicken and dumplings are the best," Caleb says, his cheeks bulging like a hamster's.

"Don't talk with your mouth full," Tiff says.

Mommy reaches over and ruffles Caleb's hair.

"You don't have to worry about minding your manners here," Mommy says. "We're family."

"I was raised to believe you should always mind your manners," Tiff says.

I've seen this tension between Tiff and Mommy before. Mommy feels like she's Caleb's real mother because she gave birth to him, but Tiff is the one who does all the day-to-day parenting.

"Well, even if he said it with his mouth full, I've got to agree with Caleb," Jay says. "I believe these are the best chicken and dumplings you've ever made, Momma."

"Thank you," Nanny says. "I'm just glad to have everybody here. I know everybody's busy, but we should try to get together for at least one Sunday dinner a month."

"That's a great idea," Tiff says. "But you don't always have to cook. Sometimes it could be at me and Jay's house."

"We could do it at my place, too," Mommy says, "after I get back on my feet."

I try to imagine a Sunday dinner at Mommy's broken-down trailer with its overflowing ashtrays and piles of garbage and dirty laundry. I don't even know if she knows how to cook anything.

"Seems to me that right now you need to be worried about eating instead of cooking," Uncle Jay says. "You ain't got enough food on your plate to bait a mousetrap."

Mommy does have just about a tablespoon of chicken and dumplings and green beans, and she's been taking the tiniest, slowest bites imaginable, washed down with big swigs of iced tea.

"I'm still having a hard time keeping food down," Mommy says, spearing a single green bean. "It's like all the bad stuff has to leave my body before I can put good stuff in."

"It's like that movie we watched where the demon gets inside the girl and they have to bring in an exorcist to get it out of her," Jay says, smearing butter on a hunk of cornbread.

"That was cool," Caleb says. "She puked up black stuff."

"You let him watch scary movies?" Nanny says, giving Jay a look.

"It was educational," Jay says. "You've got to let kids know there's evil in the world because they're gonna grow up surrounded by it. It's different from when you was growing up, Momma. Shoot, it's even different from when me and Amanda was growing up. People have got to keep God in their hearts because it's worse out there than it's ever been." He takes a bite of cornbread and chews thoughtfully. "The Internet's to blame for a lot of it, but I think most of it's on account of them taking God out of the schools."

"Well, you've got a point there," Nanny says.

"Back when me and Amanda was in school, the Ten Commandments hung on the wall of every classroom," Jay says, poking a forkful of chicken and dumplings in the air for emphasis. "You can bet some kid who was planning on shooting up the school would think twice if he looked up at the wall and saw 'Thou Shalt Not Kill' hanging up there."

I remember the preacher saying the exact same thing at church.

"You really think that?"

It takes me a second to realize these words came from Mommy.

Jay might be a little startled, too, because it takes him longer than it should to say, "Yeah, I do."

"You mean," Mommy says, her eyes narrowed, "you think somebody who's mean enough or crazy enough to shoot up a school would see the Ten Commandments hanging on a wall and think, 'Oh, well, I guess I'd better not'?"

"I think the Lord could put it in their hearts," Jay says.

"What do you think, Tiff?" Mommy asks. This is a side of Mommy I've never seen before. She's a person who's alert enough to have opinions.

Tiff smiles real pretty. "Oh, I don't know. I was just thinking about how good these dumplings is." She gives Jay a playful nudge with her elbow. "I don't pay no attention to nothing Jay says."

Jay laughs and looks at her with love. "Well, that's the truth."

Nanny laughs, too. "And that's the secret to a happy marriage. I didn't hear half of what your daddy said the thirty-two years we was married."

After dinner, Caleb asks me if I'll play catch with him in the yard. I know he's restless from sitting still so long, so I say yes even though I know I'll suck at it.

Caleb pitches a softball at me. I don't mean to, but I bring up my hands to shield my face.

"What in the Sam Hill is wrong with you, Kody?" Caleb says. "You act like you're scared of the ball."

"I kinda am," I admit. "What if it breaks my nose or something?"

"I ain't aiming it at your nose," he says. "I'm aiming it so you can catch it. Here, let me move closer. Now hold out your hands and relax them. You can't be all stiff."

I hold my hands like he shows me. He throws me the ball, and to my surprise, I catch it. I toss it back to him. My throw's a little lopsided, but he catches it easily.

"You throw like a girl, but I don't know how to fix that," he says, tossing the ball back to me.

"Some girls are good ballplayers," I say, catching the ball again.

"Yeah, well, you don't throw like none of them," Caleb says.

I laugh because he's right. Still, we've fallen into an easy rhythm of toss, catch, toss, catch. I don't see what's so interesting about it, but I'm happy to do it because it makes him happy.

"Is Mommy getting better?" Caleb says, catching my girly throw.

"She's trying to," I say. "She's trying harder than I've ever seen her."

He holds onto the ball after he catches it. "Do you think if she gets better, we'll live with her again?"

"I don't know, buddy," I say. "We'll see."

"I can't remember living with Mommy," Caleb says. He throws the ball again.

I catch it but just barely. "I know. You were a baby."

"If Mommy gets better and we live with her, do you think she'd drive me to all my games and practices?"

It's a good question. Neither of us can remember Mommy before she was an addict, so it's hard to say how responsible she'd be if she was clean. "I can't really say. But if she didn't drive you, I would."

This seems to make him feel better. "Okay," he says. "Thanks, bro."

Jay and Tiff come out of the house, Tiff carrying plastic containers of all the food Nanny's making them take home.

"Hey, Caleb, you go hug your Nanny and Mommy's neck before we go," Uncle Jay says.

Caleb runs inside, and Uncle Jay drapes his arm around my shoulder. "Your Nanny says you're working to save up for a car."

"That's right." I hope he might have some work for me.

"You want that old white pickup that's been sitting in my driveway for going on five years? I ain't found nobody that wants to buy it, but it runs good."

The truck's not a beauty, but I wouldn't be able to afford anything that was. "How much do you want for it?"

"How about we say a hundred dollars? You can give me twenty dollars a month."

"Are you sure? That's almost nothing."

"Well, I ain't making nothing with it sitting in my driveway. And I thought it might be handy to take your mommy to her meetings." He grins. "And that way you wouldn't have to beg to use your Nanny's car if you was wanting to go out on a date or something."

I let the date thing slide. "That's nice of you, Uncle Jay."

He shrugs. "Well, I ain't got no use for it, but you do. If you want to ride back to the house with us, you can drive it on home. Your Nanny says it's all right with her."

I can't stop smiling on the ride to Jay and Tiff's. I can't believe I'm going to have a truck.

Chapter 13

It's AMAZING HOW MUCH A THING as simple as having a vehicle has changed my life in the last seventy-two hours. As soon as I got it home on Sunday, I got the hose and a bucket and some rags and washed off all the dirt and leaves and bird poop that had built up from the car sitting in Jay and Tiff's driveway for so long. I scrubbed off the "MAKE AMERICA GREAT AGAIN" and "FRIENDS OF COAL" bumper stickers that Jay had put on the bumper. I'm not an enemy of coal, but I'm not a friend either. I don't feel like I can be when my papaw died of black lung.

Yesterday I skipped school because Mommy felt like she needed one more day at Nanny's with somebody staying with her. In the afternoon I drove her to the Dairy Queen for a cone, and we rode around with the windows down, and even though Mommy couldn't finish her ice cream and lit a cigarette instead, somehow just driving around with her like that felt hopeful.

And this morning I didn't have to wake up before the roosters to catch the school bus. I slept an hour later and drove myself.

It's hard to explain, but I feel like other than Papaw's old record player, this ugly old truck is the only thing I've ever had that's really for me. So what if they're both hand-me-downs? They're mine now, and that's all that matters.

Now I'm driving back to the head of the holler to pick Mommy up for her meeting. I honk the horn, and she comes out looking like she's actually made an effort to be presentable. Her hair is clean and brushed, and she has on clean jeans and a cream-colored top. She's started wearing earrings again, little silver studs.

"You look nice," I say when she gets in the car.

"That's good to hear because I feel godawful," she says. "TMI, I know, but I spent the whole day on the toilet. I knock out one symptom, and another one pops up to take its place." She lights a cigarette. Her hands are shaking. "I reckon having the trots keeps you from relapsing. I can't go buy dope if I can't get off the pot."

I laugh. "Are you okay to go to this meeting?"

Mommy nods. "I've got to go to it. I'll wear a diaper if I have to."

I sit in the car while Mommy goes to her meeting. I've learned my lesson about going to the park. Remembering I have a signal since I'm in town, I take out my phone and text Macey.

> Me: Hi Sis.
>
> Macey: Hey bro.
>
> Me: Caleb calls me that sometimes.
>
> Macey: I guess I can call him that when I meet him.
>
> Me: Yeah. He's real different from me. He made me play ball with him the other day. He says I throw like a girl.
>
> Macey: Like that's a bad thing

Me: In my case it is. Hey my uncle sold me his truck for almost nothing. It's a beater but it runs. Maybe that means I can come see you more often.

Macey: That's awesome! I wish somebody would give me a car but I guess I need to learn how to drive first LOL How is our mom doing? It feels weird to type that. OUR mom.

Me: She's still detoxing. It's hard but she's trying. She's in her meeting right now.

Macey: Good. I can't wait to meet her.

Me: Give it a couple more weeks. If she stays clean she'll be ready.

Macey: Cool. I have to go write a stupid paper.

Me: Is that part of the assignment, that it has to be stupid?

Macey: yes

Me: I guess that kind of takes the pressure off.

Macey: LOL I love you bro.

Me: I love you too

When Mommy gets in the car, she's crying and holding a big wad of Kleenex. There's nothing to say but "Are you okay?"

She sniffs and nods. "It was hard but it was good." I stood up and talked. I told everybody I'm a drug addict which, I mean, yeah, of course I am, or why would I be there? But you're supposed to stand up and admit it, so I did."

"That's great." I reach over and squeeze her hand. "I'm proud of you."

"God, I need a cigarette. My nerves is shot."

"Do you want to stop for a root beer?"

"Not with the way my guts is acting. I'd better get back to where I can be close to my best friend, the toilet. Maybe next week, okay?"

"Okay."

"People were real nice to me tonight, Kody. That's what got me to crying. After the meeting, a bunch of people came up to me and told me they remembered how hard it was when they first got clean. A couple of the women hugged me and told me they'd be praying for me. And Brian—he's the guy who runs the meetings—gave me my first chip for being clean for twenty-four hours. I get a new one once I've been clean thirty days if I make it that long."

"You will," I say.

"I want to."

"That's why you will."

I drop Mommy at her trailer and head back to the house. It's after nine o'clock and since Nanny goes to bed with the chickens, I figure I'd better be quiet in case she's already asleep. This plan is ruined by the dogs on the porch who bark at me like I've been away from home for a couple of years instead of a couple of hours.

When I come in, Nanny's still up. She's sitting in her recliner, but she's not knitting or crocheting. She's not doing anything. The TV isn't on. It's weird. Nanny never sits and does nothing.

"Kody," she says. "Me and you need to have a talk." Her voice sounds tired and old and sad.

I'm scared. What if Nanny's sick or something? "What's wrong?"

"A lot's wrong. A lot that I didn't know about. Sit down."

I sink into the couch.

"I went to Walmart's while you took your mommy to that meeting," Nanny says. The tone of her voice is flat. "While I was there, I ran into L.J."

My stomach lurches. I'm catching on to the fact that whatever this is, it's going to be about me. "How's she?" I try to sound casual, but my voice comes out thin and strained.

"Well," Nanny says, "I asked her that. And I asked her what she thought about the Bible college you took her to see, if she was thinking about going there. And she said, 'Kody never took me to look at no Bible college.' So I said, 'What about that praise music concert he took you to?' and she said, 'Kody never took me to no praise music concert.' And then she said, 'Mrs. Prewitt, I feel it's my Christian duty to tell you there's a lot of things Kody ain't telling you the truth about. He's got a lot of secrets he's keeping from you.'"

Okay. So this is what I get for waiting so long to talk to Nanny about Macey. I let it drag out, and now things are all messed up and confused, and it's my job to fix them. "I know it was wrong for me to lie to you, but I can explain why I did it," I say.

"I ain't done talking yet," Nanny says. Her voice is cold like I've never heard it.

"Yes, ma'am," I whisper.

"So all the way home I'm thinking, *What secrets? What could he be hiding?* I wondered if you might be drinking or smoking dope but I didn't think you would be on account of your mommy's problems. I thought you might be hiding some magazines with picture of naked women like I caught your uncle with when he was your age. So I searched your room—"

"Oh." The sound comes out of me without me meaning for it to, like air being let out of a tire.

"'Oh' is right," Nanny says, getting up from her chair. "Because nothing prepared me for what I found under your bed." She picks up a box from behind the recliner and drops it on the couch beside me. I don't know why I bother looking down because I know what's inside it: my canary yellow robe, the cheap blonde wig, the foundation and lipstick and eyeliner and mascara and eyeshadow and blush that I've bought secretly over time. All these things have brought me so much joy, but looking at them right now it seems like such a pitiful collection, like things a little girl wouldn't even want in her dress-up box.

There are tears in Nanny's eyes. "At first I tried to tell myself there was a girl. There's a girl, I said, and she comes over while I'm still at work, and Kody likes her to make herself up like a harlot, and they mess around in the bed. But that's not it, is it? These is your things."

The time for lying is over. L.J. was right about that anyway. "Yes, ma'am," I say, through tears.

"So you're what—some kind of he-she? Some kind of pervert?"

"No!" It hurts to hear those words coming out of the mouth of the person I've loved best in the world. "It's . . . it's playing dress-up. Like I did when I was little. I put on the makeup and the robe, and I put on a Dolly album, and I stand in front of the mirror and move my lips to the words . . . like I'm her, performing."

Nanny is looking at me like she's never seen me before, like I'm an alien that just stepped out of a spaceship. "But why?"

"I don't know why, really. I mean, I love Dolly, the songs she writes and the way she sounds and looks. Dressing up like her and pretending . . . it makes me feel good."

"Most of the temptations the devil puts in your way make you feel good," Nanny says. "You feel good then and there, but it's a trick because the cost is that you'll burn in hell for all eternity."

Maybe it's because it's all too much. Maybe I've gotten hysterical, but I feel a laugh bubbling up in my throat. Burning in hell because I dress up like my favorite country diva seems so silly. "But who does it hurt, Nanny? Until you went through my stuff, nobody even knew about it."

There are tears in Nanny's eyes. "It hurts God, Kody. He knows what you're doing. You can't keep secrets from him."

"So when I put on makeup and act like I'm singing 'Jolene,' it hurts God's feelings? Don't God have bigger things to worry about?"

"God worries about all our sins."

Surely the worst kinds of sins are the kinds that hurt other people. Before I even plan to say it, I say, "I know about Macey."

Nanny's face switches from anger to confusion. "What?"

"Macey. My sister. I know about her. That's where I was when I told you I was with L.J. I went to Knoxville to see her. It wasn't right that I lied to you about where I was, but it wasn't right that you kept her a secret from me my whole life."

Nanny sinks into her recliner. "How . . . how did you find her?"

"She found me. On the Internet."

"Now that . . . that's a tool of a lot of evil in this world. That Internet," Nanny says.

"You think it was evil for my sister to find me?"

Nanny looks her age and more. "I don't know what I think."

I scoot forward on the couch and look her right in the eye. "Nanny, when I talked to Macey's Aunt Diane, she said you wanted to get rid of Macey as fast as you could once you saw she wasn't white."

"I didn't want to get rid of her!" Nanny hardly ever raises her voice, but she does now. "I wanted to make sure she was taken care of. I just wanted her to be raised by her own kind, somewhere she'd feel comfortable. Not like here."

"What does 'her own kind' even mean? Isn't she our kind since she's our blood kin?"

"Not to look at her, she ain't."

I look at Nanny—really look at her. It's almost like she's been taken over by another person whose words are coming out of her mouth. But really, I know that person has been a part of her all along. I've just loved her so much I've never allowed myself to see it. "But that's on the outside," I say. "Aren't you always saying that it's what's inside people's hearts that matters?"

"Kody," Nanny says. "You're young, and you ain't seen much of life yet. You don't know what people's like around here. It was hard enough that everybody knew my daughter's a dope addict and that I had to raise the baby she had out of wedlock. Can you imagine what people would've said if I'd had to raise another one of her babies, this one colored?"

"Nobody says *colored* anymore!" Now I'm yelling, too. It's the only time I've ever raised my voice to my nanny, but it kills me that she thinks of Macey as a color, not a person.

"It's better than what I was raised to say," Nanny says.

"Just because you was raised narrow-minded don't mean you have to stay that way." I look at Nanny. I love her. I know I will always love her just like in the Dolly song. But can I stay with her and be the person I need to be . . . the person I really am?

"My mother and daddy didn't raise me to be narrow minded," Nanny says. "They raised me to follow the Word of God."

I'm not mad anymore, just sad. "Nanny," I say. "There are all kinds of different people in the world. Different colors and different religions and different"—I struggle with how to talk about my own differences—"ways of being. But you know who made them all like that? God. The Bible says God made man in His own image, so don't that mean we're all images of God? Black and white and in between? Gay and straight and in between?"

"I will not have you blaspheme in my house," Nanny says.

"I'm not blaspheming. I'm just thinking out loud. Or is it blaspheming to think?"

Nanny puts her head in her hands. "Kody, I thought I knew you. I thought I understood you. But the things you're doing and saying don't make no sense. The devil's got ahold of you some way."

"Did the devil get ahold of you when you decided not to tell me I had a sister?"

"It was better for you not to know. Now everything's all confused, and it can't go back to the way it was. Was Macey the one who got you dressing up like a woman?"

"No! I've been doing it since I was three years old. If you wasn't seeing what I was like, it was because you didn't want to see it." Nanny looks small sitting in her chair. Small in her body but small in the way she sees things, too. "Nanny, I can't stay here right now. I've got to figure some things out—"

"We'll figure them out together," Nanny says. "We'll go out in the yard, and we'll burn them things. Then we'll pray, and tomorrow we can go see the preacher—"

"No." I stomp into the kitchen and grab a paper sack. "I don't want to burn my things, and I don't want to go see the preacher. I'm sorry I lied to you when I went to visit Macey, but other than that, I ain't done nothing wrong." I go to my room and start grabbing underwear and socks, jeans and a few shirts and stuffing them into the sack. Nanny is standing in the doorway.

"One sin leads to another, Kody. If you walk out of this house, you're gonna wind up in the streets or on dope just like your mommy."

Those words sting. I've already promised myself I'll never touch drugs or alcohol because I don't want to risk ending up like Mommy. "Nanny, I'd like to think you know me better than that."

Nanny looks away from me like she can't stand to meet my eyes. "Well, I reckon I don't know you as good as I thought I did."

I'm having a hard time looking at Nanny, too. Somehow, I had hoped that when I told her about Macey, everything Diane said would have been a big misunderstanding and that she'd welcome Macey to the family.

I even let myself believe that when she found out I was gay, she'd somehow be okay with it, even though there was no reason to believe somebody raised the way she was would be. I guess I just wanted to believe in her the way she wants to believe every word in the Bible even though some of it don't make sense in today's world. "I don't know you as well as I thought I did either," I say.

I pick up my paper sack and walk out the door.

Chapter 14

FOR ABOUT THIRTY MINUTES, I DRIVE the country roads, burning gas and trying to stop crying. My choices about where to go are pretty limited. It's not like I can go to Uncle Jay's and say Nanny and me had a fight because she found out I like to put on women's clothes. And my bridges are definitely burned with L.J.

Finally, I do the only thing I can think of to do. I turn the car around and turn back into the holler. I drive past Nanny's house and park in front of Mommy's trailer.

I grab my paper sack and go knock on the door. There's no answer.

What do I do if she doesn't come to the door? Sleep in my car in the school parking lot?

I could call Macey, but I don't know what kind of help she could be. She's there, and I'm here.

Finally, Mommy comes to the door, wearing ratty plaid pajama pants and a white tank top so thin I can count her ribs through it. "Kody?" she says, like she's not sure it's me.

"Sorry if I woke you up," I say. "Could I come in? Me and Nanny had"—what? It wasn't a fight, exactly—"a disagreement."

She nods. "Sure. Come on in."

Mommy may be clean, but her trailer sure isn't. Cereal bowls and saucers on the coffee table are overflowing with ashes and cigarette butts. Dirty clothes are strewn all over the floor and furniture. I'm afraid to glance over at the kitchen, and when I do, I see I was right to be afraid. Dirty dishes and pots and pans are piled on and around the sink. The trash can is overflowing and buzzing with flies. An open package of bologna sits on the counter next to a pile of eggshells.

"Your nanny and me used to have lots of 'disagreements' when I was your age." Mommy grabs a pile of dirty clothes from the lumpy couch and throws them on the floor. "Here, have a seat."

Her kindness is making me cry again. This is the first time I can remember Mommy taking any sort of care of me. I sit down. "Nanny found some things of mine that are . . . private." I might as well tell the truth. Lying sure hasn't done me any good lately, and Mommy isn't exactly in a position to judge anybody. "See, sometimes when I listen to records, I like to put on makeup and pretend I'm Dolly. I know it sounds silly—"

Mommy sits down next to me. "It doesn't. You always liked to play dress-up. When you was three, I couldn't keep you out of my closet."

"Well, I reckon I'm out of the closet now," I say, and we laugh.

"Hell," Mommy says, "when you said she'd found some private stuff of yours, I thought it might be gay porn. I was trying to imagine your nanny's face looking at something like that."

It is pretty funny to think about Nanny looking at pictures of naked men doing whatever they do in those kinds of magazines. "Where would I find gay porn in Morgan?"

"I don't know," Mommy says. "The same way I always found drugs, I reckon. You just have to know the right people to ask."

"Well, I don't know them people."

"No, of course not. Your nanny raised you to be a little church boy. Did she kick you out, Kody? Because if she did—"

It feels strange for Mommy to be so protective of me. Strange but kind of good, too. "No, I left. She gave me the choice of staying, but it meant agreeing to a lot of things I don't think I agree with."

Mommy nods. "That's the way she was when I was dating Calvin. She said just when she thought I couldn't bring any more shame to the family, I'd found a way to bring even more. Well, I'm ashamed of a lot of things in my life, but dating Calvin ain't one of them. And you shouldn't be ashamed of dressing up like Dolly either."

"Thanks," I say. "Is it okay if I stay here a little while, just till I can figure out what I'm doing?"

Mommy squeezes my hand. "You stay as long as you want. I'm glad for the company."

"Thanks," I say again, meaning it. "And maybe while I'm here, I can help clean up a little. If you can focus on staying clean yourself, maybe I can focus on getting the house clean."

"That would be real nice, Kody. We'll take care of each other, okay?"

The room I end up sleeping in has a bare mattress on a floor piled with dirty clothes, chip bags, and old Mountain Dew cans. There's a musty-smelling blanket and a pillow with no case on it. But at least I'm somewhere I'm wanted.

* * *

"How was school?" Mommy is sitting on the couch
smoking a cigarette. Some trashy talk show is on the TV. A girl
about my age in a skimpy top is arguing with her mom. The
words "Help! My Daughter Slept with My Boyfriend!"
are printed on the screen.

"It was okay," I say. If I was going to describe school honestly, the word I would use would be "lonely." Without L.J.,
there's nobody to talk to, and at lunchtime I gobble up my
sandwich and go to the library until the bell rings for class.
"Are you ready to clean?"

Mommy looks around at the mess surrounding her. "I
don't know where to start."

"Well, I do," I say. "How about I get you some trash bags
and you go through the house and pick up all the garbage?
While you do that, I'll get started on the dishes."

I don't usually mind doing dishes, but there are so many
of them. And they're not dishes from a meal you just ate
either. These are old dirty plates, crusted with hardened
cheese or egg, cups half full of coffee that's grown blue
mold. I fill the left half of the sink with hot, soapy water.
There's nothing to do but start.

As I scrape and scrub and rinse, I wonder if Macey will
call. And then it hits me. She could be calling Nanny's
number right now. I dry my hands and pick up the landline phone.

"Hello?" It's Macey's voice.

"Hey, sis, it's me."

"Bro! I've been trying to call you."

I balance the phone on my shoulder so I can keep on
washing dishes. "Yeah, you'll want to use this number to call

me for the time being. I'm staying with Mommy. Me and Nanny had a falling out, I guess you could call it."

"Oh, no. I hope it wasn't over me."

"Not all of it. It was about me, too. She's got as many problems with a grandson who's a sissy as with a granddaughter who's—'colored' is the word she used."

"How modern," Macey says. "That's rough. I'm sorry."

"Nothing for you to be sorry about. I'm helping Mommy get her place clean, making sure she's staying clean. It's all good."

"I just had an idea."

"What's that?"

"Well, if you don't have to tiptoe around your grandmother anymore, there's no reason you and I can't see each other more often. Why don't you come to Knoxville this weekend and bring our mom if she's up for it?"

I'm not used to being spontaneous. It feels good but also a little scary. "Is it okay with Auntie Diane?"

"Hang on. Let me check." Until Macey said it, I hadn't really thought about how not living with Nanny gives me the freedom to see Macey whenever I want to. The freedom to do a lot of things, I guess. It's kind of sad I didn't recognize freedom until somebody else told me that I had it. "Hey," Macey says, "Auntie Diane says why don't y'all come on Saturday and spend the night?"

My world feels so big right now I can barely imagine it. "We could do that?"

"Sure. Why not?"

Why not? "Okay, let me talk to Mommy, and I'll text you tomorrow from school."

I dry my hands and go find Mommy in her bedroom, which looks like it could be in some kind of anti-drug ad:

This is what an opioid addict's bedroom looks like. Don't let your bedroom look like this.

"Hey," Mommy says, emptying out a saucer filled with cigarette butts, "I'm working on my third trash bag."

"All right," I say. "I guess after we get all the trash bagged up we'll load it in the truck and take it to the dump."

Mommy grins. "Road trip."

"Well, now that you mention it, we've got the chance for another road trip if you're interested."

"Is it better than a trip to the dump?"

I've still not gotten used to the new Mommy who is alert enough to make jokes. "Yep. I just talked to Macey. She wants us to come visit her in Knoxville on Saturday. Her aunt says we can spend the night."

A bunch of expressions seem to pass over Mommy's face all at once. "Really? Wow, Kody. This is big. A big, big step." She sounds more scared than happy. I'd been hoping for happy.

"We don't have to do it if you're not ready."

She wipes under her eyes. "Well, how about if I make myself get ready? I mean, fifteen years without meeting your daughter. That's a lot of time."

"It is."

"I don't reckon I should waste any more of it."

"No, you probably shouldn't."

A tear trickles down her cheek. "What if she hates me, Kody?"

"She won't. She's been dying to meet you for a long time. She came looking for you. That's how she found me."

"And she didn't want to find me so she could tell me to go to hell?"

"I can't imagine Macey telling anybody to go to hell."

"Well, I've already been there and bought the t-shirt anyway," she says, smiling through her tears. "Let's do it."

* * *

WHEN I GET HOME FROM SCHOOL, Mommy's laying on the couch, staring straight ahead with glassy eyes. My first thought is that she's using again, but if she was, she probably wouldn't look this sad. I set down my backpack and go sit on the edge of the couch. "What's the matter, Mommy?"

"I can't go," she says, her voice coming from some deep, sad place.

"Why not?"

"Well, I'm still in withdrawal so I feel like crap. Literally. I spent all day in the bathroom. It wouldn't be so bad if I didn't look like crap, too. But Kody, I was looking at my clothes, and the only thing they're fit for is begging on the side of the road. I can't meet my daughter for the first time looking like that."

"We can buy you an outfit. I've got babysitting money." I've sat for the Jenkins' hell spawn two more times, and it's gotten a little easier each time. "I mean, it'll be a Walmart special, but it won't be old and raggedy."

"Hey," Mommy says, sitting up. "People at group the other night was talking about that thrift store downtown. It's part of a program that gives jobs to recovering addicts to help them get back on their feet. We could go there."

"We could," I say. "Nanny would never let me go to thrift stores. She always said she was raised with too much pride to wear a stranger's hand-me-downs."

"Yeah, she's weird about thrift stores, so she buys cheap new crap at Walmart that wears out fast instead of buying good quality used stuff that'll last for years. Wanna go shopping now? I'm going kind of stir crazy being in the house all day."

"Sure." I grab my keys. There's still a lot of cleaning to do in the trailer, but I know the dirt will still be there when I get back.

It kind of hurts my heart to drive past Nanny's house, especially when the dogs bark like I was any other stranger driving through the holler. I'm tempted to stop and pet them to remind them that they're my dogs, too.

"Mommy?" I say.

"Mm?"

"Do you think it's weird that Nanny ain't checked on me since I left? She has my cell number. It's not like she doesn't know how to get ahold of me."

"No, that's the way she is. She's waiting for you to crawl back and apologize."

"I apologized for lying to her. I feel like now it's her turn to apologize to me."

Mommy chuckles. "Well, I wouldn't hold my breath."

"It looks like she'd at least want to know I'm okay." Or maybe not. Maybe finding out the truth about me turned off her love just like turning off a faucet.

"Oh, I've seen her car drive up to the head of the holler. She's seen your truck. She knows you're with me."

This makes me feel a little better. At least she wants to know I'm still alive. "I'm not much good at being a runaway, am I? I didn't even make it out of the holler."

Mommy cracks the window and lights a cigarette. "Hell, I was way better at it than you. I made it all the way up to Cincinnati. It was three weeks before the cops picked me up, and by that time I had a taste for beer and weed, and I wasn't a virgin no more. They shipped me back home, and your papaw gave me an ass whipping and made me go to church every time the door was open. But they had already lost me. You can't taste freedom like that and then go back to being a good little church girl. It's like being a wild animal locked up in a cage."

I've never heard this story before. "You were a rebel."

"I was. I rebelled in stupid ways probably, but I didn't know any smart ones."

The thrift store is bigger than I expected. It's in a space that used to belong to what Nanny always called the dime store. Once we start looking, I see Mommy's point about used clothes. Lots of the stuff on the racks is name brand and looks like it's barely been worn. Mommy finds a cute knee-length dress with purple floral print and a green paisley peasant skirt with a green scoop-necked top that looks like it was made to go with it. On a whim, I browse through the men's section and find a pair of Levi's that have been washed just enough to lose their stiff newness. And then Mommy pulls out two real Ralph Lauren polo shirts for me, a red one and a blue one. I can't believe I can afford her clothes and mine and still have money in my pocket.

The cashier is a bleached blonde with a pretty but weathered face. "Hey!" she says when she sees Mommy. "Good to see you out and about."

"You, too," Mommy says. To my surprise, the woman comes out from behind the counter and hugs her.

"This is my son Kody," Mommy says.

The woman smiles. Her teeth are broken black nubs, but her smile is still kind. "What a good-looking boy!" She holds out her hand. "I'm Brandi."

"Nice to meet you," I say.

"Brandi's in my group," Mommy says, then clamps her hand over her mouth. "You don't mind me telling him that, I hope?"

"Shoot, no, I ain't got no secrets. Say, after you're ninety days clean, you ought to apply for a job here. It's pretty sweet. Just minimum wage, but you get first pick of all the clothes that come in."

I can see that Mommy likes the idea but also that it makes her nervous. "I've got a long way to go before I hit ninety days," she says.

"Hey, one day at a time, right?" Brandi says.

Once we're out of the store, we pass the Kut 'n Kurl, which has a sign advertising $8 haircuts. Mommy pauses.

"You wanna get a haircut?" I ask.

"I don't remember the last time I got one," Mommy says. "I've just been trimming the ends myself, usually when I'm high, which ain't the best idea. We got eight dollars?"

"I've still got forty."

The woman in the Kut 'n Kurl looks about Mommy's age, but she's got on a lot of makeup and seems to be testing all the hair dyes on herself. Chunks of it are blonde, brown, and red. "Amanda Prewitt, is that you?" she asks.

"It's me," Mommy says. I can tell she's self-conscious about her looks compared to the primped-up hair stylist.

"I was one year behind you at Morgan High. Tracy Holcomb—I was Tracy Silcox back then."

"Oh, yeah, hi," Mommy says, but I don't think she knows this lady from Adam's housecat.

"So how've you been?" I can tell from the look on her face that she knows good and well how Mommy's been. Who's On

Drugs is probably one of the favorite topics of gossip at Morgan High School class reunions.

"Well, I've been bad, but I'm doing better," Mommy says and looks surprised when Tracy whoops with laughter.

"That's a good line," Tracy says. "You ought to needlepoint it on a cushion or something."

"Thanks." Mommy looks over at the stylist's chair. "Can I get a haircut?"

"That's what I'm here for. Have a seat." She looks over at me. "Will you be wanting one, too, sweetie? I know the shop looks kinda girly, but I can do girls or boys either one."

It sounds like she's coming out as bisexual, and I have stifle a giggle. "No, thanks," I say. Nanny always made me get my hair cut shorter than I want it. Mommy won't care if I let it grow out a little.

I do love sitting in the beauty shop, though. The pictures of beautiful women on the wall, the hair and makeup magazines with the "before" and "after" photos—all those images of glamour and transformation. When I was little, my favorite Disney movie was *Cinderella*. It wasn't because of the love story part. The handsome prince was about as interesting as a piece of light bread. It was the transformation that did it for me—seeing Cinderella go from being a plain girl in rags to the belle of the ball in her powder blue gown and sophisticated updo. Those glass slippers had to be hell on her feet, but they were totally worth it.

I think that's part of the excitement of Dolly Dress Up Hour—the transformation. A sign in the beauty shop advertises free makeovers, and I wish I could ask for one. I wish I could see my face made up by somebody who knows what they're doing.

Talk about transformation! When Tracy is through with Mommy, her chestnut hair is in a cute shoulder-length bob, angled so it has some swing to it. Mommy looks fresh and young. New.

"You're gorgeous!" I say.

Tracy turns Mommy's chair around so she can see herself in the mirror. "I love it," Mommy says, sounding like she might start to cry. "I really love it."

Back at the trailer, I fix us grilled cheese sandwiches and heat up a can of tomato soup. As we eat at the little card table in the kitchen, Mommy says, "It's getting so food tastes good again. The first week I was clean when I tried to eat, it felt like I was stuffing cotton in my mouth."

"Well, if you think of something that sounds good, let me know, and I'll try to fix it . . . as long as it's not too hard to cook and we can afford it." A worry pops into my head. If Nanny's rejected me, she's probably mad at Mommy for taking me in. Does that mean she'll stop buying Mommy groceries? My babysitting money won't stretch far when it comes to feeding two people.

"Cook me a lobster," Mommy says and laughs. "Actually, I don't know if I like lobster or not. I've never had it."

"Me neither," I say. "But they kind of look like big cockroaches."

"Eew," Mommy says and dunks a corner of her grilled cheese into her soup. "You know, I might like to work at that thrift shop. When I've been clean and sober long enough, I mean."

"That'd be great," I say. "You could put away all the good stuff for me."

"I would, too," she says. "Hey, I was thinking . . . I don't think I've put on any makeup since high school. But I thought

I might wear a little this weekend to look nice for Macey. Since you like that kind of thing, could you help me?"

My heart feels all warm and gooey, like a fresh-baked brownie. Mommy doesn't judge me for liking makeup any more than she'd judge Caleb for liking sports. "Sure. Maybe we can practice with it once we're done eating?"

We go in the bathroom since it has the brightest lights. Mommy sits down on the toilet lid and I stand over her. A lot of the makeup I use is too bright and gaudy for regular day-time use, but I figure it'll be okay if I go light on it. I shake a small puddle of liquid foundation on my palm and dot it on Mommy's forehead, nose, cheeks, and chin. I use a sponge to smooth it over her face. It's just enough to even out her skin tone and make her look a little less pale. I dab a brush in my little compact of blush and apply it lightly along her cheek-bones for a little color.

"That tickles," she says.

I get out the mascara and say, "Now here's the tricky part. Keep your eyes wide open and don't blink."

Mommy blares her eyes. I've never really seen her eyes up close, and they're beautiful—ocean blue with flecks of green. "Your eyes are so pretty," I say.

She laughs.

"What is it?"

"Haven't you noticed?" she says. "Your eyes and mine are exactly the same. When I look at you, it's like I'm looking at myself."

Chapter 15

"YOU'RE A GOOD DRIVER," MOMMY SAYS. She's leaned back on the passenger's side. Her shoes are off, and her feet are propped on the dashboard. Unlike when she was using, they're clean, with trimmed, pink-polished toenails.

"Thanks. Being between these two semis makes me nervous, though."

"You're doing good. You're a naturally cautious person. I don't know where you got it from. Not from me and sure as hell not from your daddy. I'm learning how to be more cautious though. I want to get my license back one day."

"That's be great." Mommy lost her license years ago on account of having too many DUIs.

When we cross the state line into Tennessee, Mommy says, "I can't remember the last time I was out of Kentucky. Maybe that time I told you about when I was fifteen."

"Really?" I shouldn't be surprised. People in my family tend to stay put.

"Yeah." She takes out a cigarette. "Kody, I'm real nervous."

"I know you are."

"I mean, what do you say to somebody who was your own child and you gave her up?"

"'Hi' is a start."

Mommy puts her face in her hands. "Lord, I don't know if I can do this, and I sure don't know if I can do it clean."

"Clean is the only way to do it."

"I know, I know." She sucks on her cigarette like it's the only thing keeping her alive. "Do I at least look okay?" She's asked me this at least a dozen times since she got dressed this morning.

"You look great."

It's true. Her fresh-cut hair is washed and blown dry so it's full and shiny, and she's wearing the cute floral dress she got at the thrift shop and just enough makeup to give her a little bit of color. She looks nice. Like she could be somebody's mom.

* * *

ONCE WE GET TO THE KNOXVILLE city limits, I get a little nervous myself because the traffic gets thicker, and I'm worried I won't be able to find my way to Macey's house. I take out the directions I wrote down and give them to Mommy so she can talk me through them step by step. I can't afford a GPS, so she'll have to do.

And then, on the side of the road overlooking the Knoxville skyline, I see it: a billboard with her beautiful, smiling face on it. Dolly is wearing a red and white gingham shirt, fitted to show off her full bust and tiny waist, and holding a guitar. The red of her lipstick is the exact same shade as the red in her shirt. The sign says *Dolly Welcomes You to Her East Tennessee Home*, and my heart feels like it doubles in size.

"There's your girl," Mommy says.

I'm too choked up to speak. It's a sign—I mean, I know it's a sign on the interstate—but it's another kind of sign, too, a sign that we're in Dolly's country now. She's watching over us, and our time here will be as happy as her smile, as golden as her hair. Well, her wig, anyway.

Macey's house is a pretty little stone cottage, almost like a place dwarves or bears might live in a fairy tale. I guess because it's in the city I was imagining it to be on a crowded, busy street, all concrete and pavement, but there's a nice yard with trees and shrubbery, and the houses on either side aren't crammed in too tight and have nice yards, too. As soon as we pull into the driveway, I hear Mommy take a deep breath.

"I need a minute," she says.

"Okay. But it's gonna be fine, you'll see."

After more than a minute, I open the front door of the car, get out, and go over to the passenger side. I open the door and hold out my hand for Mommy to take.

"Come on," I say. "You've got this."

She blinks hard, then nods and lets me help her out of the car. We walk together to the front door, holding hands.

The door swings open almost immediately after I ring the bell. Macey's standing in the doorway. As soon as she sees Mommy, she puts her hands to her mouth, and her eyes sparkle with tears. Then she spreads out her arms and gathers Mommy in a big hug. "Mommy," she says. When she pulls out of the hug, she says, "I thought I was going to call you Amanda when I met you, but when I saw you 'Mommy' just kind of came out, maybe because that's what Kody calls you."

Mommy wipes her eyes. "'Mommy' is good."

Macey hugs me next and whispers, "Thank you for coming, and thank you for bringing her."

Auntie Diane appears in the doorway. "Macey, aren't you going to let our guests come all the way inside the house?"

Macey grins. "Sure. Sorry."

Auntie Diane gives me a hug. "Good to see you, Kody. Welcome." She holds out her hand to Mommy. "Hello, Amanda. It's been a while."

Mommy shakes Auntie Diane's hand. "It has."

"I'm just happy you're here now and looking so well," Auntie Diane says. "Why don't y'all sit down in the living room, and I'll get us something to drink?"

The living room is beautiful. The walls are a buttery yellow, and the couch and armchair are sky blue. One wall is filled with built-in bookcases. I've never seen so many books outside of a library.

"Have a seat. Get comfy," Macey says.

Mommy and me sit on the couch under a painting of black ladies in big hats who look like they're going to church. Macey sits in the armchair across from us. She can't take her eyes off Mommy.

Mommy can't take her eyes off Macey either. "I can't believe how pretty you are," Mommy says. "I can see a lot of your daddy in you."

"Thank you," Macey says. She sounds shy, which is weird for her.

Things are awkwardly quiet for a minute, but then Auntie Diane comes in with a tray filled with glasses of lemonade. A little white dog is keeping pace with her, toenails clicking, but then all of a sudden, he jumps into my lap and licks my face, which makes everybody laugh.

"That's Theodore," Auntie Diane says. "Pet him as much or as little as you want. No matter how much you pet him, it won't be enough to suit him." She passes around the sweating glasses of lemonade.

"Theodore is our emotionally needy pet," Macey says. "You'll only see the cats when they decide they're ready to be seen."

"They're very regal," Auntie Diane says. "Unlike Theodore here, who has no shame."

Theodore is laying on his back in my lap while I rub his belly. "I love animals," I say.

"You always have," Mommy says. "When you was real little, you'd even want to pet bugs. I used to have to say, 'Don't pet that bee! It'll sting you!'"

Everybody laughs. I've never heard this story before. I don't know many stories about Mommy actually trying to take care of me. I wish I did.

"The lemonade's good," I say.

"I figured you'd like something cold after your long drive," Auntie Diane says. She looks at the empty rocking chair for a minute like she might sit down, but then she doesn't. "Well, I'm going to get started prepping things for dinner." She looks over at Macey. "I know y'all have lots to talk about."

That's the thing. There's lots to talk about, but nobody is talking. After Auntie Diane leaves, Mommy and Macey and me just sit holding our glasses of lemonade. I'm still petting the dog. I guess the awkwardness is understandable. How do you break fifteen years of silence? Where do you even start?

Finally, Mommy and Macey say, "So," at the exact same time and laugh.

"You start," Macey says.

Mommy takes a deep breath. "So . . . I could sit here apologizing all day for everything I missed about your life, but it wouldn't bring any of that time back. And I could tell you what I've been doing all that time, but not much of it is good." She sniffles a little, and I take a break from dog petting to reach over and squeeze her hand. "I guess what I'd like is just to get to know you a little bit."

Macey nods. Her eyes are all glittery with tears again. "Hey, how about we look at some photos? Auntie is crazed for scrapbooking."

"Okay," Mommy says.

Macey goes over to the bookcases and comes back with three huge photo albums. "These things weigh a ton," she says. "I tell Auntie that people just keep their pictures in their phones now, but she says she doesn't like to look at them that way. 'Memories should have weight,' she says. Here, let me skootch in." She sits on the couch between Mommy and me and opens the first scrapbook which is labeled *Macey Calvina Henderson, Ages 0-4.*

The three of us sit on the couch, flipping through photos, watching Macey grow from a chubby-cheeked baby to a toddler in pigtails, to a grinning first grader with two missing front teeth. We see her go from baby-fat cute to coltish to beautiful, posing with her dance team in glittery costumes. She tells stories about the different pictures, and two hours pass like two minutes.

When Macey closes the last book, Mommy says, "Thank you for that, Macey. Kody, if you'll give me the keys to the truck, I'll go out and get our stuff."

I hesitate for a second. What if she takes off in the truck to try to score some dope? But she's really trying to do better, and I know I have to learn to trust her. She's probably just emotional and needs a few minutes to herself. I hand her the keys.

"Wanna see my room?" Macey asks.

"Sure."

"I've got to warn you—the walls are still pink from when I was little. I was all about pink then. Now, not so much." We walk down a small hallway past more family photos. "I wanted to repaint the walls black, but Auntie said it would make her feel like she was living with a serial killer. So I've got to decide on something else. Purple, maybe. Auntie might agree to that. She loved Prince."

I don't know who Prince is, so I just say, "Purple's nice." It never occurred to me to ask Nanny if I could paint my room a different color. Maybe because I never really felt like the house was mine, too. It was more like she was letting me stay there.

Her room is the color of the inside of a seashell. The two cats are curled up together on her big double bed. I sit down to pet them. They don't open their eyes, but they purr. "It's been a long time since I petted a kitty. I had forgotten how soft they are."

Macey smiles. "They are super soft. Have you ever had a cat of your own before?"

"I've fed a stray that hung around for a while, but Nanny doesn't like cats inside the house. She says they're sneaky."

Macey laughs. "Sneaky how? What do they do? Steal your stuff and sell it on eBay?"

I laugh. "Maybe."

Macey looks over at the snoozing cats. "Well, I have had some stuff come up missing lately."

"I guess that explains it." I look around the room. There

are shelves full of dance trophies and a bookcase full of books. An old picture of a ballerina—one I feel like I've seen before in a book or something—hangs above her bed. "I like your room," I say.

Macey flops down on the bed next to me. "Well, it needs updating. It's too little girly. I've just been too lazy to change anything."

"You can't be that lazy if you won all them trophies."

"That's different. I love to dance. I'm not lazy about that. I'm lazy about everything else. Just ask Auntie."

One of the cats opens an eye to see who's petting it, then closes it and goes back to sleep. "So what do you think of Mommy?" I ask.

Macey picks up a pillow and hugs it to her chest. "I like her. I mean, I feel like I should say I love her, but I just met her, you know? And there's something about her that seems so fragile. Like a delicate piece of crystal. It's like the slightest touch could make her shatter."

"Yeah." I know what she means. To me, Mommy seems like a vase that's been broken, but somebody'd glued it back together piece by piece. It's kind of fixed, but the cracks show and you know how easy it would be for it to fall apart again.

"She's been outside a while," Macey says. "Do you think she's okay?"

"Well, I haven't heard the truck start up, so I don't think she stole it," I say.

"I hope that's a joke."

"It is, mostly. She's out there smoking a cigarette, I guarantee it."

Macey frowns. "Smoking's bad."

"It is, but it won't kill you as quick as Oxys will. I don't think we can expect her to kick more than one bad habit at a time."

* * *

WE EAT SUPPER—AUNTIE DIANE AND MACEY call it dinner—in the dining room. The table is big—there are six chairs around it—and made of some kind of dark, shiny wood. There's barbecue chicken, corn on the cob, a big green salad, and some kind of really good bread that's brown and crusty on the outside and soft and pillowy on the inside. We eat off pretty blue plates and drink our iced tea out of glasses with blue trim that matches the plates. Everything's fancier than I'm used to, but somehow it feels homey, too.

"This is all delicious," I say. "I wish I had more room so I could eat more."

"You're not doing so bad. That's your third piece of chicken," Macey says.

"Teenage boys can eat," Mommy says, smiling at me. "It is all delicious, Diane."

I notice, though, that she's left a lot of food on her plate.

"It's my Pop-Pop's barbecue sauce recipe," Auntie says. "It's a closely guarded family secret, but since y'all are family, I might let you in on it one day."

To my surprise, Mommy gets teary-eyed. "That's sweet of you to say."

Auntie looks confused. "What, that I might give you my barbecue sauce recipe?"

"No," Mommy says. "That we're family."

"Well, of course you are," Auntie says. "What else would y'all be?" She gets up and starts clearing plates. "Now we'll take half an hour or so for our food to settle, and we'll have some of the dessert Macey made."

"Banana pudding," Macey says.

I can't imagine ever being so full I wouldn't have room for banana pudding. "Really?" I say. "That's my favorite."

"Mine, too," Macey says. "It must be genetic."

We eat Macey's banana pudding out of blue bowls while we sit on the front porch listening to the crickets and the other night critters tune up. "This is real peaceful," I say. "It's not how I imagined living in a city at all. There's grass and trees and crickets—"

"And you were expecting nothing but skyscrapers and concrete like some kind of urban dystopia?" Macey says, grinning.

I'm not sure what the last word she said means, but I say, "Something like that, yeah."

"Well, Knoxville's just a medium-sized city," Auntie Diane says. "Sometime when you visit, we'll have to take you downtown. There's some fun stuff to do there."

"I got a look at downtown driving in," I say. "I saw the big Dolly billboard."

Auntie Diane smiles. "That's right—you love Dolly. Well, another time when you visit, we'll have to drive to Sevierville so you can see the big Dolly statue they've got downtown. I don't think the face is a very good likeness, but they got her proportions right!"

"And then we could drive to Pigeon Forge and go to Dollywood," Macey says.

"We could do that," Auntie Diane says. "Maybe in the summer."

It's like they've said they're going to take me to heaven. "I can't even imagine what that'd be like."

Macey reaches over and pats my arm. "Well, you don't have to imagine it. We'll go there."

"Unfortunately," Auntie Diane says, getting up from her rocking chair, "where I need to go right now is bed. I've got a shift starting at seven in the morning."

"That's rough," Mommy says.

"Yeah," Auntie says, "but I'm a glutton for punishment. Amanda, I'm glad you came to see us. Kody, give me a hug."

I stand and open my arms. Auntie Diane is tiny but strong. She stands on tiptoe to kiss my cheek and whisper "love you" like we've been close my whole life.

"Love you too," I say.

Mommy and Macey and me stay out on the porch listening to the night noises. After a while, Macey says, "Mommy, what can you tell me about my dad?"

Mommy takes a deep breath. "Is it okay if I smoke a cigarette?"

"Sure, now that Auntie's gone," Macey says.

Mommy lights a cigarette and stares off into the distance for what feels like a long time. "Your dad," she says with a little quaver in her voice, "was the nicest guy I've ever been with, and that includes Kody's daddy. No offense, Kody."

"None taken." Honestly, saying somebody is nicer than my daddy isn't paying them much of a compliment.

"He was having problems when I met him. The same kind of problems I was having." Mommy takes a long drag on her cigarette. "But he was still sweet and funny and made me laugh. One time I remember we got high at his place, and I started to nod out. I didn't want to waste my buzz being asleep, so I went to splash some cold water on my face. It smeared my mascara so I had black all around my eyes. Your dad called me Amanda

Panda, and at the time it seemed like the funniest thing in the world. That turned into his nickname for me. Amanda Panda. Nobody ever gave me a nickname before that."

Macey is smiling, but it's a smile mixed with sadness.

"Macey," Mommy says, "me and Calvin didn't know it was his baby I was carrying. I had moved back in with Kody's dad. I was scared to leave him, and I thought the baby was probably his. I'll tell you something, though, if Calvin knew he was gonna be a daddy, he would've been real happy. And he would've been real proud of you."

Macey wipes away a tear. "Thank you for saying that."

Mommy has tears in her eyes, too. "I said it because it's true."

Macey sniffles and says, "I'm gonna have to go get some tissues. I'll be right back."

After Macey disappears into the house, I ask Mommy, "Are you okay?"

She nods. "I'm good. She's a sweet girl, isn't she?"

"She is."

Macey comes out with a whole box of Kleenex and offers some to Mommy who grabs a handful. Once Macey sits back down, she says, "Were you with him . . . when he died?"

"Lord, it's a good thing you got the Kleenex," Mommy says. "Are you sure you want to talk about this?"

"I need to know." There's a hardness in Macey's voice, like she's toughening herself up so she'll be strong enough to listen.

"Okay," Mommy says. "But I'm gonna have to smoke another cigarette."

"Whatever it takes," Macey says.

Mommy lights a cigarette and draws on it hard. "I was there when it happened. Kody, you was there, too, asleep in your little toddler bed."

Finding this out gives me that weird, chilled feeling that Nanny always says means somebody's walking over your grave. Macey's daddy's grave.

"Yeah, your nanny was working on getting custody of you, but she hadn't gotten it yet. And Macey, I guess in a way you were there, too, because you were already growing inside me. But I was the only one in the room who knew you were there. Calvin had come over because Robert had just got some new stuff in—he was dealing pretty heavy by then—and Calvin wanted to score. They decided they was gonna shoot up some of the new stuff. I snorted just a taste, but I didn't shoot up. I told myself snorting was safer than shooting up, but of course I had no business doing either one of them things when I was pregnant."

I can tell Mommy's struggling to go on with her story, so I take her hand and hold it.

She takes a deep breath. "So Calvin, he shot up first, and he kind of flopped back on the couch with his eyes closed, smiling. He looked like an angel. But then something wasn't right. He slid from the couch to the floor almost like he had no bones. His lips and his skin looked gray, like the ashes in an ashtray. I got down on the floor and put my hand to his mouth. I couldn't feel any breath. I felt for his pulse. I barely felt one, or maybe I didn't feel one at all. I just wanted it to be there so bad I told myself it was." She takes another deep breath. "Macey, honey, are you okay? Do we need to take a break?"

"Keep going," Macey says. She has stopped wiping the tears that keep sliding down her face.

"Okay," Mommy says. "I learned CPR in high school, so I started doing it, but I was so high I don't know how good a job

I did. I told Robert to call 911, but he said no, that the cops would show up and we've got an obvious OD and all this dope in the house. Calvin wasn't coming to, and time was wasting, so finally Robert agreed that we could drive him to the emergency room, drop him at the entrance, and drive off."

"Good Lord," I say. I can't help it. It's such a terrible plan.

"I know," Mommy says. "So Robert basically drags him out to the car and puts him in the back seat. We're about to pull out of the driveway, and I say, 'Oh, shit! The baby!' and run back in the house and get you, Kody. I didn't want to put you in the back with Calvin so you just rode on my lap and went right back to sleep."

It's weird to be a character in this story, sitting on my junkie mom's lap with my junkie dad behind the wheel and a dead body in the backseat.

"It's about a fifteen-minute drive to the emergency room. Sometimes I wonder if it would've made a difference if we could've gotten there sooner. But Robert dragged him out so he was laying in front of the door. I ran into the waiting room and screamed help, then ran back to the car. Robert gunned it. When I looked back, I saw that people had came out and was trying to help him. But of course it was too late."

For few moments, nobody says anything except for the crickets.

Finally, Macey nods. "Thank you for telling me."

"I'm sorry it happened—sorry I couldn't save him," Mommy says. "But I want you to know he didn't suffer for one second. He just fell asleep and didn't wake back up."

"He was just twenty-two," Macey says. "That's barely an adult."

"I know," I say. Maybe Calvin didn't suffer when he died. But he left behind a lot of people who have suffered more than their fair share.

"Listen, that wore me out," Mommy says. "Can you show me where I'll be sleeping?"

We go inside, and Macey takes Mommy to the guest bedroom. When she comes back, she says, "I can help you fold the couch out into a bed if you want, but I'm not tired yet. Are you?"

It's weird. In some ways I feel as tired as I've ever felt, as wrung out as an old washrag. But I also know that if I went to bed, I'd lay there wide awake. "I don't think I can sleep yet."

"Me neither," Macey says. "You wanna hang out in my room for a while? We can have a slumber party."

"Okay." It feels strange to have something as silly as a slumber party after such a serious conversation, but somehow it feels right, too. "I've never been to a slumber party before."

Macey smiles. "Well, you have to put on your pajamas."

"And then we giggle and talk about boys?"

"If you like, yeah."

Mommy and me had to pack our pajamas and toothbrushes in grocery sacks because we don't have suitcases. You don't need a suitcase if you never go anywhere. I go in the bathroom and change into what passes for pajamas, an old white T-shirt that's been washed so many times it's as thin as Kleenex and a pair of gray sweatpants. I knock on Macy's door.

"Come in," she says.

She's sitting on the bed wearing light blue pajamas printed with pictures of playing cats. The real cats are still asleep on the foot of her bed. "Do they ever move?"

"Sure. When it's time to eat."

"So what do you do at a slumber party?"

"Well, first you get comfy." She pats the spot on the bed next to her.

I sit propped up on a pillow with my legs stretched out.

"That was hard," Macey says. "Hearing about my dad. I needed to hear it, but it was hard."

"I know. It was hard for me to hear, and he wasn't even my dad."

"Do you ever just need to take a break and not think about things?" Macey says. She's lying next to me, propped up on one elbow.

"Sure. That's when I put on a Dolly record." But the Dolly records and the record player are back at Nanny's. I miss them terribly.

"That's when I eat chocolate and watch stupid stuff on YouTube." Macey reaches over to the nightstand and opens the drawer. "Behold the secret chocolate stash."

There are Reese's Cups and Snickers but also kinds I've never heard of before, dark chocolate with sea salt, with orange, with toasted almonds. "Impressive," I say.

"What kind do you want?"

"I'll try a little of the sea salt one." What's the point of being someplace new if you don't try new things?

"Good choice." She pulls out a bar and hands it to me. "Toasted almond for me, I think. And now . . . YouTube."

She opens up her laptop, and we watch some videos of cats being silly. The chocolate is delicious—rich and bitter-sweet, with a salty bite.

"Hey," Macey says. "I know another kind of video you'd like." She types in "makeup tutorial" and a huge list of videos appears. "Wait . . . there's one person in particular I want you to see."

The video shows a thin, pretty man with a shaved head. In a soft, gentle voice he says he's going to demonstrate his favorite makeup technique. He makes up his face, layer by layer, while talking through each step. It's like he was a blank canvas, and now he's a beautiful painting.

My first thought is wow, I have a lot to learn about doing makeup. But underneath that, I feel something deeper. "So he's here on YouTube, doing his makeup out in the open?"

"He is. And he has over a million subscribers, so that's definitely out in the open."

I feel choked up all of a sudden. "That's beautiful, isn't it? To see somebody be their whole self like that."

"It is," Macey says. She takes my hand and holds it. "Kody, I want you to know you can always be your whole self with me."

It's the nicest thing anybody's ever said to me.

Chapter 16

I WAKE UP IN MACEY'S BED and realize I never made it back to the couch. We ate chocolate and watched videos and talked till we fell asleep side by side. It felt natural, like the way a litter of kittens curls up in a furry knot.

But now Macey's side of the bed is empty. I get up and stop to use the bathroom and try but fail to make my hair look less crazy. I find Macey in the kitchen. She looks better having just rolled out of bed than I've ever looked in my whole life.

"Hey," she says. "I made some coffee. You want me to toast you a bagel?"

"Sure. Thanks." I've never had a bagel before but I know it's bread, so how bad could it be?

I sit down at the kitchen table and she brings me a steaming mug with pictures of cats on it. "It smells good. Thanks." I can tell it's too hot to drink. "You know, this is the second Sunday in a row that I've not been to church. I don't think I've ever missed two Sundays before."

Macey grins. "You're turning into a regular heathen, aren't you?"

"I reckon I am." But I have to say I feel better sitting in this sunny kitchen with Macey than I ever did sitting in church. Maybe I really am a heathen.

Macey sits down next to me with her mug of coffee. "We go to church maybe once or twice a month, but a lot of Sundays Auntie has to work. I think our church is really different from yours, though. Our church welcomes everybody. We've got gay and lesbian couples and families. The music director is trans."

I can't even imagine what this would look like. "I didn't know a church could be like that."

"There are all kinds of churches. But maybe not where you live." A bell rings. "Our bagels are ready."

I watch Macey spread cream cheese on her bagel, and then I do the same. When I bite into it, the outside is crunchy, but the inside is soft and doughy. I like it. "This is my first bagel," I say.

"Oh, I had no idea you were a bagel virgin." Macey grins. "Laying out of church, losing your bagel virginity. Clearly I'm a bad influence on you."

We must sit for an hour at the table, drinking coffee and joking around. Mommy still hasn't come out of the guest bedroom, so I figure I'd better go check on her.

I knock on the door gently, then a little harder. When I hear a grunt, I decide it's an invitation to come in.

She's still in bed, with the covers pulled over her head to block out the sunlight pouring through the window. "Mommy? It's almost eleven o'clock. You want to get up?"

"No," she whines, like a little child.

I know mornings are the hardest times for her. She says she wakes up sick and hurting then she remembers she can't take anything to make the pain go away and so she feels crushed and helpless. I don't know how many days of the week she manages to get up when it's still actually morning. A lot of days when I come home from school, I get the feeling she hasn't been up very long.

"There's coffee," I say. "Want me to bring you some?"

"Coffee," she says, so I take that for a yes.

"You want anything to eat?"

"No," she says like I just offered her a dish of rat poison.

"Okay, just coffee then."

When I come back with her coffee, she props up in bed. Her eyes are red and puffy, and her hands shake as she lifts the cup to her mouth. "I need to go home," she says.

"Okay. I'll take a quick shower while you drink your coffee. Then you can get cleaned up and ready to go."

She nods.

To tell the truth, I'd like to stay longer, till after lunchtime at least. But I can tell Mommy has reached her sell-by date. She put on a good show yesterday, but it took a lot out of her.

When I come back to check on her, she's gotten dressed in the same clothes she had on yesterday. She hasn't showered, and her breath smells stale. "Let's go," she says.

Macey is laying on the couch playing with her phone. The dog and both cats are asleep on her.

"Hey, I think we're gonna head out," I say.

"Oh, no. So soon?" She sits up, making the pets scatter.

"I've got school tomorrow, and Mommy's tired. Thanks for everything, though. It's been great."

"You have to give me hugs, or I won't let you out the door," Macey says.

She hugs Mommy first. "I'm so happy to finally get to meet you," she says. "Promise we won't make it another fifteen years till we see each other again, okay?"

"I promise," Mommy says.

Macey hugs me and says "I love you, bro."

"I love you, sis."

* * *

MOMMY IS QUIET IN THE CAR, staring blankly out the window and smoking.

"You okay?" I ask.

"She's a sweet girl," Mommy says.

"She is."

"I'm glad I got to meet her. It's just . . . it made me think about a lot of things I ain't thought of in a long time."

"You want to talk about them?"

"No. Just thinking about them's hard enough."

I drive and leave Mommy with her thoughts.

When we get home, there's a white envelope taped to the door. It says *Kody* in Nanny's handwriting. I take it down and take it inside. I feel nervous but hopeful to have something from Nanny. It could be a note telling me I'm going to burn in hell, but it could also be an apology saying she wants to work things out and that I'm welcome back at her house.

I open the envelope and pull out a folded sheet of notebook paper. When I unfold the paper, three twenty-dollar bills fall out. The paper has two words written on it: *for groceries.*

Well, at least she isn't going to let us starve.

* * *

MOMMY WANTED TO SLEEP AS SOON as we got home, so I've left her to nap and come to Walmart with the grocery money. Thanks to growing up with Nanny, I'm pretty good at stretching a dollar till it squeals, as she says. I study the prices carefully, doing the math in my head. I pick out bread, milk, orange juice, cheese singles, bologna, cornflakes, bananas, apples, some blue box mac and cheese, and a few cans of vegetables since the fresh ones are too expensive. I've been trying to get Mommy to eat more vegetables.

It's weird. I feel grateful to Nanny for teaching me things like how to buy groceries, but then I remember the way she looked at me the night she found my dress-up clothes, the way she talked about Macey for not being white. How could somebody who's taught me so much know so little?

When I go to the checkout, I'm so startled I let out a little gasp. Nanny told me she saw L.J. at the Walmart, but she didn't tell me L.J. was working here.

But there she is, in an ugly blue vest, at register number five, the only register without a line.

I feel a sudden burst of courage. L.J. and me have gone for weeks of not talking, with her acting like if she ignores me, I'll go away. If I go to her register, she'll have to talk to me, even if it's just to say how much money I owe the Walmart corporation.

At first, she doesn't even look at me, but when she does, she lets out the same kind of gasp I did when I saw her.

"I didn't know you worked here," I say.

"Yeah, part-time, a couple of days after school and on weekends. Daddy got laid off, so—" She trails off like she's suddenly remembered she's not supposed to talk to me. She focuses on scanning my items.

"I'm sorry to hear that," I say. It seems like jobs around here get scarcer and scarcer. "Listen, L.J., I feel like we really need to talk to each other. Even if we're not going to be friends anymore, I feel like there's still stuff we need to say."

She doesn't look at me. "I don't know if that would be such a good idea."

"Just a ten-minute conversation? To kind of clear the air?"

She sighs and looks up at me. I can tell she's trying not to cry. "I get off in twenty minutes."

"I'll wait for you in the parking lot. I'm in a white Ford truck, the one that Uncle Jay used to drive."

* * *

WHEN L.J. GETS IN THE PASSENGER side, she says, "I had to go hide in the bathroom and pray about whether talking to you is the right thing to do or not."

"And is it?"

She shakes her head. "I don't know. Lots of things don't feel like the right thing anymore. Like working on a Sunday. Walmart don't care that the Bible says it's a sin. I won't let them schedule me till the afternoon so I can go to church, but I'm still not honoring the Lord's day like I should."

Hearing L.J. talk, I feel less mad at her than I've been. She truly does try to live by her faith, and I know she told on me to Nanny because she couldn't stand the thought that I had lied to her. "I miss you," I say.

She holds up her hand. "Don't say that."

"Why not? Don't you miss me, too? Can you honestly say you have more fun hanging out with Brianna than you do with me?"

She doesn't look at me. She looks down at her hands which are folded in her lap. "Brianna is a good Christian. She wouldn't do what you done, dragging me into your lies, saying you was going somewhere so you could sneak off and do sinful things with some other boy—"

"Stop right there," I say. "It was wrong of me to lie, and it was real wrong of me to bring you into my lies. But I wasn't sneaking off to meet some boy. I was sneaking off to meet my sister."

L.J. looks at me like she's looking at a crazy person. "You don't have a sister."

"Yes, I do, L.J. I just ain't had the chance to tell you about her yet. That girl you saw in the picture on my phone—the one you thought was my girlfriend? That was my sister, Macey."

L.J. looks at me like I'm trying to pull one over on her. "Kody, that girl was *colored*."

Has nobody in this town ever heard the word *Black*? The more time I spend with Macey and Auntie Diane, the more I feel like this place is frozen in an earlier time. Or part frozen, anyway. It has the drugs and joblessness of modern times, but it's like the civil rights movement wasn't even a thing that happened. "L.J., surely you know that sometimes people have relationships with people whose skin in a different color from theirs."

"Well, when they do, it's a sin," L.J. says. She's staring out the windshield, probably so she doesn't have to look at me.

"I'll pass that on to Mommy," I say. "I'm sure she'll think it's useful information." I don't mean to be sarcastic with L.J., especially when I'm trying to mend things between us. But she's so sure the answer she has for everything is the right one. "Years ago, Mommy had a relationship with a guy who happened to be Black. She had Macey and gave her to the guy's sister to raise."

"Where's Macey's daddy?"

"Dead. An overdose. I think one of the reasons him and Mommy got together was they had a lot of the same hobbies."

L.J. nods. "Sad."

"Yeah. But I've been getting to know Macey, and that's been real good. I wanted to tell you about her, but then things between you and me got . . . complicated."

L.J. wipes away a tear. "That's how it is, isn't? Things get all twisted up, and then you don't say what you need to say. Like, I should've told you a long time ago how I felt about you. That way you would know, and you could've told me we'd never be together the way I wanted us to. I would've knowed sooner that way, and it would've saved me a lot of hurting."

"I'm sorry for all that hurting," I say. I want to touch her—pat her shoulder or squeeze her hand—but I'm afraid she'd just jerk away from me.

"It's not your fault. I should've seen the way things was. The way you was. I just didn't see it because I didn't want to."

"Yeah." For two people who were supposed to be best friends, there was a lot about ourselves me and L.J. didn't show each other.

"I'm still not over you," L.J. says. She's really crying now, not just shedding a tear or two.

"That kind of thing takes time," I say, like I have all this romantic experience to draw on. "But do you think that once you've had some more time, we could be friends again? And not like before. We'd be the kind of friends that tell each other everything."

L.J. turns around in the seat to face me. "Kody, I do miss you, and I'd love to be your friend again. But the only way I can is if you get help."

A lump forms in my stomach. "Help for what?" I know what, but I want to make sure I'm right.

"You *know*," L.J. says. "You need to get your plumbing fixed. I've been reading and praying about it a lot, and probably the reason you think you like boys the way you do is you've never had a strong male figure in your life. You've stayed with your nanny and done needlework and watched *The Golden Girls* and it's made you confused."

"You think *The Golden Girls* made me gay?"

"Not just *The Golden Girls*. It's that you've had too much feminine influence and not enough masculine influence." She looks me in the eye for the first time in this conversation. "But you know what? Jesus is the best masculine influence there is. If you pray, if you start going to church again, you can get on the right path." She sounds so sure it makes me sad.

"L.J., I've been praying and going to church my whole life, and I'm still the gayest thing you've ever laid eyes on."

"But you've never prayed for help with your problem. God can help you." She's still looking at me. Somehow her gaze is soft and hard at the same time. "And Kody, if you'll let me, I'll help you, too. I've been praying a lot about this, and I . . . I can help teach you how to like girls." She reaches for my hand, and I pull away. L.J. and me have held hands thousands of times since we were in kindergarten, but this time it doesn't feel right. It feels like it would mean something else.

"L.J., I do love you," I say. "Just not the way you want me to."

"But we can change that together," L.J. says, her face sad and pleading. "You and me and Jesus."

"No, we can't," I say. "Not even with Jesus. L.J., God made me the way I am, and I've got to believe that He knows what he's doing. But if you can forgive me for the lies I told and accept me the way I am, we can still be friends just like before."

L.J. shakes her head. "I forgive you, but I can't accept you because what you are is an abomination."

An abomination. I take a deep breath. "Okay, I guess that's all the answer I need. Goodbye, L.J. You take care of yourself."

She touches my arm. "I hope you find salvation, Kody. I really do."

"And I hope you find somebody who makes you real happy," I say. I also hope she learns the world is bigger than Morgan, Kentucky and the church she was raised in, but I know it wouldn't do any good to say it.

L.J. slides out of the truck and closes the door. I turn the key and leave her standing in the Walmart parking lot. I cry a little as I drive away, feeling the distance increase between us.

Chapter 17

MOMMY ISN'T OKAY. USUALLY SHE'S PRETTY chatty when I drive her to her Tuesday night meeting, but tonight she's quiet.

"You all right?" I ask even though I've already come to the conclusion that she's not.

She nods. "I'll be all right. The cravings has hit me real bad again. Ever since we got back from Knoxville."

"I read online that the withdrawal gets worse after about twelve days. That's around where you are." It seems cruel that the cravings get worse again before they get better and go away. If they ever go away. "So you're normal anyway."

"I ain't heard that much in my life," Mommy says, smiling a little. "Just cause it's normal don't make it any easier."

"I know." I decide to change the subject. "Macey texted me today. She can't stop talking about how glad she was to meet you."

I thought saying this would cheer Mommy up, but instead she lets out a little choked sob.

"She's got a nice life, don't she?" Mommy says. "Diane's got a good job, and they've got that pretty little house. She don't want for anything."

"I guess not," I say, because I'm not sure what Mommy is getting at.

"She's got a better life than you've got. Or Caleb's got. I've been thinking about that ever since we went to see her."

I thought it would make Mommy happy to see how good things had turned out for Macey. "Me and Caleb have good lives, too. You can't just compare one person's life against another like you was comparing brands at a grocery store."

Mommy takes out a cigarette and lights it. "Think about it, Kody. She's there in Knoxville where she's got all kinds of opportunities. You and your brother are stuck where there's no jobs and no future. Nothing to do but church or drugs. Jay and Tiff do their best with Caleb, but they barely make enough to get by. And you . . . I left you to be raised by somebody so narrow minded she acts like you're a serial killer when she finds out you've been playing with lipstick." She wipes away tears with her fist. "It would've been better if I'd put you two up for adoption, let you get raised in a city where you'd make something out of yourselves."

We're in downtown Morgan now, and I turn into the Hardee's parking lot so I can look right at Mommy when I talk to her. I put my hands on her shoulders to make sure she's paying attention to me. "I never want to hear you say that again," I say. "I wouldn't trade my time with you for nothing. And you know what? Caleb's doing great. He's one of the best ball players his age in Southeastern Kentucky. He's in 4-H and the Boy Scouts. And me . . . " I'm what? "Maybe this isn't the easiest place to grow up being the way I am, but you know what? It's made me strong."

Mommy nods. She's still crying. "You are strong."

The truth is, I don't feel strong. Between Nanny and L.J., I feel like a piece of paper that keeps getting wadded up and thrown away because people don't like what's written on it. "Let's get you to your meeting," I say.

* * *

USUALLY WHEN MOMMY LEAVES THE MEETING, she walks out alone, sniffling, holding a balled-up piece of Kleenex. But tonight she's with somebody, a guy a little younger than she is, with shoulder-length sandy blonde hair. Cute, if you like the biker type. He says something to her, and she laughs and play-slaps him on the shoulder. She's still smiling when she gets into the truck.

"Who was that tall drink of water?" I ask.

She laughs. "That's Tyler. He's like the class clown in the group. The leader gets mad at him, but damn, sometimes, you just need to laugh, you know?"

"So do you have a little crush on this class clown?"

Her face turns red, which is all the answer I need, but she says, "No! No way am I ready for anything like that. You hush, Kody!"

I start the truck. "A hit dog hollers, that's all I'm saying."

She smiles. "That better be all you're saying, mister."

* * *

I WAKE UP TO A LOUD clatter and Mommy's voice saying, "Shit!"

I throw off the covers and get up from my mattress on the floor.

Mommy's in the kitchen. She's breaking eggs into a bowl, one after another, and not doing a very good job of it. Her hands are slimy, and there are pieces of eggshell in the bowl.

"Mommy, what in the Sam Hill are you doing?"

"Oh, shit, I woke you up. I was making you a cake. It was supposed to be a surprise. For your birthday."

I'm so confused I wonder for a second if I'm dreaming. "It's not my birthday."

"For your pretend birthday, then," she says, like this makes perfect sense.

"We don't even have all the ingredients to make a cake. Why don't I just put this bowl of eggs in the fridge and we can scramble them for breakfast in the morning?"

"But what about your birthday?" Mommy says.

The pretend birthday makes me think of the Mad Hatter and the March Hare and the other crazy characters having an Unbirthday party in *Alice in Wonderland*, a movie I liked when I was little. I remember reading that the author of the *Alice in Wonderland* book was high when he wrote it.

All of a sudden, things start to make sense. "Mommy, are you high?"

"What? No!" she says with a nervous laugh.

But her face tells another story. Her eyes are droopy-lidded and glassy. There's a dopey softness to her expression that puts me in mind of a cow.

She knows I know.

"Don't be mad at me, Kody." She puts her hands on both my cheeks. "I love you so much."

"Of course I'm mad." I gently grip her wrists and take her hands from my face. I'm about to ask her where she got the pills, but then I realize I know. "It was that guy in the parking lot, wasn't it? He sold it to you."

"He *gave* it to me," Mommy says, "because he likes me." She wanders out of the kitchen and flops on the couch. "He really, really likes me, if you know what I mean."

I feel sick. I'm pretty sure the guy didn't give her the dope as a gift so much as payment for services rendered, possibly in a supply closet in the Methodist church. Classy. "If he liked you, he'd want you to stay clean."

She leans back on the couch. "It's hard. Staying clean. Too hard. There's just so much pain."

I sit down next to her, not because I want to be close to her but because there's no place else to sit. "Mommy, that car wreck happened when I was little. The doctors say there's no reason for you to still be in that much pain."

"It's not that kind of pain," Mommy says. "It's the pain here." She puts her hand over her heart. "And the pain in here." She brings both hands up to her head. "It's too much."

"Everybody hurts, Mommy. Right now I'm hurting because of Nanny. Because of L.J. Because of you."

"I loved her daddy, you know," Mommy says.

At first, I don't understand because her words don't have anything to do with what I just said. But then it clicks. "Macey's daddy?"

She nods in an exaggerated way, like her head is extra heavy. "I loved him, and now that I know her, I love her, too. And you know what?"

She's waiting for me to say "what?" so I do.

"I sat there in that sweet little girl's pretty little house, and I lied to her like it was nothing."

"What do you mean you lied to her?"

Mommy looks at me, but her eyes are unfocused. "When she asked me how her daddy died, I lied to her. And you

know what's scary? That lie spilled out of me just as easy as if
it was the truth. That's what they say in group. Being an
addict makes you a liar. You lie to yourself and you lie to
other people. Especially to people you love."

"Wait a minute. I'm confused. When did you lie to Macey?"

"You remember when I told her how her daddy died?"

I nod.

"That was when I lied to her."

I feel like I'm getting more confused by the second. "You
mean the story you told wasn't what really happened?"

"Some of it was true. What I said about how sweet Calvin
was and how he would've been happy if he'd known I was
carrying his baby. And how he would've loved Macey." She
stops talking and seems to stare at nothing.

I prompt her. "But the way he died?"

Mommy nods. "I smoothed it over to save Macey some pain."

I don't understand how what Mommy told Macey could be
any less painful. "Tell me."

"I ain't never told nobody."

"And it feels bad, doesn't it? Walking around with a secret
you're afraid to tell even the people you love?" It's a feeling I
know something about.

"It eats at you," Mommy says.

"So tell me." And I say what I wish Nanny and L.J. could've
said to me. "I love you no matter what."

"Okay," Mommy says. "Can I have a glass of water?"

I bring her the water and she takes a long drink, then
closes her eyes. "Calvin did come over that night to make
a buy." Her voice sounds far away and floaty, like she's
speaking from a dream. "Robert told him he had something special he wanted Calvin to try. He fixed it for him

in the kitchen so I didn't see what he put into it, but he came back with the works all ready, and Calvin tied off and shot up. And then the same thing happened that I told Macey. Calvin looked real peaceful and happy for a minute, but then he turned gray and slid off the couch onto the floor."

I'm confused. "I don't understand how this is any different from the story you already told."

"Here's where it's different," Mommy says. "I was panicking and checking to see if Calvin was breathing and your daddy said, 'I know you've been carrying on with that—' I won't say the word, but I'm sure you know what it was. He said, 'That's what you get, you whore. What you both get.'"

It's more than my brain can take in. "Wait, are you saying that—"

"Let me keep going," Mommy says, sounding exhausted. "If I stop, I won't be able to tell you the rest. It'll be too hard to start again."

I nod. I feel numb, like my body's shut down.

"I picked up the phone to call 911, but Robert grabbed it and smashed it against the wall. I tried to do CPR, but Robert pulled me off of him. I told him he was a murderer, that he would go to jail for murder, and he called me a whore again and said nobody was gonna worry about one more dead—" She trails off and shakes her head, like she's trying to shake off the memory. "Anyway, by this time there was no doubt Calvin was dead, so your daddy started talking about all the abandoned mines in the county, deep holes where you could drop a body, but I said no, Calvin had people who loved him and they'd look for him. I was the one who said to drop him at the emergency room door. That way I figured his body would at least be treated with respect, and when they saw it was an OD, they wouldn't suspect murder. So Robert drove us to the hospital with you in the front seat on my lap and Calvin's body in the back. When we got there, Robert dumped the body right at the door to the ER and drove off."

There's so much to take in here I don't know where to start. "So you helped Robert"—I can't call him my father right now, let alone *Daddy*—"dispose of the body? And you covered everything up. Why?"

"I was high and I was scared. I was scared of what Robert would do to me. I saw what he done to Calvin."

"But later you still could've gone to the police."

"Kody, me and the police have never been the best of friends. I already had a record back then. Shoplifting, possession, a couple of DUIs. I figured they wouldn't believe what I had to say anyway." She picks up her pack of cigarettes from the coffee table and shakes one out. "Besides, a week later, your daddy got arrested for a DUI. He was holding when they caught him. It wasn't the first time he'd been busted, and he had enough Oxys on him that it counted as intent to sell. A felony. I thought good, he's going to prison. Problem solved."

I can't follow her logic, if you can even call it that. "Problem solved? But he wasn't being punished for murder. Didn't he just do a year or two? If they got him for murder, he would've gotten life."

"At the time, I thought a felony's a felony. It seemed like pretty much the same thing to me."

"But it's not."

"No. But I was young and high all the time and scared and confused, so it seemed like it was. And then when you was still little and Caleb was just a baby, your daddy got it in his head that it was a good idea to rob the Gas 'n Go. That's when they got him for armed robbery plus possession. He'll be doing that sentence for another five years at least." She's quiet for a minute, smoking and staring off somewhere glassy-eyed. "You know, as the years went by, I thought less and less about Calvin and what happened to him. Too much pain, you know? But when you told me you'd met Macey, it all came back." She looks at me. "So you told me you'd love me no matter what. Do you still love me?"

I feel crushed by the weight of what she's told me. I know it's true, but my mind can't accept it. My daddy killed Macey's daddy, I tell myself. My daddy killed Macey's daddy.

Do you love me? Mommy wants to know. I look at her, small and fragile, unable to handle the pain life keeps throwing at her. At all of us. I think about the secrets she's carried, the lies she's told. And now, too late to help anybody, is the truth.

I can't look at her anymore. Not tonight. It's two-thirty in the morning, and I have to be up for school in four hours. Nothing feels real.

"I love you, Mommy, but I can't talk about this anymore tonight. I'm going back to bed."

"Okay," she says. "But hang on a second." She reaches in her jeans pocket and holds something out to me. At first, I think it's a coin, but then I see it's like a poker chip. She presses it into my hand. "I'm sorry I slipped today," she says. "Backslid, your nanny would call it. But tomorrow's a new day. I'll start over and I'll do better."

"Okay. I'll keep this for you." I want to believe her so much, but I don't know what to believe.

I crawl under the covers on my mattress. I vacuumed and shampooed the carpet in this room three times, but it still smells musty. Maybe there are some things you just can't get clean.

Tomorrow is a new day, Mommy said. But it's already tomorrow, and I don't know how to face it.

Chapter 18

WHEN I GET HOME FROM SLEEPWALKING through school, Mommy's still in bed. I know I should probably wake her, try to keep her on some kind of schedule. But the ugly truth is, I just can't deal with her right now. Last night was too much. Plus, since she used again, she'll be dopesick once the last of the dope has worn off, and she'll have to detox all over again.

It's like one of those video games Caleb and Uncle Jay like to play. When you die, you lose all the progress you made and have to start all over.

I wish, for about the millionth time since I moved here, that I could just lay in bed and listen to Dolly. I wouldn't even want to dress up today. I'm too tired to go to the trouble. I would just let Dolly's sweet voice soothe me into a nap.

I decide maybe I'll lay on the couch and turn on the TV when the phone rings. I dive for it so it won't wake Mommy up.

"Hello."

"Hey, bro."

Macey's voice is so happy and light it makes me feel extra weighed down by everything I know that she doesn't.

"You sound funny. Are you okay?"

I decide I can at least tell her a small part of the truth. "Last night was rough. Mommy fell off the wagon."

"You still use wagons in Kentucky?"

At first, I think she's joking. "Oh—it's an expression. I mean, she used again last night. Got high."

"Oh, no. I'm so sorry to hear that. From what you said and from meeting her this weekend, it seemed like she was doing better."

I can hear the sadness in her voice. There's so much more sadness I have the power to bring her, and right now I can't deal with being the person who does that to her. "Listen, Macey, I'll call you soon, okay? Now's not the best time to talk because of the shape Mommy's in."

"Okay, but promise you'll let Auntie and me know if there's anything we can do to help."

"I promise."

"I love you, bro."

"I love you, too."

I hang up and lay back down on the couch. My head aches, and my stomach hurts. If Mommy has to reset and start over, then I wish I could reset things so I don't know what I found out last night.

I'm too agitated to watch TV, so I decide I might as well go to the kitchen to see what I can get started for supper. I stare inside the cabinets and the refrigerator, not even really seeing what's there.

The knock on the door makes me jump like there's been an explosion. Nobody ever comes to the door of this trailer, not even Jehovah's Witnesses.

When I open the door, Nanny's standing there holding a cooking pot with something wrapped in tinfoil balanced on the lid. She's not smiling or frowning either one.

"Hey," I say, like it hasn't been weeks since we've spoken.

"Hey," she says. "I made a pot of chili and some corn-bread and thought I'd bring you'uns some. I'm not used to cooking for one person, and I've been making too much food ever since you left."

"Well, thank you," I say, taking the pot out of her hands. "Do you want to come in?"

"If that would be all right," Nanny says.

It's like she's asking me for permission, which is weird. "Of course. Come on in."

She steps inside and looks around. "Well, you've got this place looking better than I would've thought you could," she says.

I set the pot of chili on the stove. "I think I bought every cleaning product they sell at Dollar General," I say. "You wanna sit down?"

She sits on the lumpy couch. "How's your mommy?"

I sigh. "She was better for a while. Then last night, not so good."

"She use again?" Nanny asks.

I nod.

"She'd been clean about two weeks?"

"About that, yeah."

Nanny shakes her head. "She always backslides after about two weeks."

"Well, she did feel bad about it." I sit on the opposite side of the couch from Nanny. "She said she wasn't gonna do it again, that she was gonna start over fresh today."

Nanny gives a knowing nod. "She always says that, too."

I want to feel like I'm helping Mommy, that me being here is at least giving her a chance. "Maybe this time—"

"Maybe," Nanny says. "I'm praying for her. I'm always praying for her." She's quiet for a minute, then says, "Management called all of us girls in today and told us they're shutting the factory at the end of the year."

"Shutting it?" Nanny has worked in the uniform factory since she was around my age.

"Moving operations overseas like every place else," Nanny says. "They don't have to pay them a decent wage over there."

"What are you going to do?" Except for one place that makes automotive parts, Lyon Uniform is the last factory operating in this part of the state.

Nanny shrugs. "I don't know. Put on one of them ugly blue vests and work at Walmart's if they'll have me. But the hours are crazy, the pay's not near as good, and I'd have to be on my feet all the time." She sighs. "Kody, I'm old and tired."

"You ain't that old. You're not even sixty-five yet."

"But I am that tired. Listen, I didn't come over here to talk about my problems. You and me need to talk about what happened the night you left." She's picking at a loose thread on the couch instead of looking at me. "I was wondering . . . maybe you could come over Sunday morning? Your mommy will still be asleep. I'll fix us a big breakfast. All your favorites."

I am getting pretty tired of my own sorry excuses for cooking. "Biscuits and gravy?"

This is the first time she's smiled since she walked in the door. "Biscuits and gravy, eggs and sausage, grits. And we can talk about things. And maybe you can come to church with me just like always."

Just like always. The longer I stay away from church, the

weirder it is to think about going back. "Yes, to the biscuits and gravy and the talking. Maybe to the church part."

"All right," Nanny says. She stands up. "Well, I guess I'd better be getting back. The dogs'll be wanting their supper. They miss you."

I know this is the closest Nanny can come to saying she misses me. "I miss them, too."

* * *

WHEN I STEP ONTO THE PORCH at Nanny's house, the dogs bark and wag so much I'm afraid they're going to lose their voices . . . or their tails. Dolly, Loretta, Tammy, and even lazy old George Jones are all over me, acting like they've never been petted before in their lives. I scratch ears and rumps and talk total foolishness. "I've missed my babies, yes I have!" I say, and they eat it up like fresh kibble.

I knock gently on the door before I push it open.

"Since when did you have to knock?" Nanny hollers from the kitchen. "Get on in here."

The house smells like baking biscuits and savory sausage. It smells like a warm welcome.

Nanny is wearing an apron with a picture of a chicken on it over her church clothes. "Go on and sit," she says. "The biscuits is just about ready. You want your eggs fried hard?"

"Yes, ma'am." I sit down at what's always been my place at the table.

Nanny smiles and shakes her head. "I still don't understand why you'd want to ruin a perfectly good egg by cooking it to death."

"Runny yolks are nasty." I've always thought so. It's something about the way you cut into the egg and the yolk bleeds out like it's turning your plate into a gory crime scene.

Nanny breaks an egg into a sizzling pan. "But you can't sop your biscuit with a dried-up egg."

"That's what gravy's for."

Everything's delicious. The biscuits are brown and flaky on the outside and pillowy soft on the inside. The gravy is creamy, and the eggs have those brown, lacey edges I love. "You know," I say, cutting into a sausage patty. "I think this food tastes extra good because I've only been eating my own cooking the past couple of weeks. I can keep Mommy and me from starving, but I'm definitely limited. Lots of grilled cheese and tomato soup."

"Well, there ain't nothing wrong with a grilled cheese and tomato soup," Nanny says. "But there is something wrong with a boy having to cook for his mommy and clean up after her. She ought to be taking care of you, not the other way around."

"Yeah," I say. "But there's a big gap between how things ought to be and how they are."

Nanny nods and sips her coffee. "In this world, that's the truth. You know, the law says I've got custody of you. You ain't supposed to be living with your mommy."

"I know," I say. "But Mommy don't judge me for who I am. Maybe because she's sunk so low, she don't have room to judge anybody."

"Maybe." Nanny pushes her plate away. She hasn't eaten much, but I'm still shoveling it in. "I hope you don't have it in your head that I kicked you out of the house. You chose to leave."

I set down my fork. The lyrics to "I Will Always Love You" float through my mind. "I chose to leave because I didn't feel like I could live here and be who I am."

Nanny's eyes look wet, but no tears fall. "And if that changed, would you come back?"

"I would. But I'd still want to help Mommy all I can."

"You're not how I thought of people like that."

"Do you mean gay people?" We might as well put the word out there and call it what it is.

"Yes." She looks nervous and won't meet my eyes.

"Nanny, have you ever met anybody who's gay besides me?"

"Not that I know about."

"Then how can you know what gay people are like?"

"The way I know everything else. From the Bible and church."

I touch Nanny's arm. It's the first time I've touched her since I left her house, and it feels strange and familiar at the same time. "Nanny, do you know that in Knoxville Macey and her aunt go to a church where a lot of gay people go? Some of them are married and have kids even."

"Is it . . . a colored church?" she asks.

I cringe at the word "colored" but decide to let it go. "It's a church where everybody is welcome."

Nanny's brow is knitted. "I ain't never heard of a church like that."

"Nanny, one thing I've been learning is that there's lots of things in the world I've never heard of. But that don't mean they're wrong or bad."

"I know there's a lot that I don't know," Nanny says, staring down into her coffee cup. "I quit school when I was sixteen because I was in such a hurry to work and start making money. Now I wonder what I was in such a hurry for. I had a whole lifetime of work ahead of me."

It seems like she's at least listening to me. I look down at my plate. "It's kind of like eggs," I say.

She looks at me like I've lost my mind. "What's like eggs?"

"Me being gay. See, you like your eggs runny, and I like mine cooked hard. We like different things, but it's okay."

"I never heard Pastor say it's a sin to like your eggs cooked hard," Nanny says.

"No, and if he did, you'd think it was silly. Because different people like different things, and that's normal."

Nanny rubs her eyes. "What you're saying goes against the way I was raised and what I've been taught my whole life. But I hear the words coming out of your mouth, and you're my grandson, and I know you've got a good heart. So I don't know what to think anymore."

I reach across the table and take both of Nanny's hands. They're strong from all those years of hard work. "What I want is for you to try to understand. Think about it. Pray about it. If it turns out you can't understand, that's okay. But I want you to try."

Nanny squeezes my hands. "Okay. I'll try."

"Thank you."

Nanny stands up. "Now come over here and give your nanny some sugar."

I hug her neck and kiss her on the cheek. Nanny isn't much of a hugger, so when she asks for a hug, it feels like it means something. Like she's making a promise.

When we pull out of the hug, she says, "Kody, will you go to church with me this morning?"

I was feeling so much calmer, but now a little flutter of nerves comes over me. "I don't know, Nanny. It's awkward there with everything that happened between L.J. and me. And I've been thinking a lot about things on my own. I think it's been good for me to take a break from church for a little while."

Nanny's eyes narrow. "You been taking a break from God? Backsliding?"

"No, I ain't been taking a break from God. Just from church. They're two different things, you know."

Nanny looks at me like she's searching for something. "You've been sitting beside me at church every Sunday morning since you was an itty-bitty boy. It's been real hard the past couple of weeks, sitting in that pew with an empty space beside me and everybody asking where you're at."

I'm sure she's right about everybody asking where I am. If somebody misses one Sunday, everybody acts like they need to fill out a missing person's report.

When Nanny looks at me, I know she's seeing me at every age I ever was, from baby to toddler to little kid to big kid to whatever I am now. I know having me beside her at church means a lot to her. I also know we're each going down a road where that might not be possible. I can't always give her what she wants, but I can give it to her today. "Okay," I say. I look down at my jeans. "I ain't really dressed for it, though."

She smiles. "Jesus don't care what you've got on as long as none of your private parts is hanging out."

I laugh. "Well, I guess I pass Jesus's dress code then."

* * *

THE FIRST PEOPLE WHO COME UP to me at church are the Jenkinses. Last week when I babysat for them, they asked why I hadn't been in church, and I said it was because I was taking care of Mommy. When they see me, they say, "Good to see you, Kody. Is your mama doing better?"

"Some better," I say, not really sure if I'm telling the truth or not.

Jay and Tiff and Caleb come up next. Nanny doesn't care for how Tiff dresses for church; she always says her skirts are too short and her makeup is too heavy, but I think she looks pretty. Tiff hugs me and says, "I've been praying for your mommy."

Jay claps me on the back and says, "How's that truck running for you?"

"Real good," I say. "Having it's a big help."

Caleb talks to me for a while about his basketball team, and I smile and nod like I know what he's talking about.

After that, it's a blur of faces coming up to me and saying, "we've missed you" and "good to see you're finally back." It seems like there are two ways to think about words like these: the nice way is to think these people you've seen all your life but still don't know very well truly missed you while you were gone. The way it feels to me, though, is that they think if you missed church, especially more than one Sunday in a row, it must've been because you were up to something.

I sit next to Nanny on the same pew we've sat on all my life. In the row in front of us, L.J. is sitting with her mother and daddy and brother. I see her see me, but we don't speak.

The service starts with Mrs. Sutton banging out the opening bars of "Bringing in the Sheaves" and everybody standing up to sing. I actually like this hymn. To be honest, I don't know what sheaves are, and I'm too lazy to look it up, but the song talks about spending the day sowing seeds of kindness, which is a nice idea.

After the hymn, Pastor Jack takes his place on the pulpit. He is a small, wiry man, full of energy. He always starts off the service in a jacket and tie, but by the end he's always jacketless and tieless with his shirtsleeves rolled up, sweat stains spreading under his arms. It's like for him church is some kind of athletic event.

"Brothers and sisters, let us pray," he says.

It's the usual prayer, thanks to the Lord for His beautiful creation, followed by calls for help for the sick, the sinful, and those who haven't come to Jesus yet, ending, "In Jesus' name we pray, Amen."

Then there's a hymn I don't like much, "Nothing but the Blood of Jesus," which is too gory for my taste, and the passing of the offering plate. It's a poor congregation, and when the plate comes around, most of the money in it is one-dollar bills and pocket change. Nanny puts in a dollar.

When Pastor Jack takes the pulpit again, he's holding up his Bible in the air like a sword. "Brothers and sisters," he says, looking around at the congregation, "when I turn on the TV and watch the news and see all the sin and fornication and degradation, I think how much better our world would be if people would just follow the words of the Apostle Paul."

"Amen," somebody behind me says.

"Turn in your Bibles," Pastor Jack says, "to Romans, chapter one, verse twenty-six."

I don't have a Bible with me, but Nanny has hers and flips to the right page almost immediately.

Pastor Jack looks down at the Bible and reads, "*For this cause God gave them up to vile affections: for even the women did change their natural use to that which is against nature. And likewise, also the men, leaving the natural use of the woman, burned in their lust for one another . . .* "

There are other words, but I'm too upset to hear them. As soon as Pastor Jack closes the Bible, though, he looks right at me.

I don't even think. I just stand up, excuse myself past the other people in the pew, and stride down the aisle to the exit. It's all I can do not to run.

As soon as I'm outside, I do break into a run. I get into the truck and lock the door like I expect the Baptists to come after me like a bunch of zombies.

I stare at the church door, hoping to see Nanny coming out of it. But I know she won't. She would never walk out and make a scene.

But what if it's more than that? What if she asked Pastor Jack to preach on that passage? What if she thinks turning to Jesus will cure me of being gay the way she wants turning to Jesus to cure Mommy of her addiction?

The difference is that Mommy needs curing. I don't.

If I drive away, I know Nanny could get a ride from somebody, but I also know that if I left her, we would lose all the progress we made this morning.

I need to talk to her about what just happened. I also don't want to be the kind of person who abandons old ladies in parking lots.

I sit and wait.

When Nanny finally does come out with the rest of the congregation, I can tell she's upset even though she's trying to hide it. She gets in the truck and says, "I thought you might've drove off."

"I wouldn't leave you." I turn toward her. "I've got to ask you, though. Did you talk to Pastor Jack about me being gay?"

Nanny nods. "I had a private counseling session with him. I needed to talk to somebody, and he's my pastor."

I wish she had talked to somebody else, but I can't say it.

"Okay. Did you tell Pastor Jack to preach on those verses from Romans because I was gonna be here this Sunday?"

"No!" Nanny says. Her eyes are wide with shock, and I know she's telling the truth.

Nanny may have some blind spots and some passages in her mind that are too narrow for comfort, but she isn't a liar. "I believe you," I say. "But did you see when he finished reading that verse he looked right at me?"

Nanny nods. "He ought not to have done that. What I told him was supposed to be private."

It's the first time I've ever heard her say that Pastor Jack might have done something wrong. It's progress. "I guess he thought it was more important to condemn me than to keep his promise to you." I start the truck.

"I've got half a mind to call him and give him an earful this afternoon," Nanny says.

"I'm sorry if I embarrassed you by walking out." But I'm not sorry I walked out.

"I was embarrassed at first. But then I closed my eyes and started praying on it. I stopped paying attention to what Pastor Jack was saying, and I kindly went inside my head and talked to God. And I realized you matter more to me than anybody in the church and what they think."

My eyes brim with tears. "Thank you."

Nanny dabs at her eyes, so she must be tearing up, too. "From now on, anything that has to do with you is between you, me, and the Lord. All right?"

"All right."

"Now when are you moving back into the house?"

I feel ready to move back right now, but I can't leave Mommy in such a fragile state. "Let's give Mommy a couple of days to be clean again. I'll take her to her N.A. meeting on Tuesday night, and then we'll see."

"So Wednesday," Nanny says. "You'll come back home on Wednesday. I'll cook a big supper, and we can watch *The Golden Girls*."

I've missed watching *The Golden Girls* with Nanny. "Okay."

We're quiet for the rest of the ride home, but it's a comfortable quiet. Driving away from the church feels much better than driving toward it.

Chapter 19

"YOU'RE GONNA TELL THEM, RIGHT?" I say. I'm driving Mommy to her meeting. She's been quiet the whole way, smoking and staring out the window like there's something to see besides the usual fields and cows, houses and trailers.

"What?" she says like she's been a million miles away.

"At the meeting. You're gonna tell them you used again."

"I ain't gonna lie about it if that's what you mean." She keeps staring out the window.

Somehow this doesn't seem the same as saying she's going to tell them. Ever since she used again the other night, it's like I'm a little suspicious of her. When she was clean, I was starting to trust her. Now I'm not so sure. "But you've got to admit it. You can't just sit at the meeting like a bump on a log and not say anything. Sometimes not saying anything is the same as lying."

Mommy laughs, but it's not a happy laugh. "Sometimes you sound so much like your nanny it gives me chills. I tried to get away from her, but I ended up giving birth to a male version of her."

I'm not ready for this hostility. "I don't think that's fair. I love Nanny, but you know her and me have our differences. I'm a lot more open minded than she is, for one thing."

"You are. But you're both still busybodies."

I drop her at the church door and make sure she goes straight inside, then find a space in the parking lot. I love her, but I'm happy to have a break from her even if I am just sitting in the truck doing homework.

Poor Mommy. She needs somebody to take care of her so she won't make terrible mistakes, but because she wants to get high and make terrible mistakes, she ends up getting mad at whoever's trying to take care of her.

I hope she tells them the truth tonight. But the truth is, I'm not being that honest either. I've been sitting on the story of how Macey's daddy really died, not saying anything to Macey or Auntie Diane because I'm too scared of what will happen if I do. I'm not scared that they'll press charges against my daddy because I've come to believe that he's earned every bad thing that happens to him. But what if the horribleness of what I have to say ruins my relationship with Macey? What if she can't see me as a brother anymore but only as the son of the man who killed her daddy?

Telling her might ruin our relationship, but so will lying by not telling her. I take my phone out of my pocket.

"Hey, bro!"

"Hey, sis." Her voice sounds so happy it's tempting to start off with some chit-chat, but I try to resist. "Listen, I've got some stuff to tell you—some stuff about our family—but I don't want to do it over the phone." I need to tell her face to face even if it means it'll be the last time I see her.

"Are you okay?"

"Yeah," I say even though I'm trying not to cry. "I just need to tell you some stuff Mommy told me the other night. Since you're my sister you've got as much of a right to know as I do."

"Okay," she says, but she sounds nervous. "I've been pestering Auntie to bring me to Kentucky. She says I won't like it, but I want to find out for myself. Hang on a second. Let me go talk to her."

I wait, part of me hoping they won't come too soon so I'll have Macey in my life a little while longer.

When she comes back, she says, "Auntie says we can come up on Saturday but just for the afternoon. We won't trouble you by spending the night or anything."

"It wouldn't be trouble," I say, but what I'm thinking is *You won't want to spend the night after you hear what I have to tell you.*

* * *

WHEN IT'S ALMOST TIME FOR THE meeting to let out, I walk up to the church steps. I want to escort Mommy to the truck to make sure nothing sketchy happens in the parking lot.

When Mommy comes out, she's with an expensively dressed middle-aged man I've never seen before and a vaguely familiar blonde lady. It takes me a minute to place the lady, but then I remember her from the thrift shop. "And there's your handsome son," she says, smiling. "Hey, Kody!"

"Hey—"

"Brandi," she says before I have to admit I have no idea what her name is. "I just remember your name because your mommy talks about you in group. Usually, I'm awful with names."

"She does talk about you in group," the man says. His hair is silver at the temples. He's what gets called distinguished-looking. He seems much too fancy to be in any group Mommy's a member of. "And it's always nice things. I can tell you're a big help to her, Kody."

"Thank you, sir," I say. The "sir" comes out of my mouth without me even thinking about it.

"I'm Jeremy Carr, by the way," the man says, holding out his hand.

I take his hand to shake it, and he covers it with his other hand. He's wearing a gold signet ring studded with diamonds and engraved with the letters "J.C."

"Your mom did a very brave thing in there," he says.

"She did," Brandi says. She turns to Mommy. "Give me a hug now."

Mommy isn't a big hugger, but she lets herself be hugged.

"I'm praying for you, baby," Brandi says. "One day at a time, right?"

"Right," Mommy says.

In the truck, I say, "I'm proud of you for telling them."

Mommy nods. "It was hard."

"I know it was." I start the truck.

"But it's easier to talk to people who're all going through the same thing," Mommy says. "Like that Jeremy guy, he's probably the richest man in the county, and he still goes through times when he has to come to meetings to stay clean. It's not just screwups like me that have these kinds of problems. It's important people, too."

"Just because you're not rich don't mean you're not important," I say. "You're important to me." I take a deep breath. If Mommy was brave tonight, I should be, too. "Listen, after you went in to your meeting, I started thinking about what a hypocrite I am, asking you to tell the truth and then not doing the same thing myself."

"What are you talking about?" Mommy lights a cigarette and cracks the window.

"I need to tell Macey what you told me about how her daddy died."

"No!" Mommy grabs my arm which isn't a great idea since I'm driving. "You can't tell her! That was private information I told you!"

"It should never have been kept private. It was a crime. It should've been reported to the police."

"And that's what Diane'll do if she finds out. Your daddy will end up on Death Row, and I'll go to prison. Is that what you want?" Mommy's eyes are wide and terrified.

"No, of course I don't want you to go to prison, but I don't think you will anyway. You tried to save him. It was just too late." I take a deep breath, try to calm myself down, and hope that calm is contagious. "But I do want Macey to know what really happened. You lied to her, Mommy. We need to set the record straight."

"There is no 'we' here, Kody. There's just you. I'm sticking to my story that I already told Macey."

"The lie, you mean?"

"Sometimes a lie goes down better than the truth."

Once we pull in front of the trailer, I say, "Mommy, there's something else I need to tell you. Nanny and me had a good talk on Sunday, and I think it's time I move back in with her. Since she's got custody of me, we could get in trouble if I stay with you for too long."

"Fine." She spits out the word. "Leave me like everybody else does."

The unfairness stings, but I don't want to get into any more of an argument than I already have. "I wouldn't be leaving you, Mommy. I'd still see you every day. I'd come over here, and you could come to Nanny's whenever you wanted to."

Mommy's face is red and streaked with tears. "So she can judge me and criticize me? And don't think she won't be judging you and criticizing you, too. She don't think Jesus loves the little gay boys, so she won't love them neither."

My hands are still clutching the steering wheel even though we've been parked for a good five minutes. I loosen my grip. "Nanny and me had a good talk. She said she was gonna try to understand. I'm gonna give her a chance."

Mommy wipes her eyes with her fists. "Yeah, she always gets a chance. Nobody ever gives me a chance."

I've given Mommy so many chances. But I know I can't say this. "Listen, let's not sit in the truck and argue all night. Let's go inside and get some rest. We can talk more when I get home from school tomorrow."

"No," Mommy says. "You've made your decision. You ain't coming back in my house. You wait right here." She gets out of the truck, slams the door, and then disappears into the trailer. In a couple of minutes she's back, throwing jeans and t-shirts and underwear out the front door and into the scrubby little patch of grass that passes for a yard. It's so weird that it takes me a second to realize what she's throwing is my stuff. I get out of the truck and start picking it up. I'm glad there are no neighbors to see me. "Mommy, is all this drama necessary? Why can't we just talk?"

"There's nothing to talk about. You've made your choice, and I've made mine." She slams the trailer door closed, and I hear the lock click.

I finish picking up my things and put them in the truck. There's nothing like picking your underwear up off the ground to make you feel like your life is in a great place. I don't have my toothbrush, but I don't guess I'd want to use it after she threw it in the yard anyway. I drive the quarter mile to Nanny's house. As soon as I pull into the driveway, the dogs start barking.

Nanny answers the door in her nightgown, the high-necked one I used to make fun of, asking her if she got it at Victoria's Secret. "Kody, are you okay? Is she—"

"She kicked me out. I'm back here to stay if you'll have me."

"Of course I'll have you. Get in here." She holds the door open. "You want some hot chocolate? I was just about to fix me some."

"Sure."

"Sit down. You look like your nerves is shot."

"They are." I sit on the couch and take my shoes off.

"She gets mad, but she won't stay mad," Nanny says as she busies around in the kitchen. "She needs you too much."

I wish she had said "loves" instead of "needs," but "need" is probably closer to the truth. In a few minutes, Nanny hands me a steaming mug.

"With extra marshmallows," she says.

I look down at the mug. The marshmallows are the pastel-colored kind that taste a little fruity. It feels nice to have somebody fix something for me. "Thank you."

"I've been saving that bag of marshmallows for when you came home." Nanny sits in the recliner with her own mug of hot chocolate.

I take a sip. It's perfect. "Me and Mommy got into an argument about Macey. She told Macey some stuff that wasn't true, and I want to straighten it out, but she doesn't." I hope Nanny doesn't ask for details because as I am talking, I realize she probably doesn't know the truth either, and I'm way too tired to go into it tonight.

"Well, your mommy's been lying to everybody so long I think she's about forgot how to tell the truth. And that includes lying to herself."

All of a sudden, I realize something that almost makes me choke on a marshmallow.

I must look panicked because Nanny says, "What's the matter?"

"Macey and Auntie Diane are supposed to drive up here on Saturday. There's some stuff we need to talk about. I was gonna have them come over to Mommy's because I wanted her to be a part of the conversation, but that's not gonna happen now."

After a few seconds, Nanny says, "They can come over here if Diane is willing. I know I ain't exactly her favorite person, but I'll put out cookies and lemonade and stay out of the way so you can talk."

"You'd do that?"

Nanny nods. "You know, ever since you and me had . . . our differences, I've been thinking a lot about the way I was raised. There was a lot that was right about it, but there was some that was wrong, too. I'll go to my grave believing in the Ten Commandments and that it's right to say 'ma'am' and 'sir' and 'please' and 'thank you.' And I believe in treating other people the way you want to be treated.'" She sets down her mug on the coffee table. "See, Mother and Daddy preached that, but they didn't always practice it. Like Daddy hit us kids oftener and harder than most people would say was right these days. That's why I've never been big on whipping you. And then there was the way Mother and Daddy was about colored people—talking about them like they wasn't as good as us."

I let the word 'colored' go. I know she's saying things she's been thinking hard about, and I don't want to interrupt her thoughts.

"I know now that wasn't right. And when management told us they was shutting the factory down, I started thinking about Priscilla losing her job, too. She started working there when she was still a teenager just like I did, and she raised her kids while she was working that job just like I did. And now she has grandkids like I do, and she goes to her church on Sunday, and I go to mine. So how are Priscilla and me that different just because her skin's darker than mine? It's like thinking somebody's not as good because of what color eyes or hair they've got."

"Exactly." I'm surprised to feel tears springing to my eyes. It's been an emotional night.

"Well," Nanny says, getting up from her recliner. "I'd better get to bed. But you tell Macey and Diane to come here on Saturday. Tell them they're welcome."

"Yes, ma'am," I say.

My room looks the way it did when I left it. Papaw's LP player is still in the corner with the Dolly albums lined up beside it. I put *My Tennessee Mountain Home* on the turntable and put on my headphones so I won't bother Nanny. Hearing Dolly's voice again is the best kind of homecoming.

On impulse, I get down on my knees and look under the bed. My cardboard box is there. I pull it out. Inside is my yellow silk robe and wig and makeup. Nanny could have thrown it all away. She could have burned it like they burned witches in the old days. But she put it right back where she found it.

Chapter 20

IT FEELS WEIRD TO ANSWER THE doorbell at Nanny's house and see Macey and Auntie Diane standing there with the dogs wagging all around them.

"Hey, bro," Macey says and hugs me. When she pulls back, she says, "This place is in the middle of nowhere. What do you *do* here?"

"You know, the usual," I say. "Whittle. Play my banjo. Tend to my moonshine still."

Auntie and Macey both laugh, but Auntie seems nervous. I can tell she doesn't like being here and that she has a suspicion that what I tell them isn't going to be good.

Once they come in, Nanny steps out of the kitchen. "Look at how pretty you are!" she says to Macey.

"Thank you," Macey says, sounding a little shy.

"Diane," Nanny says.

"It's been a long time," Auntie says. Her tone isn't cold, but it's cautious.

"It was a long time ago, and it's not a time I'm particularly proud of," Nanny says. "But I'm glad y'all are here now. There's cookies and lemonade in the kitchen. I just wanted to say hello, but I'll clear out so you can talk."

I look at Nanny. It seems crazy to tell Auntie and Macey what I'm about to tell them and not tell her, too. Our family doesn't need any more secrets. "Maybe you should stay, Nanny. If it's okay with Macey and Auntie Diane."

"Of course it's okay," Auntie Diane says. "It's her house, isn't it?"

"Is Mommy going to be here?" Macey asks.

"No. We had . . . a disagreement. She don't want me to tell you what I'm about to tell you." I take a deep breath. "Why don't all of y'all sit down?"

Macey and Auntie take seats on the couch and Nanny sits in her recliner. None of them look comfortable. They're all perched on the edge of the furniture like they could jump up and bolt away any second.

"Okay," I say. I'm too nervous to sit. "When Mommy got high the other night, she told me how your daddy died, Macey."

Macey looks confused. "She already told me. You were there."

"What she told you wasn't the truth. Not the whole truth, anyway. Your daddy did OD, but not the way she said. My daddy knew that your daddy and Mommy had been carrying on. He fixed the shot that killed your daddy. It wasn't an accident."

Macey's eyes are huge, but I can't read Auntie Diane's expression at all.

"So you're saying Robert *murdered* Calvin?" Nanny asks. She's leaned forward in her seat.

"That's what Mommy said." I wonder if Macey and Auntie Diane will get up and walk out, if they'll never want to have anything to do with me again.

Nanny nods. "Well, I knew Robert was the sorriest SOB that ever lived, but I never took him for a murderer." Saying SOB is the closest I've ever heard Nanny come to cussing.

"Your dad . . . killed . . . my dad," Macey says, like she's trying to wrap her brain around it. There are tears in her eyes.

"To be honest, I'm not surprised," Auntie Diane says. Her eyes are dry. "I told him if he moved here, he was gonna get himself killed."

"You told him he was gonna get killed just for moving here and being . . . Black?" Nanny says.

At least she didn't say "colored."

"I was right, wasn't I?" Auntie Diane said. "When he told me he was coming to school here, I went to the library and made a copy of an article talking about how Morgan had been a sundown town well into the sixties. I had been writing a paper about sundown towns for a history class, and Morgan had kept coming up in my research."

"I don't know what 'sundown town' means," Macey says.

"I'm sure Mrs. Prewitt knows what it means," Auntie Diane says.

Nanny nods. "I remember when I was little there used to be a sign as you went inside the city limits. It said, 'Ni**er, don't let the sun set on you in this town.' Now when I think about that, I see how wrong it was. But back then I guess I didn't know enough to ask questions."

I can't believe I've lived in Morgan my whole life and this is the first time I've heard about this part of its history.

Auntie Diane nods. "I showed the article to Calvin, but he said times had changed, that I was just being paranoid."

I wonder if Auntie is right, if Calvin was killed because he was Black. If Mommy had been carrying on with a white man instead, would Daddy have gotten mad enough to kill him? I might be wrong, but I don't think he would've. There would have been an old-fashioned hillbilly fist fight, and both men would have walked away bruised and bloody. But both men would have walked away.

"I feel like I should apologize," I say, looking at Macey and Auntie Diane. "For what my daddy did, for y'all being kept in the dark about what really happened." My voice is breaking, and I feel like I'm breaking, too. "I love you both, and I don't want this to change anything between us. But I feel like it's changed everything."

Macey is on her feet and has her arms around me before I even know what's happening. "It doesn't change anything between you and me. I love you, bro."

Auntie is right behind her and hugs me, too. "Nothing has changed," she whispers in my ear.

"Are you gonna call the law on Robert?" Nanny asks.

"I don't see what good it would do," Auntie Diane says. "It would be hard to prove. Plus, he's already doing a fifteen-year prison sentence. If he were out walking the streets it would be different. But he's not."

"A lot of folks would want to see him dead for what he done," Nanny says.

"Yes," Auntie Diane says. "But it wouldn't bring Calvin back, would it? And besides, Mrs. Prewitt, I don't think revenge is particularly Christian."

Nanny looks at Auntie with an expression I can't quite read. "Wanda," Nanny says. "Call me Wanda."

"I will. Wanda," Auntie Diane says. The feeling between the two of them isn't warm, but it's gone from cold to cool, like a pond that's been frozen over, but now the ice has started to thaw.

"Should I call you Wanda, too?" Macey asks.

"If you want to," Nanny says. "Of course, Kody and his brother call me Nanny, so if you wanted to call me that, too, it'd be all right."

We sit quietly for a few minutes, but it doesn't feel quiet because so many things are swirling around us: this shared knowledge that's just between the four of us and that we're planning to keep that way.

After a while, Nanny says, "Who wants some lemonade?" We all troop into the kitchen like we're grateful to have something specific to do, and everybody takes a glass of lemonade and a store-bought sugar cookie, and it's weird because it's kind of like a party even though the reason we're together is to talk about Macey's dad's murder at the hands of my own father.

But the cookies and lemonade still hit the spot.

Outside, the dogs start going crazy. Our weird almost-party is interrupted by a banging on the door. Nanny and me share a look.

"I'll get it," I say.

Nanny raises an eyebrow. "You sure?"

"Yes, ma'am." I go to the door hoping that if it's her, she's here to apologize.

As soon as I see her, it's obvious. Her eyes are unfocused and heavy lidded. She's swaying where she stands. She has on a lime green tank top with no bra and Daisy Dukes that show off too much of her skinny, pale legs. On her left arm I can see the bruise that's forming where the needle went in.

"Mommy," I say.

She beckons me with a curled up index finger. "Come out here and talk to me for a minute," she half whispers.

I go out on the porch and try to calm the dogs down. Mommy's so unsteady on her feet I'm afraid one of them might knock her over.

"I wanted to say . . . " Mommy's speech is slow and slurred, and she seems to be having a hard time putting thoughts together. "I wanted to say I'm sorry for throwing you out the other night. You just hurt my feelings is all."

"Well, you hurt my feelings, too, so I guess we're even."

Mommy looks back at Auntie Diane's car in the driveway. "They're here, huh?"

I nod.

"You didn't tell them, did you?" She wobbles a little and steadies herself on the porch railing.

"Mommy, you're high."

She looks at me, but I can tell it's hard for her to focus. "You're changing the subject. That's not what I came here to talk about."

"I'm not going to talk to you about anything when you're high."

Mommy rolls her eyes. "Can you at least tell me if you told them or not?"

"They know, but they're not gonna say or do anything about it. They promised."

"People don't always keep their promises," Mommy slurs.

I almost laugh. "You're telling me."

"What's that supposed to mean?"

"I think you know what it means. You made a promise to stay clean, and you're not keeping it."

She grabs my hand in both of hers. "I try, baby. I really try. It's just so hard."

No drug can take away the pain that's in her eyes. "I know it is."

The door opens behind us. "Hey," Macey says. She walks out on the porch.

Mommy drops my hand and finger combs her hair and tugs at her clothes. It would take a lot more than that to make her look presentable. "Hey," she says back.

"I thought I'd come out and say hi," Macey says. I can tell she's trying not to show her shock at how bad Mommy looks.

"There's my pretty girl," Mommy says. "Come here and give me a hug."

Macey hugs Mommy, then pulls away and looks at her. Mommy reaches out and strokes Macey's hair. She grabs a curl, stretches it out, and watches it spring back into place. "I wish you could've grown up with me," Mommy says, all slow and dreamy. "I could've braided your hair every morning and put you in pretty dresses for school."

"Except that you wouldn't have," Macey says in a matter-of-fact tone I've never heard her use before. "You would've gotten high instead."

Mommy looks like Macey just slapped her. "You hate me," she says. "And he's been telling you all this stuff that makes you hate me more."

"I don't hate you," Macey says. "But I've got to be realistic about what the situation was when I was born, and clearly Auntie Diane was in better condition to raise a child than you were. I'm glad I'm getting to know you, though."

"I'm glad I'm getting to know you, too." Mommy's all weepy now, and she gives Macey another hug which I'm not sure Macey wants.

"I don't guess I get a hug because you're mad at me," I say.

"I'm mad at you but I still love you," Mommy says.

"I love you, too, Mommy. But I'm mad at you for using again."

Mommy puts a finger to her mouth. "Shh. She don't know," she whispers, nodding toward Macey.

"I know what a person on drugs looks like," Macey says.

Mommy shakes her head. "You kids today are too damn smart." She holds onto the railing as she walks cautiously down the porch steps. "I'd better go on home before your nanny catches me and bawls me out," she says.

"I'll come see you tomorrow," I say. "Tomorrow you're starting over and staying clean. One day at a time, right?"

Mommy walks away unsteadily. "One damn day at a time, one damn hour at a time, one damn minute at a time."

After Mommy's out of earshot, Macey says, "Wow, she's messed up."

"Yep. Welcome to the family."

She smiles a little. "Thanks."

"Hey," I say, "Would you like to go for a walk?" I feel a sudden need to be alone with Macey and away from all the drama.

She crinkles her nose. "Are there snakes?"

"It's kind of early in the year for it to be too snakey," I say.

"All right," she says. "But if there's a snake you have to protect me from it."

I picture myself as a knight with a sword, slaying a copperhead like a dragon. "I promise," I say.

We walk down toward the creek with the dogs trotting behind us. The sun is shining through the trees. Loretta and Tammy jump into the creek and play in the water, splashing around and nipping at each other. Macey smiles at them. "Pets always make things better."

"They do," I say. Animals' lives seem so much happier and so much less complicated than ours. "Are you okay with what I told you about your daddy?"

She shrugs. "Well, I mean, it's not okay, the way he died. But it doesn't change things between you and me if that's what you're worried about."

I breathe a big sigh of relief. "That was what I was worried about."

"Nope," Macey says, taking my hand. "We're good."

We walk alongside the creek holding hands, watching the dogs splash and play.

"It's pretty here," Macey says.

"It sounds like you were about to say 'but,'" I say. "Like 'it's pretty here, but—'"

"Well, I wasn't going to, *but* I guess I have no choice now," Macey says. "It's pretty here, but have you ever thought about living somewhere else?"

"Well, I'd like to travel more and see some places—like Dollywood—but I guess I never thought about living someplace else. Mommy needs me close by, and it'd break Nanny's heart if I left."

Macey looks at me kind of funny. "But isn't that what kids are supposed to do? Grow up and leave?"

"It's different around here." I point out a neighbor's property, a white frame house sitting between two trailers. "You see over there? The parents live in the house, and each of them trailers belongs to one of their grownup kids. You see that all the time here. Part of it's on account of people not having much money, but it's also because people like to stay close."

Macey stops walking and turns to face me. "But Kody, don't you have anything you just want for yourself? Like dreams?"

"Most of my dreams have been wasted on wanting Mommy to get better so she could be a real mother to Caleb and me.

But you saw her today, so you know how far them dreams went. What about you, Macey? Do you have dreams?"

Macey smiles and nods. "I want to get a scholarship to go to UT and be on the dance team. And I want to major in communications and be a news anchor on TV."

I can totally see it. "That's not just a dream. You're going to make that happen."

"I'm going to try to."

"You're gonna work your butt off to make your dreams come true just like Dolly did," I say. "I don't really have any dreams like that. I guess I always figured after I graduated, I'd get on at the uniform factory where Nanny works. She always said there was a job waiting for me there. But now that it's shutting down, I'm going to have to figure out some other way to get by."

Macey is picking up pebbles and tossing them into the creek. "Life should be about more than getting by, Kody. What makes you feel happy and alive?"

"Well, you do, for one thing," I say.

Macey grins. "Right back 'atcha. What else?"

I throw a few pebbles into the creek, too. "Well, I know it's weird, but when I put on my makeup and blonde wig and move my lips to Dolly, I feel . . . different. Like there's some part of me that's usually in the dark that I'm letting out into the light and air. Like I'm free, I guess."

"Yes!" Macey says. "That! You need more of that."

"More dressing up like Dolly? I can't see how there'd be much of a future in that."

"Well, sure, more dressing up like Dolly, but maybe more things in your life that make you feel free. You know, there are at least three gay bars in Knoxville where drag queens lip synch to songs onstage and people pay to see them."

I try to imagine having the courage to do what I've always done in private in public. "People pay to see them?"

"They do."

I laugh, trying to picture myself prissing around and moving my lips to "Jolene" in front of an audience. "Well, I don't know if I'd have the courage to perform myself, but I'd sure love to see one of them shows."

Thinking of myself going into a nightclub feels crazy, like something out of a movie. But it does make me smile. "You make me think about doing things I'd never think about on my own."

"Good." Macey throws a pebble in the creek. It makes a surprisingly big splash. "Somebody needs to. Because you need some new dreams."

Chapter 21

I GO INTO THE LIVING ROOM and find Nanny sitting on the couch, still in her housecoat, drinking a cup of coffee and reading. She looks up and says, "Mornin'. I made a can of them cinnamon rolls you like."

"Thanks," I say, but I sound as confused as I am. "It's Sunday, right?"

"It is."

"Well, shouldn't you be getting ready for church?" I can't remember a Sunday morning when Nanny didn't have her hair fixed and have on one of her three good church dresses.

She grins. "Lord, you're the last person I'd expect to be fussing at me for not going to church."

"I'm not fussing. I'm just curious. You not going to church on a Sunday is like the moon coming out in the morning."

Nanny sets her cup down on the coffee table. "Well," she says, "it's like this. Pastor made me mad last week singling you out the way he did. And I know he's a human and imperfect like all of us, but I've been praying on some things and studying on some things—things I've been taught my whole life but now I'm not so sure about anymore. This morning it felt like the right thing to do was to stay home and read my Bible."

I see that what she's been reading is the black Bible with the gold-lined pages she always takes with her to church. "I think that's a good idea, Nanny."

She smiles. "The best part is that the Lord don't mind that I'm still in my housecoat."

"Hey, back in Jesus's day, they dressed in housecoats all the time." I've thought about this before. Why is it a sin for boys to wear dresses when that was pretty much what Jesus wore? His hair was long, too.

"After you get you some breakfast, would you sit and read Scripture with me?" Nanny says.

Somehow this seems a lot better than going to church. We can sit and read together, but nobody is going to tell us what to think. I go to the kitchen and eat a cinnamon roll and drink some orange juice. Then I wash the sticky frosting off my hands and go to my room to get the little blue Bible Nanny gave me when I got baptized.

I sit down next to Nanny. "What are we reading?"

"New Testament," Nanny says. "You know how these Bibles put everything Jesus said in red letters? Right now I'm going through the Gospels and reading everything in red. What he said, not what somebody else said about him. I figure that's a good place to start."

I turn to the Book of Matthew. I've always found the Bible hard reading, so I go through it slowly. I read all the red lettered parts in Matthew, Mark, Luke, and John. There are three things I notice:

There aren't that many things that we know Jesus said.

Everything he did say that somebody wrote down was really good, about loving each other and not judging other people because somebody else might judge you.

Jesus never said a word about it being a sin to be gay. He never said a word about gay people at all. Not one word.

I close my Bible. "I think that was the best church service I've ever been to."

"Amen," Nanny says. She pats my knee. "Let's get us another cinnamon roll."

* * *

I KNOW THERE'S NO POINT IN checking on Mommy until afternoon because she won't be awake. Nanny fries us some hamburgers for lunch and fixes an extra one for Mommy so I can take it to her. It's a challenge to smuggle a hamburger past the dogs on the porch, but I manage it.

I knock on the door of Mommy's trailer. There's no answer, so I bang on it. When that does nothing, I try the door. It's unlocked.

Mommy is sprawled on the couch, her eyes closed, one arm dangling down so her fingertips touch the floor. She's pale and still.

I'm afraid.

I set the paper plate I'm carrying on the cluttered coffee table and shake her by the shoulder. "Mommy? Mommy? Can you wake up?"

Finally she grunts and opens her eyes, but just so they're tiny slits. It's like somebody raising the blinds on a window just enough to let a crack of light in.

"Kody," she croaks.

"Hey. I brought you lunch. Nanny made hamburgers."

Mommy wrinkles her nose like I just offered her a plate of worms. "No. No food. Too sick."

The dope's worn off. Now there's just sickness to wait out one day at a time. "Is there anything I can get you?"

"Ice water," she says like it's her last request.

"Coming up," I say, too cheerfully. I don't know why I'm the happy servant girl all of a sudden.

Even though I've not been gone from Mommy's long, things have started to pile up again—soda cans and over-flowing ashtrays. The kitchen sink is full of dirty dishes. I have to wash a glass to get her water.

"Thank you, baby," she says when I bring her the water. She still has on the same clothes she was wearing when she showed up at the house yesterday.

"Why don't you see if you can sit up to drink it?" I say.

Slowly, she manages to pull herself up. The half circles under her eyes are so dark they look like bruises. She takes the glass, gulps down half the water, then gags.

"Slow down," I say. "Small sips."

She takes a tiny, ladylike sip. "Sorry I'm such a mess."

Right now or always? I want to ask but I don't.

"Must've caught a bug or something." She takes another tiny sip.

I can't just stand here and let her lie to me and to herself. "Mommy, we both know you don't have a bug. You used again, and it wore off, and now you're dopesick."

She bursts into tears. "I know. I'm such a loser. I never even got a second chip."

"You'll get it this time," I say, trying to sound more hopeful than I feel. "After you finish your water, why don't you take a shower?" I figure this is a more positive thing to say than *you stink.* Which she does.

She nods. I look around the floor at the scattered dirty clothes. "You got laundry that needs doing? If you can pick it up and put it in a basket for me, I'll take it to Nanny's and wash it."

"I don't know if I can. When I bend over, I get dizzy."

I sigh. I know a lot of moms complain when they have to pick up their kids' dirty underwear off the floor, but in what kind of a world does a son have to pick up his mother's dirty panties? "Okay," I say. "I'll pick it up."

She grabs my hand. "You're a good boy, Kody. You're always doing nice things for me. Now I'm gonna do something nice for you."

"What's that?" It's hard to think of what she could do for me since I'm not sure she can even stand up.

"See that piece of paper over on the coffee table?"

A wadded-up scrap of paper is beside the overflowing ashtray. I unfold it and see the name Jeremy Carr and a phone number. "Jeremy Carr? That name sounds familiar."

Mommy lights a cigarette. "That's cause you met him. He's that rich guy in my group. We was talking the other day and he was saying he needed somebody to do some yardwork and to help him with moving some stuff around the house. He said you seemed like a good worker and asked me to give you his number. He's loaded, Kody. He'll pay you real good."

I'm surprised that Mommy was so thoughtful. I put the slip of paper in my pocket. "Thanks. This'll help me pay off the truck."

"He said the sooner the better," Mommy says.

"I'll call him tomorrow right after school."

Finally Mommy gets in the shower, and I go through the trailer picking up her dirty clothes and stuffing them in a trash bag so I can carry them back to Nanny's to wash. I'm not thrilled to be picking up her dirty things, but I do feel better because she thought of me for that job. Even if it doesn't work out, at least it means that for a minute or two,

Mommy was thinking about me instead of dope and how to get it.

As soon as I get to the outskirts of town, my phone buzzes. Once I'm in the school parking lot, I check my messages. There's one from Macey:

> *Hey Auntie Di and I think u should come stay with us in Knoxville for the summer. What do you think? Our neighborhood has a pool. We'd have a blast. #dreams*

I laugh. It's a crazy idea, and I don't think Nanny would agree to it. Besides, I wouldn't even know how to act in someplace like Knoxville. I wouldn't have the right clothes. I wouldn't know what to order if we went to a nice restaurant. Plus, it wouldn't be good for Mommy if I was that far away.

Still, a picture pops into my head of Macey and me lounging beside a big blue swimming pool, wearing matching sunglasses like movie stars, and I can't help but smile.

In social studies we're watching a war movie I saw in another class freshman year, so my mind starts to wander. I think about how pole-axed I probably acted when Macey asked me about my dreams for the future, about how all my life has been just trying to get through the day I'm in. With the sewing factory and all the other good jobs gone, what's left here for me? Walmart? Fast food? Figuring out a way to draw a disability check from the government?

No wonder people here take pills. Taking pills gives them something to do. Something to look forward to.

On the way to lunch, I surprise myself by knocking on the guidance counselor's office door.

"Come in," she says.

Mrs. Reeves is a thin, nervous-looking woman with straight mousy brown hair cut in a shoulder-length bob. She always wears the kind of long, loose floral-print dresses that Nanny says look like flour sacks. She looks surprised that somebody has come to see her. "How can I help you?" she says.

"Hi," I say, feeling shy. "I was wondering . . . do you have any information on places you can go after high school? Like other schools?"

"Like colleges?" she asks.

"Maybe." I feel my face heating up from embarrassment. I should probably just leave. I don't even know what I came in here to ask for.

"Remind me of your name," she says.

"Kody Prewitt."

"Eleventh grade, right?"

"Yes, ma'am."

She smiles at me. "Well, it's definitely time for you to be thinking about these things. Do you have a minute to sit down?"

"Yes, ma'am." I sit across from her desk, which has lots of pictures of cats on it. The cats are pretty. I feel less nervous.

"So you're thinking about college but you're not sure?" she asks. She actually seems glad I'm here, like she was bored and lonesome and is happy for the company.

"Yes, ma'am. I guess I've not thought about my future much before, and I'm trying to change that."

She gives me an encouraging smile. When she smiles, she's almost pretty. She's one of those barefaced women. A little mascara and foundation and lipstick would do her a world of good. "So what kind of things are you interested in, Kody? What do you like to do?"

I figure saying I like to dress up like Dolly Parton and kind of perform as her isn't what she's looking for, so I manage to say, "Well, I'm interested in doing makeup and hair, that kind of thing." It comes out softly, but it does come out.

I expect Mrs. Reeves to call me a freak and tell me to get out, but instead she smiles again and says, "Perfect! That gives you a lot of options, Kody." She gets up from her desk and starts digging through filing cabinets. She finally finds everything she's looking for and comes at me with a stack of pamphlets.

The pamphlet on top is called "A Career in Cosmetology." The cover shows a lady (of course!) smiling as she fusses over some other smiling lady's hair. The rest of the pamphlets are about specific schools, the Bluegrass College of Hair Design and Aesthetics in Lexington, the Tennessee School of Beauty in Knoxville. "Thank you," I say.

She gives me a little pat on the shoulder. "I tell you what. You look these over and let me know if you might be interested in talking to anybody from any of the schools. And next year, if you decide to apply, I can help you with that, too. There's financial aid available if you need it."

"Okay, thanks," I say, getting up to leave.

"Kody," she says, "I feel like this could be a really good option for you. And I feel like in that field you'd meet a lot of friends you'd have things in common with. Girl friends and guy friends, too."

I'm pretty sure the guidance counselor just told me she knows I'm gay and she's fine with it.

In the cafeteria, I can't help looking over at the table where L.J. is sitting with Brianna and a bunch of other churchy kids. My heart gives the same little tug it always does when I see L.J., but I make myself walk past her.

In the back left corner of the cafeteria is a new kid who's been sitting by himself all semester. He could be sitting alone because he's a serial killer, but chances are he's sitting alone because he's new and country kids aren't always very welcoming to kids who "ain't from around here."

I walk up to the kid's table. "Anybody sitting here?"

"Just my imaginary friend," the kid says. He's got glasses and curly brown hair he wears longer than most boys around here.

"Can I sit in his lap?"

The kid smiles. "Go for it."

"I'm Kody."

"I'm Miles." He definitely doesn't have a Kentucky accent.

"Where are you from, Miles?"

"Illinois. Outside Chicago. We moved here because my dad got a job teaching French at Randall."

I nod. "It must be different here from what you're used to."

He nods. "Yeah. Like, other planet different."

I unwrap my peanut butter and jelly sandwich. I think about how long I was friends with L.J. without telling her who I really am.

"Miles, I want to tell you something about myself, so if you have a problem with it you can go ahead and let me know."

He looks interested. "Okay."

"I'm gay."

He shrugs. "That's cool. I'm straight, but my sister's gay. I'm glad she's already off in college so she didn't have to move here with us. I don't think it would be easy here."

"It's not." But somehow it feels like it's getting easier.

Chapter 22

JEREMY CARR'S HOUSE IS LIKE NOTHING I've ever seen except on TV. It's a huge white two-story with black shutters and white columns, like something out of *Gone with the Wind*. It sits on acres of land surrounded by the kind of black wooden fences they use in the Bluegrass part of the state. The fancy part. Which this isn't.

But Mr. Carr has made his little spot fancy all the same. I called him on Monday and he said Mommy had told him all about me, that it sounded like I was the responsible kind of guy he needed to help him around the property.

It's weird to think of Mr. Carr sitting in the N.A. group meetings in the church basement with Mommy, about him having the same kind of problems she does. What would Mr. Carr need to escape from? His life is clearly going great.

I pull into the long, paved driveway, feeling a little self-conscious about parking my crappy truck beside his Mercedes. I swallow my nervousness, get out of the truck, and go up on the front porch, which is set up like a sitting room with white wicker furniture. It all looks like something off the cover of *Southern Living* magazine.

I ring the doorbell. It's the kind of door you'd expect to be answered by a butler in a tuxedo.

Mr. Carr opens the door wearing a yellow golf shirt and khakis. When I met him before, I didn't notice what piercing blue eyes he has. "Hi, Kody," he says, smiling. His teeth are straight and white. "I'm so glad you could come out today."

"No problem," I say.

"Well, come on in, Kody, and let's hammer out a business deal."

I step inside. The ceilings are higher than in any house I've ever been in, and the hardwood floors shine like mirrors. The curving staircase looks like Scarlett O'Hara might come flouncing down it any minute. "You have a beautiful home," I say because I don't want to just stand here gaping.

"It's a money pit," Mr. Carr says. "Me, I could've gone with something simpler, but my ex-wife said, 'If you're going to make me live in this god-forsaken part of the state, the least you can do is build me a decent place to live.' So I did, but guess what? She left me anyway." He laughs. "Why don't we sit down in the living room?"

The living room also looks like it could be on the cover of a magazine. I'm afraid to touch anything, but I perch on the edge of the butter-yellow couch. Mr. Carr sits across from me in a sage green wing-backed chair. The paintings on the wall are floral designs that match the colors of the furniture.

"Oh, I almost forgot," Mr. Carr says, snapping his fingers. "Can I get you something to drink? Iced tea? Lemonade?"

I picture myself spilling iced tea on this couch, which probably cost more than every stick of furniture in Nanny's house. "No, thank you," I say.

"Well, let me know if you change your mind. I want you to feel comfortable here, like you can come and go as you please and help yourself to whatever's in the fridge. I know the surroundings look formal, but I'm really a very informal person."

"Okay. Thanks," I say, trying to sound a little more casual.

"So right now I'm thinking of a first mow for the yard. It's a little early in the season, but I like to start out with everything nice and even," Mr. Carr says. "How much do you usually charge for your mowing services?"

"Usually between twenty to forty a yard, but I've never mowed a yard this big before."

Mr. Carr smiles. "Oh, this is a hundred-dollar yard at least. And then I thought for other little jobs I might have you do around the place, ten dollars an hour. Does that sound reasonable?"

"That sounds great." Lots of people don't want to pay kids a decent wage. I guess they figure we're too young to know better.

"Good, good. Well, if you'd like to come out to the garage with me, I'll introduce you to the lawnmower. I'm sure you'll become good friends."

He leads me through the kitchen, which is huge and has counter tops made of some kind of shiny rock. We go to the garage, and he shows me a riding lawnmower which is almost as fancy as his car. "You think you can work with this?" he asks.

"Yessir."

He touches my shoulder. "Please, call me Jeremy."

Mowing on the riding lawnmower isn't like working at all. I just drive back and forth in straight lines across the yard, and it does all the work for me. I sing Dolly Parton songs because I figure the motor's loud enough that nobody can hear me.

It takes me about three hours to finish the whole yard, but a hundred dollars for three hours of light work isn't bad at all.

I knock on the door to let Mr. Carr—Jeremy—know that I'm done. When he opens it, he's holding a sweating glass of lemonade. "I heard you finishing up and thought you might be ready for something to drink."

"Thank you," I say, taking the glass. I am thirsty, and the lemonade is perfectly tart and cold.

"Come on in," Jeremy says, "and I'll get your money."

I stand in the foyer, and he takes out his wallet. "Are twenties okay?"

I try not to grin like an idiot. "Twenties are great."

He peels them off and hands them to me. "Thank you, Kody. You did a great job. I can tell you're somebody with standards. I appreciate that. Say, before you go, would you like a tour of the house? You seem like you have an appreciation for beauty. Not many boys your age have that."

"Not many of them," I say.

"I remember high school," Jeremy says, shaking his head. "All those meathead boys talking about sports and hunting and fishing and girls they wanted you to think they were having sex with when they really weren't."

I smile. "That all sounds pretty familiar."

"I bet it does," he says. "Here, let me show you around."

I'm starting to understand something about Jeremy Carr that may explain why he needs to go to N.A. meetings even though he seems to have all the money in the world. He's lonely.

I follow him down the hall. "This is the study where I think all of my great thoughts," he says, rolling his eyes so I'll know he's joking.

The room is lined with shelves of books. There's a huge antique desk with a computer on it and a comfy-looking leather chair. At the end of the hall, he says, "This is the den." The room has, unbelievably, a full-size pool table, a leather sectional sofa that could probably seat ten people, and a TV that takes up most of one wall. "You're always welcome to hang out here when you need to take a break," he says. "There's cable and Netflix and a couple of different video game systems."

"Thanks," I say. He probably thinks I'm all excited about the video games, but what I'm really doing is wondering what it would be like to watch *The Golden Girls* on a TV that size. Betty White's head would be huge.

"And now the upstairs," he says.

I follow him up the elegant, curving staircase. The first room we peek in has pink walls, a canopy bed, and little plastic horses everywhere.

"My daughter's room," he says. "She's off at college now. UK." We look at another room, this one a soft green with a brass bed. "The guest room," he says. "But the master bedroom's the one you need to see."

The huge room is painted gold, with a king-sized bed piled with pillows and a walk-in closet that's about as big as my room at Nanny's. Its racks are full of dress shirts in a rainbow of colors. "The bathroom is the best part," Jeremy says.

The bathroom floor seems to be made of marble. There's a sink that looks like a big stone bowl and a shower stall with a clear door so I can see there are multiple shower heads that spray every which way. Against the back wall is a tub that would be big enough for two people.

"It's the prettiest bathroom I've ever seen." It's a weird thing to say, but it's true. It may actually be the prettiest room I've ever seen.

"I know, right?" Jeremy says. "You know what? You've got grass clippings all over you, and I'm sure you're sweaty. You ought to take a shower and then relax in the jacuzzi for a while. If you fill the tub and then push the button, the jets will massage all your tension away."

Is it normal for people to invite the person who was just mowing their lawn to use their bathroom like this? Maybe it's normal for rich people. I've never even seen a jacuzzi before, let alone sat in one. People like me don't usually get the opportunity to experience this kind of luxury. But it's already past suppertime, and I know Nanny must be getting restless since I'm not back home yet. "Thanks, but—"

"I've got a pair of shorts and a t-shirt you can change into if you don't want to put your old clothes back on," he says.

The room is so beautiful, and I do wonder what a jacuzzi bath would feel like. I decide I'll rinse the grass clippings off in the shower, sit in the tub for fifteen minutes, and then I'll hurry up and get dressed and go home. "Okay, you've talked me into it," I say. "Thanks."

"Great! Let me get you that change of clothes." He comes back a few minutes later with a pair of running shorts and a Kentucky Wildcats t-shirt. "I'll give you your privacy," he says. "Enjoy."

The shower feels like standing under a waterfall if a waterfall was hot and steamy. I run the tub almost full, thinking of

how Nanny would fuss at me about the water bill. I guess rich
people don't have to worry about using too much of anything
because they always have plenty.

I climb into the huge tub and scoot myself down so I'm up
to my neck in hot water. I push the button Jeremy showed
me. Some kind of motor starts up, and jets of water pound
into my shoulders and lower back. This may feel better than
anything I've ever felt before.

I close my eyes and lay back. I didn't know how tense I was
until the water started working out the knots. For the first
time in a long time, I let my head clear and just float.

When the jets stop, I'm tempted to push the button again,
but I don't want to take advantage of Jeremy's kindness, and I
don't want to worry Nanny any more than I already have. I pull
the drain plug, get out, and dry off. The shorts and Kentucky
Wildcats t-shirt Jeremy loaned me are baggy, but it still feels
good to be wearing clean clothes. I look for some cleaning spray
under the sink so I can clean the shower and tub, but I can't find
any. I hang up the towel I used and pick up my old clothes. I
open the door to the master bedroom.

Jeremy is there. In bed, laying under the covers, propped
up on one elbow. He doesn't have a shirt on. My stomach ties
itself in knots. I wonder what else he doesn't have on. "Isn't
the jacuzzi relaxing?" he says, smiling.

"Um, yes," I say. My voice goes up at the end like I'm
asking a question.

"You know what else is relaxing? This memory foam mattress. Would you like to try it out?"

"Are you . . . making a pass at me, Mr. Carr?" *Making a
pass.* Where did I even come up with those words? Did I hear
them on *The Golden Girls*?

"I'm doing my damnedest," Jeremy says. His smile doesn't seem friendly anymore, and now I know what his light blue eyes put me in mind of. A wolf.

I start backing toward the door. Somehow it doesn't seem safe to turn my back on him. "I ain't even eighteen yet."

"Well, as long as we're discreet, I don't think that'll be a problem. You're not the first piece of chicken that's been in this bedroom. And nobody has ever found out."

A piece of chicken. Something to be consumed. "I'm not interested, sir. I'm gonna leave now."

Jeremy sits up in bed, the cover slipping down so I can see his pale belly. The hair there is salt and pepper, too. "At least think about it, Kody. The arrangement would have some real financial benefits for you."

I think of Mommy and how I'm pretty sure she's gone to bed with men not because she's wanted them, but because she wanted something they can give her. Drugs. Money for drugs. "I'm not a prostitute!" I'm surprise to hear the rage in my voice.

"Of course not. I wasn't suggesting you were. But Kody, I have to say I'm confused. When I talked to your mother, she said she was pretty sure you would be . . . receptive. She said you would like it."

"My mother doesn't know what I like."

Too much is coming at me too fast. All I can do is run. I run out of the room and down the Scarlett O'Hara staircase and out the door. I jump in the truck, start it, and tear out of the driveway like people do in horror movies when a monster is chasing them.

My first thought is to call the police. But what would I say? He didn't force himself on me, and who would believe a seventeen-year-old gay boy like me over one of the richest men in the county?

I drive toward home, my heart pounding in my chest, blood pounding in my ears.

She said you would like it.

Mommy knew. She knew, and she arranged for me to go to his house knowing what he was.

I drive straight to Mommy's trailer and bang on the door. When she doesn't answer, I keep banging. Finally, she opens it. Her eyes are droopy with sleep, and she's wearing pajama pants and an old tank top. "Good God, Kody, you think you could knock a little louder? You pound on the door like that, you might as well be pounding on my head."

I push my way into the trailer and slam the door behind me. "Did you tell Jeremy Carr I'd go to bed with him?"

"What?" She looks confused at first but then says, "Oh, him. I didn't tell him you *would.* I told him you *might.* On account of you being gay and everything."

"So me being gay means I must be willing to have sex with a man who's thirty years older than me?"

Mommy puts up her hands. "Hey, I don't judge."

"I've never kissed a boy my own age. I've never even been on a date." Tears spring to my eyes, and I wipe them away. "Why would I—?" I can't make myself say the words to finish the question, so I ask a different one. "Mommy, did Jeremy Carr make some kind of promise to you if you'd get me to come to his house? He doesn't really go to N.A. meetings because he's in recovery, does he?"

"Don't I at least get one phone call before you interrogate me?" Mommy says.

I don't answer.

Finally she says, "Jeremy's a doctor. Well, he was before he got fired from the hospital. He's a supplier—for people who need medicine. Mostly he gets paid in money, but if you're broke, sometimes he'll take . . . favors."

"So I was a favor?"

"It wasn't like that," Mommy says. There are tears in her eyes. "It was like a date—a blind date. You didn't have to do anything if you didn't like him."

"And what was you gonna get out of it? Tell me, Mommy. How many pills am I worth?"

She's really crying now. "I wouldn't have done it if I'd known it'd upset you so bad," she says through her sobs.

"But you would've. You would've if you thought it would get you some dope. You would've sent Caleb to him if you heard he liked them younger."

I turn to leave, and Mommy grabs me by my shirt tail. "Don't leave me, Kody! You know I love you!"

And I do know that. But I also know that dope means more to her than love.

I gently pull her hands off me. "Let me go, Mommy. You need to let me go."

She's still hollering as I get in the truck and drive away.

When I walk into Nanny's house, she takes one look at me and says, "What's the matter?"

I can't talk about it yet, so I just say, "Mommy did something that hurt my feelings."

"That's what she does," Nanny says. "We just have to remember she ain't in control of herself."

"The meetings aren't working, are they?" I say.

Nanny shakes her head. "No, they're not enough. Nothing we try is ever enough. If we had money to pay for treatment, maybe it would be different. But maybe it wouldn't. I don't know." She takes a deep breath then says, "Hey, I made us some vegetable soup and cornbread. You'll feel better if you eat something."

"It smells good." I follow her into the kitchen.

I don't know how many times I've watched Nanny make vegetable soup since I was little. She said back then it was the only way she could get me to eat a lot of vegetables. She puts a lot of work into it, breaking up the green beans, slicing the carrots, cubing the potatoes, stripping the corn kernels right off the cob. She always does it quietly, like she's really concentrating, the same way she reads the Bible.

Maybe because it's so much work, Nanny's vegetable soup has always tasted like love to me. Love is work, the work you're willing to do for somebody else even if you don't get anything out of it yourself.

Because of her addiction, Mommy can't put in the work. I understand this about her, but it still hurts.

But Nanny can. And so can Macey and Auntie Diane. And Caleb will probably be able to once he grows up a little. I crumble up cornbread over my soup. Hillbilly croutons. "Nanny?" I say.

"Hm?"

"After I graduate from high school, if I was to move somewhere else for a while to go to school so I can get a good-paying job, would that be all right with you? It'd just be for a while."

She's quiet for a minute. It's probably not a whole minute, but it feels like one. "Well, honey, it don't really matter what I think. By that time you'll be eighteen and I won't be able to tell you what to do no more."

"I still want to know what you think, though."

"All right." She's fiddling with her soup more than eating it. "Here's what I think. I think it'd break my heart if you moved off somewhere else. But I also think it's a good idea to get some schooling above high school so you won't just end up drifting from one dead-end job to another." She looks at me for a second, then says. "You know, Kody, sometimes when I think about my life, it feels like I didn't hardly make any choices at all, that my life just sort of happened to me. I don't want you to feel that way."

"Thank you," I say, reaching over to pat her arm. "You could always come with me, you know."

"What?" Nanny raises her eyebrows almost to her hairline.

"With the factory closing and all, you could come with me to Knoxville or Lexington or wherever I end up going to school. You could find a job there."

Nanny looks at me like I've just suggested she go to the moon. "Lord, I could never live in a city like that! All them people and all that traffic, I'd be scared to death all the time. Besides, I need to stay close to your mommy and Caleb. You'll just have to come visit us a lot."

"Every weekend."

Dollywood

"You ready?" Macey says as we hand over our tickets at the gate.

I nod. I'm too excited to speak, and my belly is full of butterflies which is appropriate since Dolly loves butterflies and has a song about them. Macey takes my hand.

We pass through the gate into what looks like an old-fashioned downtown. There are beautiful flower beds, and I hear Dolly's voice singing "My Tennessee Mountain Home." I can't see where the music is coming from, so it feels like Dolly's following us around and singing to us.

Nanny and Auntie Diane and Caleb pass through the gate right behind us. This is the first time Nanny's taken a vacation since her and Papaw went to Gatlinburg on their honeymoon. But since Auntie Diane found a program that matches up needy people with rehab facilities for free, Nanny has been able to take a little time for herself.

Mommy is doing sixty days in a residential rehab facility in Florida. It's another chance for her, but I don't know what she'll make of it. I'm trying to be hopeful, but it's in her hands.

"Okay," Auntie Diane says, like a person who's used to organizing things. "Macey and Kody, y'all go on and do whatever you want, but meet us here in three hours and we'll go find some dinner."

"What about me?" Caleb asks.

"You stay with Diane and me, and we'll take you to ride some rides," Nanny says. "As long as we don't have to get on none of them ourselves."

"You've got that right," Auntie Diane says, smiling.

"I want to go on the big roller coasters!" Caleb says.

Of course he does.

Macey and me walk off on our own. "How about you?" Macey says. "Do you like roller coasters?"

"I don't know. I've never been on one." The only rides I've ever been on were some old, rickety ones at an itty-bitty carnival that sets up in the Walmart parking lot some summers.

"Well, we'll have to fix that," Macey says, grinning. "But I bet you want to look at the Dolly stuff first, right?"

My heart flutters. "Please."

"You want to see her house? It's just over here."

For a minute, I'm confused. I know Dolly doesn't really live in Dollywood, but when we walk up to it, I understand. In front of me is a replica of the cabin where Dolly grew up with her eleven brothers and sisters, the same house that's pictured on the cover of *My Tennessee Mountain Home*. I'm frozen to the ground, unable to believe what I'm actually seeing.

"You want to go inside and look around?" Macey says.

"Can we?"

"That's what it's here for, silly." She takes my hand and pulls me up onto the porch. I feel strange, like I'm walking in a dream.

Inside is a hallway where you stand and look at the inside of the house, all behind glass so you can't touch anything. It's tiny, just two rooms, a kitchen/living area and a bathroom. The walls are papered with some flowered wallpaper but also old newspapers. Pots and pans are hung around the old-fashioned woodstove. There are lights in the ceiling so you can see what's in the house, but I know from reading Dolly's autobiography dozens of times that the real house had no electricity or running water. There's only one bed, and I try to picture how all the Parton kids fit in it, piled on top of each other like a litter of puppies.

Macey must be thinking the same thing because she says, "Fourteen people. Fourteen people lived in this house."

"Nanny's mama didn't grow up too different from this," I say. "It was her and her mommy and daddy and six brothers and sisters in a one-bedroom house in a coal camp."

I look at the wash basin and the butter churn, the sewing table and the fireplace and the firewood. It's strange to look at what mountain life was like back when more people farmed for a living, back before the mines shut down. A life without TV or Walmart, without cell phones or pain pills. "I wonder what it would've been like to live this way," I say.

"Hard," Macey says. "Can you imagine working like that for day-to-day necessities? Just keeping clean would've been so much effort." She points to a container next to the wash basin labeled *LYE SOAP.* "I mean, you had to make your own *soap.*"

"Yeah," I say. "You would've had to work hard, but at least everybody would be working together, and you'd know what you was working for."

"Yeah, to stay alive," Macey says. "If it's all the same to you,

I'm going to enjoy my electricity and running water and keep buying soap at the store."

I laugh. I wouldn't want to trade my electricity and running water either, but looking at the way Dolly grew up, I can't help thinking that with all we've gained, we've lost something, too. Maybe Dolly also feels this way. Maybe that's why she wants to show us the way she lived, to show us the hard work and love in the warm, dark cocoon where she transformed into the bright, beautiful creature she became.

"Let's go to the Dolly museum, want to?" Macey says, taking my hand again.

I nod, too overwhelmed to talk.

"I love taking you places, Kody," Macey says. "It's like everything is so new to you. It's going to be an awesome summer."

After our Dollywood visit, we're going to drive Nanny back home, and then I'm going to stay with Macey and Auntie Diane for the whole month of June. It's going to be an adventure.

The Chasing Rainbows Museum is full of photographs of Dolly with other stars and lots of Dolly's spangled, sequined costumes on headless mannequins with the proportions of Dolly's unbelievable figure—petite height, huge bust, itty-bitty waist. I'd try on every outfit in the place if they weren't too tiny to fit me. Just looking at those costumes and knowing Dolly has worn them, my skin breaks out in goosebumps.

"Kody! Come over here!" Macey calls. She's standing beside a glass case.

I go over to her, and as soon as I look inside the case, I gasp.

Behind the glass is Dolly's Coat of Many Colors, the real one, which her mommy stitched together from fabric scraps because they were too poor to get a store-bought coat. Next to the coat, scrawled on a dry-cleaning receipt of Porter Waggoner's, are Dolly's original lyrics to the song.

From my years of sewing with Nanny, I can see that Mrs. Parton's needlework was fine, and the patchwork coat, made so little to fit the eight-year-old Dolly, is a work of art, created with clever hands and the bold imagination to make something out of nothing. That spirit is in a lot of mountain people. It's in Nanny when she turns yarn into an afghan or some flour and milk into biscuits and gravy. It's in me when I paint on some makeup and put on a wig and am suddenly somebody else, somebody beautiful. And it was in Dolly when she took a pen, a dry-cleaning receipt, and a memory and turned it into music.

Seeing the little coat makes tears spring to my eyes when I think about the other kids who made fun of Dolly for wearing it, who couldn't see how special it was. How special she was.

I look over at Macey and see that there are tears in her eyes, too.

"It's perfect, isn't it?" she says.

I take my sister's hand in mine. "It is."

The End

About the Author

JULIA WATTS IS THE AUTHOR OF fourteen novels for adults and young adults, all published by independent presses. Her books, which are set in Appalachia and often depict the lives of LGBT people in the Bible Belt, have won a loyal following and several awards. Her novel, *Quiver*, set in rural Tennessee, received a rare "Perfect 10 Rating" from *VOYA Magazine*, and, along with several of her other novels, was selected for the American Library Association's Rainbow List. Her novel *Finding H.F.* (Alyson Press, 2001) won the Lambda Literary Award in the Children's/Young Adult category, and her historical YA novel *Secret City* (Bella Books, 2013) was a finalist for the Lambda Literary Award and a winner of a Golden Crown Literary Award. Watts was recently given the Tennessee Library Association's Intellectual Freedom Award. She lives in Knoxville and is working on a PhD in Children's and Young Adult Literature at The University of Tennessee.

RECENT AND FORTHCOMING BOOKS FROM THREE ROOMS PRESS

FICTION

Lucy Jane Bledsoe
No Stopping Us Now

Rishab Borah
The Door to Inferna

Meagan Brothers
Weird Girl and What's His Name

Christopher Chambers
Scavenger

Ron Dakron
Hello Devilfish!

Robert Duncan
Loudmouth

Michael T. Fournier
Hidden Wheel
Swing State

Aaron Hamburger
Nirvana Is Here

William Least Heat-Moon
Celestial Mechanics

Aimee Herman
Everything Grows

Kelly Ann Jacobson
Tink and Wendy

Jethro K. Lieberman
Everything Is Jake

Eamon Loingsigh
Light of the Diddicoy
Exile on Bridge Street

John Marshall
The Greenfather

Aram Saroyan
Still Night in L.A.

Stephen Spotte
Animal Wrongs

Richard Vetere
The Writers Afterlife
Champagne and Cocaine

Julia Watts
Quiver
Needlework

Gina Yates
Narcissus Nobody

MEMOIR & BIOGRAPHY

Nassrine Azimi and Michel Wasserman
Last Boat to Yokohama: The Life and Legacy of Beate Sirota Gordon

William S. Burroughs & Allen Ginsberg
Don't Hide the Madness:
William S. Burroughs in Conversation with Allen Ginsberg
edited by Steven Taylor

James Carr
BAD: The Autobiography of James Carr

Judy Gumbo
Yippie Girl

Judith Malina
Full Moon Stages:
Personal Notes from
50 Years of The Living Theatre

Phil Marcade
Punk Avenue: Inside the New York City Underground, 1972–1982

Jililian Marshall
Japanthem: Music Connecting Cultures Across the Pacific

Alvin Orloff
Disasterama! Adventures in the Queer Underground 1977–1997

Nicca Ray
Ray by Ray: A Daughter's Take on the Legend of Nicholas Ray

Stephen Spotte
My Watery Self:
Memoirs of a Marine Scientist

PHOTOGRAPHY-MEMOIR

Mike Watt
On & Off Bass

SHORT STORY ANTHOLOGIES

SINGLE AUTHOR

The Alien Archives: Stories
by Robert Silverberg

First-Person Singularities: Stories
by Robert Silverberg
with an introduction by John Scalzi

Tales from the Eternal Café: Stories
by Janet Hamill, with an introduction
by Patti Smith

Time and Time Again:
Sixteen Trips in Time
by Robert Silverberg

Voyagers:
Twelve Journeys in Space and Time
by Robert Silverberg

MULTI-AUTHOR

Crime + Music: Twenty Stories of Music-Themed Noir
edited by Jim Fusilli

Dark City Lights: New York Stories
edited by Lawrence Block

The Faking of the President: Twenty Stories of White House Noir
edited by Peter Carlaftes

Florida Happens:
Bouchercon 2018 Anthology
edited by Greg Herren

Have a NYC I, II & III:
New York Short Stories;
edited by Peter Carlaftes
& Kat Georges

Songs of My Selfie:
An Anthology of Millennial Stories
edited by Constance Renfrow

The Obama Inheritance:
15 Stories of Conspiracy Noir
edited by Gary Phillips

This Way to the End Times:
Classic and New Stories of the Apocalypse
edited by Robert Silverberg

MIXED MEDIA

John S. Paul
Sign Language: A Painter's Notebook
(photography, poetry and prose)

DADA

Maintenant: A Journal of Contemporary Dada Writing & Art
(Annual, since 2008)

HUMOR

Peter Carlaftes
A Year on Facebook

FILM & PLAYS

Israel Horovitz
My Old Lady: Complete Stage Play and Screenplay with an Essay on Adaptation

Peter Carlaftes
Triumph For Rent (3 Plays)
Teatrophy (3 More Plays)

Kat Georges
Three Somebodies: Plays about Notorious Dissidents

TRANSLATIONS

Thomas Bernhard
On Earth and in Hell
(poems of Thomas Bernhard
with English translations by
Peter Waugh)

Patrizia Gattaceca
Isula d'Anima / Soul Island
(poems by the author
in Corsican with English
translations)

César Vallejo | Gerard Malanga
Malanga Chasing Vallejo
(selected poems of César Vallejo
with English translations
and additional notes by
Gerard Malanga)

George Wallace
EOS: Abductor of Men
(selected poems in Greek & English)

ESSAYS

Richard Katrovas
Raising Girls in Bohemia:
Meditations of an American Father

Far Away From Close to Home
Vanessa Baden Kelly

Womentality: Thirteen Empowering Stories by Everyday Women Who Said Goodbye to the Workplace and Hello to Their Lives
edited by Erin Wildermuth

POETRY COLLECTIONS

Hala Alyan
Atrium

Peter Carlaftes
DrunkYard Dog
I Fold with the Hand I Was Dealt

Thomas Fucaloro
It Starts from the Belly and Blooms

Kat Georges
Our Lady of the Hunger

Robert Gibbons
Close to the Tree

Israel Horovitz
Heaven and Other Poems

David Lawton
Sharp Blue Stream

Jane LeCroy
Signature Play

Philip Meersman
This Is Belgian Chocolate

Jane Ormerod
Recreational Vehicles on Fire
Welcome to the Museum of Cattle

Lisa Panepinto
On This Borrowed Bike

George Wallace
Poppin' Johnny

Three Rooms Press | New York, NY | Current Catalog: www.threeroomspress.com
Three Rooms Press books are distributed by Publishers Group West: www.pgw.com